MURDER AT THE WEDDING

a Modern Midwife Mystery

Christine Knapp

MURDER AT THE WEDDING
Copyright © 2022 by Christine Knapp
Cover design by Daniela Colleo
of www.StunningBookCovers.com

Published by Gemma Halliday Publishing Inc
All Rights Reserved. Except for use in any review, the reproduction or utilization of this work in whole or in part in any form by any electronic, mechanical, or other means, now known or hereafter invented, including xerography, photocopying and recording, or in any information storage and retrieval system is forbidden without the written permission of the publisher, Gemma Halliday.

This is a work of fiction. Names, characters, places, and incidents are either the product of the author's imagination or are used fictitiously, and any resemblance to actual persons, living or dead, business establishments, or events or locales is entirely coincidental.

To Bob, Michael, and Andrew
Le haghaidh a chreidiúint i gcónaí

"Midwifery should be taught in the same course with fencing and boxing, riding and rowing."
—Herman Melville, *Moby-Dick; or, The Whale*

CHAPTER ONE

The first trimester of pregnancy begins on the first day of the last menstrual cycle and lasts until the end of week twelve.

Contrary to popular opinion, midwifery is the oldest profession, and I was getting older by the minute waiting for Christy Nelson to give birth. Christy had been in labor for a very long time.

She was what I called a "nuts and granola" fan. Everything about her birth experience had to be natural and pure. Christy had a long birthing wish list that began with dim lighting in the room, one hundred percent organic cotton sheets on the bed, and minimal intervention in labor. It ended with Yanni's "Live at the Acropolis" playing during the birth.

In some states, Yanni at a birth could be construed as child abuse.

Now, with her labor at twenty-six hours and counting, both Christy and I were more than ready for her baby to be born.

Christy was a first-time mother being induced at Creighton Memorial Hospital because of the baby's large size and the decreased amount of amniotic fluid seen on her last ultrasound. She strongly objected to being induced but realized it was best for her baby. Still, she had fought every intervention tooth and nail. I had spent hours repeating midwifery philosophy to her and Leon, her type-A investment banker husband. I had explained at length that I would keep their desires in the forefront but frequently reminded them our goal was a healthy mother and baby. At this point, Christy had an epidural and was making progress, and even though the birth wasn't going totally according to their plan, they were rising to the occasion step-by-step.

It was now six-thirty a.m., and the baby was beginning to crown. I estimated the weight to be a bit over nine pounds.

"Christy, you're doing great! It won't be much longer."

"How *much* longer, Maeve?"

"Very soon."

"*GIVE ME A TIME*!"

"By seven a.m., we should have a baby."

"Seven a.m.? I *caan't!*" Christy wailed.

With this, Robin, our veteran labor nurse, took over with a determined look. "Come on now, Christy…get ready…deep breath and push down…push, push…very good."

Robin was short with smooth, dark hair—a quiet, unobtrusive presence who always kept her voice low, calm, and encouraging, which I appreciated. I disliked birth rooms that sounded like a football cheering squad had taken up residence.

"That's excellent, Christy. I'm going to scrub up now and get the room ready." I walked over to the sink, and Leon quickly followed me.

"Remember," he said. "Dim the lights a bit more, and I'll start the music. Don't forget that the baby needs to be put on her chest immediately. These requests are non-negotiable."

I took a deep breath. "Leon, this is a large baby, but I'll do everything I can to make this a wonderful birth."

Leon paled, and bright red splotches appeared on his cheeks as he walked away to set up his video equipment. I wanted to give him more reassurance, but I needed to concentrate fully on the birth right now. I had already spoken to Robin regarding my concerns about the baby's size, and, as always, she was ready with backup staff on standby. I put on my gloves and opened the delivery kit. As I turned to Christy, a large portion of the baby's head was now visible.

"Christy, remember what we talked about. When I tell you to stop pushing, quickly blow out. I'll tell you everything that's happening. Listen to my voice."

"I need to push!" Christy screamed.

"Nice and easy. You're doing great."

I exerted a slight pressure on the baby's head to keep it flexed. The ears began to emerge, and then big chubby cheeks appeared. This was always a tense moment with a large baby. Would the head turn easily? And, more importantly, would the shoulders slide out? The threat of shoulder dystocia, when the baby's head is out but the shoulders get stuck, strikes terror in the hearts of all delivery-room personnel. Sometimes babies are injured, or worse, from this complication even with the best planning.

I was as prepared as I could be. Christy had a roomy pelvis, and Robin had helped her into a great position. I turned the baby's head gently to see if it would rotate easily. It did!

"Okay, Christy. Stop pushing! Blow out!"

"I have to push," Christy screamed.

"Look at me, Christy."

She held my gaze, and I nodded.

"Nice and easy. You've got this."

Christy blew out rapid breaths while Leon rubbed her shoulders. Then he turned to his equipment.

"Quiet, please, everyone," he said. "The baby needs to hear the music."

The electronic drone of a generic synthesizer filled the room.

Robin gave a slight roll of her eyes and then gave me an inquiring look.

I applied downward pressure to the baby's top shoulder and felt some resistance. The shoulders were a bit tight. I quickly moved them slightly off-center.

"Robin, can you give me a little assistance here, please."

Robin stepped onto the stool she had placed beside the labor bed. She placed both hands slightly above Christy's pubic bone and gave me steady downward pressure.

"Push now, Christy. One more strong push."

Christy pushed and exhaled loudly while falling back on the pillows.

The baby delivered slowly at first, making its way into the world by what seemed like fractions of an inch as I held my breath. Then the shoulders passed through the pelvis, and the body began to come more easily. Finally, the legs and feet slid quickly out.

"It's your daughter. She's lovely!" I told her and silently breathed a sigh of relief.

"Oh, sweetie," Christy cried. Leon burst into tears and kissed her.

"You both were amazing. Strong, strong work," I told them.

Robin stepped down from the stool. "Such a great team."

The baby was a bit blue and not crying, but her arms and legs flexed well. Robin took her and placed oxygen tubing near the infant's face while gently rubbing her back. In typical fashion, Robin already had a warm blanket ready. The baby began to pink up immediately and let out a loud screech.

"Is she alright?" Christy asked.

"She's perfect. She just needed a bit of air," Robin said as she placed the baby on Christy's chest. "Here, you need to see her."

Christy held Abigail gently and smiled as tears trickled down her cheeks. "She has your hair, Leon."

"What's Abigail's Apgar score?" a thoroughly disheveled Leon asked. The Apgar score, which measured the baby's general condition, was given at one and five minutes after birth. The score ran from zero to ten and measured heart rate, breathing, color, muscle tone, and reflexes.

"Robin, what do you give Abigail?" I asked. I always had a nurse assign the Apgar score at my deliveries. I liked to keep myself honest.

"Eight."

"What! Not a ten?" Leon sputtered.

"I took a point off for color and because she needed a whiff of oxygen. Abigail will get a ten at five minutes."

"I can't believe she didn't get a perfect score. Maybe it was from the epidural." He turned toward me.

I tried to reassure him. "Leon, an eight out of ten is an excellent score. Abigail looks wonderful, and she will certainly get a ten at five minutes." I wanted to add that this wouldn't affect her chances of getting into Harvard but kept my mouth shut.

"At least there was no episiotomy," Leon muttered.

Christy was stroking the baby now and cooing. I finished my charting on the bedside workstation and recorded the baby's weight and vital signs. Leon, the proud father, was already on his cell, alerting the world to Abigail's arrival.

I hugged Christy goodbye and complimented her again on her strength and wonderful birth. She thanked me for my help through her tears. Then I left the room and wearily stretched. Outside, the birth suite was humming with the change of staff. I said good morning to a few regulars as I passed the nurses' workstation.

"Hey, Mauve! Have a good sleep," Carl, the patient care manager, called as I passed by.

"Funny guy," I said, waving. Maeve, my traditional Irish name, was said in so many ways by so many people. I probably should carry a card that read, *Maeve, like brave with an M.*

After a quick shower in the locker room, I changed into my black jeans, a white tank, and a charcoal cotton jacket. The pants didn't quite reach my ankles, but finding tall pants wasn't always easy. I clipped my shoulder-length, blonde hair into a twist and put on some rose lipstick and blush to counteract my lack of sleep. I wanted to look at least a bit pulled together for my quick coffee date with my husband, Will. *Not too bad for an exhausted midwife,* I thought as I took a last glance in the mirror.

Traffic was heavy on Main Street in Langford. Boston commuters were on the move, and the omnipresent school buses were rolling.

I pulled up to The Coffee Cup, housed in a remodeled Victorian house in the center of town. As I entered the café area, I spotted my older sister, Meg, holding court.

Oh great. I forgot today is real estate open house day. I didn't want to see her after a night call, so I slid into a booth and pretended to study my phone.

Meg marched over to my table. "Avoiding me, Maeve?"

"Of course not." I gave a weak smile.

Meg and I were both six feet tall, but she was model thin and, this month, a flaming redhead. Thirty-six years old, she had an unbelievably well-adjusted, fourteen-year-old son and lived in a lavish Tudor-style mansion on the shores of Langford Bay, courtesy of her uber-wealthy ex. She was also a very successful real estate agent and was well respected by her colleagues and clients.

Meg had on black sheer stockings, a black silk pencil skirt, and a lime green sleeveless shell, all complemented by hair and makeup worthy of a *Vogue* cover shoot.

"I know you're bringing life into the world, but really, Maeve, do you not own a hairdryer?"

"It was a long night, Meg."

"That's what it looks like."

I sighed and held my hands up in surrender.

"Okay, okay, you're mostly hidden by the booth anyway." She grinned.

This was our typical exchange. Meg was the perpetual homecoming queen, impeccably dressed and charming her court, while I was the shy, studious, unfashionable little sister watching in the background. To her credit, Meg had tried valiantly for years to perform makeovers on me, but always to no avail. The latest fashion trends were just not my passion.

"We're about to tour homes." Meg gestured to her colleagues, who were gathering their belongings. Air kisses and hugs were quickly exchanged, and the pack of agents was off like hounds at the chase.

"Call me later," Meg sang out as she left.

"Roger that."

I sat and sipped my decaf mocha latte while engaging in some light people watching.

"Hey, beautiful!" Will, my 6'4" husband, appeared next to me. He had a lean runner's body and a head of dark brown curls and was easily the best thing to ever come out of Langford. He was everything wonderful—kind, honest, and outgoing. He also hated golf and loved baseball and me. How had I gotten so lucky?

"Hey, there." I kissed him.

"How was the night? The birth went well?"

As was typical with midwives' families, Will was well-schooled in centimeters, dilatation, and prenatal testing.

"All's well that ends well—a healthy baby girl. And I'm so glad you suggested we meet for coffee."

Will, aka William Charles Kensington III, had followed the family tradition of attending Yale. But upon graduation, he'd gone on to study culinary arts at Johnson & Wales. Afterward, he'd returned to Langford, where he'd opened a catering and bakery business to the eternal consternation of William Charles Kensington Jr., CEO of Oyster Cove Financial Services, one of the East Coast's largest private equity management firms. In five short years, Will had succeeded in making any event catered by A Thyme for All Seasons a highly prized ticket.

I leaned against him, and my entire body relaxed.

"Are you ready for the *Event*?" he asked.

The "*Event*" of this season was the wedding of Charlotte Whitaker, daughter of the chief of obstetrics of Creighton Memorial, to Brooks Hawthorne, which was to take place tomorrow at The Country Club. Just The Country Club, no other name needed. A Thyme for all Seasons had recently expanded to cater large events, and the Whitaker wedding, if all went according to plan, could really help promote the business. On the other hand, Will would have trouble repaying his sizable business loan if the reviews were less than fabulous.

Will sighed and finished his mug of coffee. "I believe *I* am. So much is riding on this wedding. If it's spectacular, it will be great for business."

"It will be great," I assured him. "You only do great." Then I hugged him.

"I hope so." He finished his coffee and slid out of the booth. "See you tonight, honey. I love you. Get some sleep."

As Will pulled away in one of the company vans, I again wondered how he was so grounded and loving, considering the rest of his family.

But that's another story.

I got into my trusty Jeep before sleep could overtake me and pointed the car toward home.

CHAPTER TWO

Certified nurse-midwives are registered nurses who have completed a graduate-level midwifery program and have passed a national certification exam.

Saturday morning dawned bright and sunny. But then, it would never rain on a Whitaker wedding. Will had left hours ago to make sure the catering was on track.

I took Fenway, my four-year-old rescue dachshund, for a quick walk and then got ready for the wedding. I slipped into my new silk, sapphire wrap dress. It displayed more cleavage than usual, but, hey, why not? It was expensive, but it was also gorgeous and looked great with my new black silk slingbacks and black beaded clutch. I donned the beautiful Mikimoto pearls Will had given me on our wedding day and was ready to head off. Amazingly, even my stick-straight hair had some loose waves courtesy of a seldom-used curling iron. *Not bad*, I thought as I went out the door.

The parking lot at St. Andrew's Episcopal was filled almost to capacity. Despite a recent visit to the car wash, my Jeep looked out of place next to all the Mercedes, BMWs, Range Rovers, Jaguars, and Porsches.

I took out and quickly scanned the engraved linen cream invitation. It read:

Matrimonial Ceremony of
Charlotte Alexis Whitaker
and
Brooks James Hawthorne IV
St. Andrew's Episcopal Church
Langford, Massachusetts

Saturday, the eighth of June, at two o'clock in the afternoon

As I approached the massive church, I saw all the pink plantings and railings wrapped in white tulle with pink peonies at precise intervals. It was a floral tour de force that must have taken an army of gardeners and florists a few days to accomplish. Inside there were pink roses, peonies, and hydrangeas everywhere. The scene was right out of *InStyle Magazine*. I wondered, *were there any pink flowers left on the East Coast? On the West Coast?*

As I squeezed into the last row, a large choir serenaded the full house in the loft above the congregation.

The choir began to sing "My Spirit Sang All Day" as Mrs. Whitaker, resplendent in a strapless, rose silk Carolina Herrera with a vibrant pink cabbage rose behind one ear and a necklace of marble-sized, green South Sea pearls, was ushered to the left front pew. *Really? Strapless for the mother of the bride? Well, she does look amazing.*

A hush fell over the crowd. The stained-glass doors closed, and the groom and his men filed to the altar.

Did one have to be six feet two, gorgeous, and ripped to be in this wedding party?

As the first strands of Wagner filled the air, the doors opened, and down the aisle came Anastasia Bleeker. She was one of the bride's four-year-old charges at Miss Bloomfield's School, where wealthy, pregnant women enrolled their offspring-to-be to claim a coveted spot. Anastasia was wearing a white tulle fairy-tale gown with a dark rose-colored sash. A circle of petite, light pink roses and baby's breath crowned her chin-length, straight, white-blonde hair. She carried a small, white wicker basket in one hand, and with the other, she started to drop pale pink rose petals down the long aisle.

Channeling Lady Di, I thought.

Next came the ring bearer, Barrington Cabot. He was another nursery school trust-fund-baby-in-the-making in white linen shorts and jacket and a head of black, curly hair. Then six breathtaking models, or rather bridesmaids, dressed in rose-colored tulle skirts and pale pink lace wrap blouses, floated down the aisle carrying white and pink hydrangeas wrapped in rose-colored ribbons. They looked like an upscale version of an ad for the United Colors of Benetton.

After a slight pause, the stained-glass doors parted again, and Dr. Whitaker appeared in his morning suit, standing at Charlotte's right side. She was breathtaking in a Vera Wang white silk ball gown glittering with thousands of tiny seed pearls. A deep rose satin ribbon wrapped around her bouquet of white peonies. Her Belgian lace veil trailed behind her down the aisle.

The ceremony went on amid candlelight, roses, and organ music. It was like being in a dream, albeit a very, very expensive dream.

Finally, vows were exchanged, there were no objections, and Charlotte and Brooks were off to the photo-taking session in a vintage, white Bentley. As they left, the guests milled about outside the church for a bit and then headed to the reception.

Evelyn Greyson, the sixtyish director of Obstetric Nursing, stood at the top of the church stairs as I exited. She was dressed in a powder blue suit with a short jacket with peplum and knee-length, fitted skirt. A pearl necklace, her ever-present pearl brooch, and small pearl stud earrings completed the look. Her graying hair was, as usual, in her trademark chignon.

"Beautiful wedding," I said.

"Magnificent," Evelyn replied. "Dr. Whitaker wouldn't have it any other way. See you at the reception, dear." And then she strode off to her car.

Evelyn always agreed with everything Dr. Whitaker said and did. She worshipped him. Did she also have an unrequited crush on him?

I quickly greeted a few colleagues but didn't linger because I wanted to see how Will was doing.

The Country Club was buzzing with activity when I drove through the porte cochère, pulled up to the main entrance, and handed my keys to a valet. The grand foyer was glittering with hundreds of candles and still more massive floral arrangements in blush pink. A string quartet played Pachelbel's "Canon in D" beside the grand staircase.

Out on the veranda, the wedding party was taking pictures before an expanse of green lawn and brilliant blue sky and sea. It would be a wedding album worthy of its own issue of *Town & Country*.

I made a quick detour to the caterer's kitchen. Waiters in black tuxedos formed a parade carrying silver trays of hors d'oeuvres and champagne. I spotted Will toward the back making a detailed inspection of the wedding cake, a tower of white and pink with fresh roses on the layers. The cake topper was a porcelain likeness of Charlotte and Brooks, complete with a replica of her gown and veil.

"Hey, Will!" I called out as I came up behind him.

He turned and looked at me for a long moment. "You look stunning, Maeve," he finally said. Then he gave me a huge grin followed by a kiss.

Will gazed around the kitchen as he quickly took measure of the dinner preparations. "Hey, Kevin, can you help pass the hors d'oeuvres, please?" Will asked.

Kevin was an old family friend who Will had recently hired. I had a hand in his hiring, although Kevin was unaware of my influence.

"Sure, Will. Hey, Maeve, nice to see you."

"Great to see you, too," I responded.

A well-run major catering event was like a ballet. Everyone and everything had to flow just right. Timing was critical.

I put my arm around Will's waist and hugged him. "You got this, honey."

"Do or do not. There is no try," Will countered.

"Yes, Yoda," I said as I kissed him on the cheek and took my leave. We both knew how high the stakes were today.

Conversations buzzed in the ballroom and on the veranda as I returned from the kitchen. Large silver serving trays were circulated among the guests, offering tiny crab cakes topped with dill aioli, mini beef Wellingtons, smoked salmon pinwheels, and tomato and goat cheese on toast points. There were massive silver bowls of fresh shrimp on ice on round marble tables.

"Maeve! Maeve! Over here!" one of the midwives called.

Looking around the ballroom, which held table settings for six hundred guests, I saw that the Creighton Memorial staff was on the right side of the room while family and friends were on the left. I waved to the midwives but walked over to the table where Grand, Will's grandmother, was sitting with Will's parents, Will's sister, Eloise, her husband, Taylor, and Will's younger brother, Teddy.

"Hello, Maeve." William stood and extended his hand. Never a hug, never a kiss on the cheek, just a handshake.

"Hello, so nice to see you all," I replied, shaking his hand as I nodded to the table. I saw that Lydia, my mother-in-law, was outfitted in a mint green silk cocktail dress with a large diamond necklace and matching drop earrings. She tilted her head toward me and smiled but said nothing.

"The Country Club is such a perfect wedding venue," I offered.

"Quite lovely," she replied.

"You look beautiful, Maeve," Grand said.

"Thanks, Grand."

"Sweet dress," Lydia said.

Sweet dress? What, am I five years old? Lydia was a master of the backhanded compliment, and she was not my biggest fan. Keep it together, Maeve.

Eloise was in a sleeveless, pale green and cream striped dress with an emerald and diamond pendant and earrings. *Like mother, like daughter.*

"Well," I said, "enjoy the meal. Will has been creating a masterpiece." I saw William's and Lydia's smiles tighten. They did not respond. They were not pleased with Will's chosen profession.

"I can't wait," Grand said.

I gave a little wave and headed over to find my table.

Scanning the room, I saw my sister, Meg, cross her eyes and raise her wine glass in a mock salute. Meg was the Langford real estate agent of choice for the wealthy and had been invited along with other top business leaders of the town. She knew I had just navigated a minefield with my emotionally distant in-laws. As soon as I reached my table, I quickly sat down and took a long drink of chardonnay.

Herend Chinese Bouquet china in pink, Gorham Newport Scroll sterling, and Baccarat crystal decorated each setting.

My gosh, they'll have to pat everyone down before they leave.

Murray Alfond, the famed orchestra leader, turned on his mic and said, "Please be seated while the bridal party arrives."

There was sustained applause as Charlotte and Brooks triumphantly paraded into the ballroom. "The bride and groom will dance to a classic personally chosen by Brooks," Alfond announced.

"The Very Thought of You" wafted through the room as Charlotte and Brooks took to the floor. They obviously had attended many ballroom dancing classes in preparation for this moment, and they danced impeccably.

Then the entire wedding party sashayed to "Fly Me to the Moon." It was like watching *La La Land*. They were all perfectly coiffed, dressed, and ready for filming. Plus, they could dance.

When they were done and returned to their seats, Alfond intoned, "Please bow your heads while Reverend Lucas Mathers says grace."

The Episcopal pastor of St. Andrew's, Reverend Mathers, was slightly rotund with flushed pink cheeks. He ran his hand through receding black hair, obviously feeling the weight of this moment. Then he bowed his head.

"Dear Holy Father, thank you for this glorious day! What a wonderful celebration! We ask you to bless Charlotte and Brooks, as well their families and friends, and we beseech you to grant this special couple a life together that is happy and blessed. We further ask you to bless this fabulous repast and grant your blessings on all present. Amen."

Gee, that was short. He must be hungry.

A phalanx of waiters served the first course of spring green and white asparagus spears with shaved red onion. As we started in on the delicate vegetables, the best man, Ry Farmington, took the microphone and asked all to raise their glasses in a toast to the couple.

"Brooks has been like a brother to me since our first day at Hollis in Harvard Yard. We've seen many adventures together—none of which, out of respect for your patience and his reputation, I will go into here."

He paused for applause and a few knowing hoots.

"In the words of the Bard,
No sooner met but they looked;
No sooner looked but they loved;
No sooner loved but they sighed;
No sooner sighed but they asked one another the reason;
No sooner knew the reason, but they sought the remedy;
And in these degrees have made a pair of stairs to marriage.

Please rise and toast to their lives together."

Six hundred guests rose and toasted the couple.

Then came truffle-scented tenderloin with dauphinoise potatoes and tender baby carrots. I snuck a look first at the Whitaker table and then at William and Lydia. They all seemed to be enjoying the meal, and I prayed that all the reviews would be excellent.

For dessert, a chocolate mousse with a crème brûlée center was placed at each setting. I knew the wedding cake would be cut and served later.

Just then, the wait staff re-entered the room. They set a Baccarat champagne flute filled with pink champagne at each place. A hush came over the ballroom. Dr. Whitaker was standing at the head table, staring the crowd into silence. Then he picked up his glass and smiled adoringly at Charlotte.

Everyone listened as he gave a long, loving toast to his daughter. Finally, he took a moment to gather his thoughts before saying, "Charlotte, your mother and I found this magnificent champagne in France a few years ago and had it shipped in for your wedding."

Mrs. Whitaker stared at Dr. Whitaker with a huge Miss America smile.

Dr. Whitaker continued, "Would everyone please rise and toast my lovely daughter Charlotte and her husband, Brooks." He lifted his crystal flute to his lips and took a sip while beaming at Charlotte.

Immediately, his cheeks turned scarlet, and he started to wheeze. The crystal dropped from his hand and shattered on the ground. He clutched at his throat while making extensive gasping attempts to pull in a breath. Then he went limp and collapsed to the floor. The room erupted into pandemonium.

CHAPTER THREE

After ten weeks of pregnancy, the embryo is referred to as a fetus.

Dr. Theodore Cydson, vice chief of the obstetrics department, ran to the table and searched for a pulse. "Get his EpiPen! Call 9-1-1!" he shouted.

Mrs. Whitaker quickly retrieved an EpiPen from her clutch. The crowd parted, and a deadly quiet overtook the ballroom as she handed the pen to him.

"Please save him!" Charlotte cried. She had spilled champagne from her flute, and a large stain ran down the front of her gown.

Dr. Cydson tried to inject the contents of the EpiPen into Dr. Whitaker's thigh. "What?" he cried out in surprise and repeated his motion with the EpiPen. "It's broken!" he exclaimed in alarm. He withdrew the EpiPen and threw it against the wall. By now, Dr. Whitaker's skin had turned a mottled blue as he lay flaccid on the floor.

"I need a new EpiPen!" Cydson screamed, looking wildly around the gathered crowd.

"Start CPR now," said Dr. Sanjay Patel, another of the obstetrics staff. He was a bit more composed as he stretched the stricken physician into position to begin chest compressions. He and Dr. Esther Wong, the emergency department chief, started doing two-rescuer CPR as sirens wailed in the distance.

One of the labor and delivery nurses quickly brought over The Country Club's defibrillator and switched it on. Immediately, it gave instructions to attach the pads to the patient.

"Analyzing rhythm. Do not touch the patient," the machine instructed. In a moment, it announced, "Shock indicated. Charging. Stand clear." Everyone stepped back as Dr. Patel pressed the button to deliver the shock, and the body gave a sudden jolt.

"Shock delivered. Resume CPR," directed the device. Sanjay Patel and Esther Wong resumed their efforts.

A frantic guest ran up to them and offered her EpiPen as paramedics came running into the ballroom. Sanjay injected the new EpiPen but got no response from Dr. Whitaker.

The paramedics replaced the defibrillator with their monitor. The jagged, irregular line snaking across the monitor showed that Whitaker's heart was fibrillating uselessly. Another shock was administered to no effect. The paramedics quickly placed an intravenous line and intubated their patient. Another dose of epinephrine was given. It, too, had no effect.

Continuing CPR, the paramedics loaded Dr. Whitaker into the waiting ambulance and sped off to the Creighton Memorial emergency room. The immediate family followed in close pursuit. In the ballroom, silence gave way to confused conversations.

"What happened? Was it something in the champagne?" asked one of the guests looking at her flute on the table.

"Maybe it was a cardiac issue," another said.

"I don't know," I said, shaking my head. It didn't look to me like a heart attack. "This is shocking."

The ballroom itself was now a picture of chaos. The head table was in shambles. Chairs were tipped over, plates and glasses were in pieces on the floor, along with debris from the CPR efforts. Stunned wedding guests were milling about and murmuring to each other. The dinner was long forgotten, and the musicians had begun packing up. Festivity had given way to numb disbelief.

I went to find Will.

He was leaning on a bar countertop with his head in his hands. "Will," I began. He turned to me, and I saw his eyes lacked focus. "Are you okay?"

"Maeve, this is unbelievable," Will said.

"Do you have any idea what happened?" I asked, taking hold of one of his hands and holding it tightly for some sense of normality.

"I have no idea. We poured Dr. Whitaker's own champagne selection in the special Baccarat flutes. The champagne was delivered to us from his private vendor."

"He grabbed his throat. I think he may have had an allergic reaction to something," I said.

"I don't see how that's possible. We had a list of everyone's allergies, and we were obsessively careful about them. Plus, he had the attack while he was drinking champagne and not while he was eating." He looked up and held my gaze. "I hope my team didn't mess up."

"I am sure it has nothing to do with you or the staff." *But was I sure?* "Dr. Cydson must have known Dr. Whitaker had allergies because he called for his EpiPen right away," I said.

"We always ask about allergies, and for this wedding, we made sure there were no nuts in any of our dishes. Anyway, he was drinking, not eating. What was wrong with his EpiPen? Was it broken?"

"Who knows?" I shrugged.

"Maeve, I need to get myself together and talk to my staff. Are you okay to drive home?" His forehead was creased with worry.

"I'm fine. Go ahead, Will. We'll talk later."

He hugged me tightly and then went back into the kitchen.

I saw Grand sitting alone at her table and made my way over. "Grand," I started. She took my hand. Her clear blue eyes stared into mine.

"Will's worried," I said, feeling panic start to overwhelm me.

"Have courage, Maeve. Be strong for Will."

I squeezed her hand and nodded.

About fifteen minutes later, Dr. Patel walked to the microphone. He raised his hand for silence. "Ladies and gentlemen, I just received a call from Dr. Cydson. Our emergency room staff was unable to resuscitate Dr. Whitaker. We ask for your prayers and thoughts for his family."

There was a collective gasp from the guests, who began gathering their belongings and heading to the exit. As they did, veteran Langford police captain Mike Petrucelli took the microphone and announced, "Good evening. Before you leave, please see Deputy Police Chief O'Reilly. He and his staff will be taking the names and addresses of everyone in attendance. I know this will take a few extra minutes, but we ask for your assistance. We will do this as swiftly as we can. Thank you for your cooperation."

Deputy Police Chief O'Reilly was my older brother, Patrick. I needed to talk to him, but the crowd surrounded him. I looked at the gathering of elegantly dressed people giving their names and addresses to the police. These were definitely not the usual suspects.

I started to follow along, filled with conflicting emotions. I was sad for the Whitakers, but I was also terrified for Will. No matter what happened, everyone would ask who the caterer was at the reception.

Maybe it would turn out that Dr. Whitaker had a heart attack, but an allergic reaction would need to be excluded. An autopsy would clearly need to be done. *And where was that EpiPen, and what was wrong with it? Why didn't it inject?* I realized that maybe the police hadn't found the pen yet. I glanced over and saw that Patrick was still knee-deep in work with the other police officers.

I walked over to the head table, where Dr. Whitaker had coded, but I couldn't see the EpiPen. I started to look under the table when a police officer approached me.

"May I help you, ma'am?" she asked, her voice stern.

"Hello, officer. I was just looking for the EpiPen. I was wondering why it didn't work."

"May I have your name, ma'am, and your relationship to the victim?"

"Oh, I'm Maeve Kensington. Uh, O'Reilly-Kensington. I, uh, I…"

She looked puzzled.

"M-A-E-V-E, it's pronounced like cave with an M." *If I had a nickel for every time I had said something like this…I think I know every word that rhymes with Maeve.*

Patrick must have finally spotted me and walked to us. "Can I help, Officer Manning?"

"Sir, this woman was looking through the crime scene. I was taking her name and particulars."

"This is Maeve Kensington, my sister. She works at Creighton."

"Sorry, sir."

"Nothing to be sorry about. You were doing your job," Pat said, then turned to me, looking not entirely happy. "Maeve, please just fill out the form, and leave the police work to us."

"Pat…"

"Maeve, I know he was your colleague, but we need to keep the crime scene secure until we fully evaluate it," Pat pointed out.

"I know, Patrick. I was just curious as to why that EpiPen didn't work." I scanned the ground one last time, hoping to spot it.

"Maeve, fill out the form, and I'll call you later. I know you're worried about Will. Are you okay to drive?"

"Yes, I'm fine. Thanks, Patrick. We can talk later."

He walked back to join the other officers.

"You will get through this, Sis," Meg said as she sidled up to me.

I let out a sigh.

"Stiff upper lip time, Maeve. Is Pat being tough on you?"

"He's just doing his job. Why didn't that EpiPen work?"

"Come on, Nancy Drew," Meg chided, steering me away from the front of the room. "It's time to call it a day. This isn't Will's fault." We got up to the table at the exit, and Meg and I filled out our information. Then we walked out to get our cars. "Call me if you hear anything," Meg said, hugging me.

"I will," I promised as I got into the Jeep.

"Or even if you don't."

When I got home, I put on my sweats and made a mug of fruit and almond tea. Grabbing a spoon and a pint of Ben & Jerry's Cherry Garcia, I snuggled under our red-and-white wedding ring quilt with Fenway. I had no idea when Will would get home, but it wouldn't be soon enough.

CHAPTER FOUR

The second trimester of pregnancy is from thirteen to twenty-seven weeks.

On Monday morning, as I pulled into the hospital garage, I saw the American flag on the lawn at half-staff. All of Creighton Memorial would be in a somber mood today.

As I sat in my Jeep, I thought back to my job interview five years ago. Arriving at Creighton, the long row of imposing redbrick buildings and immaculate lawns made me believe I had come across one of the many college campuses scattered across Massachusetts. Doctors in training at different Boston medical centers routinely rotated through the various services to get a feel for private practice. And while the excellent care contributed to the hospital's reputation, it didn't hurt that the grounds and facilities, endowed to the hilt by the town's wealthier citizens, could only be described as magnificent.

Walking into the main building, I'd nodded at the two blue-haired and deeply tanned older women sitting at the information desk. The foyer had marble fireplaces, tasteful reproduction furniture, and antique quilts on the walls. Call it Ralph Lauren's country hospital. Dr. Whitaker had been the chief of obstetrics for thirty years.

After gawking at the opulent lobby, I'd been directed to his suite and found myself in a waiting room paneled in rich, dark mahogany and furnished with maroon leather club chairs. On the walls hung scenes of naval battles and hunting dogs. It was pitch-perfect old boy decor.

I'd been greeted by a tall, slender middle-aged woman who wore a dark navy, fitted suit with a peplum jacket, a pearl circle pin on her lapel, and a starched white shirt. Her dark hair had been pulled tightly into a severe chignon, and she looked as if she'd stepped out of a 1950s secretarial pool.

She had introduced herself as Evelyn Greyson, Obstetric Nursing director, and abruptly told me that I would follow her on a tour before my interview. Even then, I'd wondered if this was the power behind the throne. During the tour, Evelyn barely acknowledged the staff except to occasionally announce I was a midwifery candidate.

It quickly became apparent that the physical plant was second to none. The patient areas were lovely, warm, and homey, with state-of-the-art equipment readily available but hidden from view. The floors gleamed, gorgeous indigo hydrangeas were on desktops, and every room appeared to offer views of the harbor. *Is this a hospital or a spa? Could a hospital make me feel underdressed?* This one had, even in the beige linen suit and white silk blouse I'd worn to the interview. That morning, as I left my apartment in Boston, I'd thought I looked calm and collected, but trailing behind Evelyn through these polished spaces, I'd felt sweaty and scraggly and wrinkled.

Finally, Evelyn had taken me through a mahogany door into Dr. Whitaker's inner sanctum, where a man with patrician good looks, a chiseled chin, and thick, steel-gray hair sat behind a massive, glass-topped desk. Under his pristine white lab coat, he had on a pale blue shirt paired with navy trousers and a navy silk tie. It suddenly felt like everything here was color coordinated from Martha Stewart's blue palette. To one side, a grouping of family portraits crowded a credenza, displaying several smiling children in various nautical settings. One large picture of a beautiful woman with violet eyes, dark brunette hair, and high cheekbones stood out from the rest—the doctor's wife, I'd later confirmed.

Dr. Whitaker had made approving comments on my recommendations and training—UMass/Amherst College of Nursing, Masters in Midwifery at Columbia, and four years at Boston General—and asked a few lightweight questions before I was summarily dismissed. As I'd correctly assumed at the time, Dr. Whitaker did not get very involved in the hiring of non-physicians. Luckily, when I met with the midwifery group, I found them to be strong, intelligent women who took Dr. Whitaker and Evelyn with a massive grain of salt.

Suddenly remembering what had happened to Dr. Whitaker, I left the Jeep and hurried in through the main door. I didn't want to be late for this quickly called department meeting.

Yesterday, I'd fielded phone calls from my mom and Meg and let the rest go to voice mail. Unfortunately, Patrick had not returned any of my calls. In part, Will had made his version of American chop suey because cooking always calmed him down. It was the perfect comfort food, and we ate it while watching the Red Sox get pounded by the Minnesota Twins, which was a fitting end to the weekend.

Stopping on the Labor and Delivery Unit, I quickly scanned the patient board. It listed six patients, all either in early labor or recently delivered. For the moment, everything was calm, and so I went on to the meeting.

In the Hadley conference room, Dr. Theodore Cydson was seated at the head of the table with Simon Peters, the urban planner turned healthcare CEO of Creighton. Evelyn Greyson sat directly to Dr. Cydson's right. Although her hair, makeup, and suit were pristine, Evelyn's face was drawn. She seemed oddly deflated and kept her gaze upon her clenched hands. Obstetricians, midwives, and obstetrical nursing managers completed the gathering around the massive oak table.

"Good morning," Simon Peters said when everyone had found a seat. "Creighton Memorial Hospital has suffered a terrible loss. Dr. Whitaker was the heart and soul of the OB/GYN department and a pillar of the hospital and the community. While we will honor his memory in due time, our immediate task is to keep up his legacy and move on as he would want us to do. Our grief counselors will be on hand for any staff who wishes to meet with them later."

"Do we know what the cause of death was?" Val, the Labor and Delivery nurse manager, asked.

"The autopsy results will be released as soon as possible."

I pray it was a heart attack.

"How is the family doing?" Dr. Sanjay Patel asked.

"As well as can be expected," Peters said. "We will offer them all the support we can." He stopped, took a breath, and continued, "I want you all to know that we will carry on as usual. The trustees and department chiefs will meet this afternoon to decide on how and when his successor will be named."

"Who will cover his patients?" Val asked.

"Well, as chief, he did not have a full clinical schedule, but his booked surgeries will be reassigned after discussion with his patients," Simon replied.

Dr. Patel put down the pen he'd been fiddling with. "Is there any word on the funeral arrangements?"

"The service schedule will be announced shortly when all the plans are finalized. I believe many of his family are coming from a distance, and, of course, the medical examiner must release the body. It will be a few days. Any further questions?"

The group was silent.

"For now, please carry on in your usual tradition of excellence. I know the Creighton family will weather this shock with its accustomed resilience. In the interim and to provide continuity and experienced guidance, Dr. Theodore Cydson has been appointed acting chief."

Dr. Cydson stood and smiled broadly at everyone in the room. A few people nodded in his direction. "I know we will all work together to show the true character of Creighton Memorial even in these darkest of hours. Thank you all for coming and for your continued support."

As staff filed out, Madeline, the Midwifery director, asked the midwives to stay for a brief meeting. Madeline was an excellent clinician, our outspoken advocate, and a lifelong yoga enthusiast. She lived with her wife, Joy, and their four kids, all six and under, plus assorted animals in an old farmhouse they were constantly renovating with the help of Joy's four brothers.

"Well, that really was the wedding of the century," Madeline said.

"What killed Dr. Whitaker? Was it an allergy? His heart?" Winnie asked. She was our older, very experienced British midwife, born in Montserrat and educated at Queen Charlotte's and Chelsea Hospital in London. As the unofficial mother to the group, younger midwives routinely told one another to "Stay calm, and call Winnie."

Madeline gave her a reproving look. "We need to wait for the autopsy."

"Why didn't the EpiPen inject?" I wondered.

"Another unknown," Madeline shrugged.

"I still can't believe this," Bev, another midwife, groaned. "Dr. Cydson, the acting chief? There will be no living with him now." Bev was a native New Yorker of Haitian heritage. Tall, elegant, and unflappable in clinical situations and life, she always managed to make us all smile with her quick wit.

"And El Cid has been in such a foul mood lately," Winnie said. Dr. Theodore Cydson, the vice chair of the obstetrics department, was commonly referred to as "El Cid" by the staff when safely behind his back.

"What happened?" Madeline sighed.

"He's been storming around the labor floor barking out orders to nurses, second-guessing everyone on fetal monitor tracings, and generally pushing people's buttons with obnoxious regularity," Winnie said.

"And this is new?" Bev asked.

"Well, hard as it is to believe, he seems worse than usual," Winnie replied.

"Doctor One-Day-This-Will-Be-Mine-All-Mine should be very happy now," I mused. "Dr. Whitaker was going to retire soon, and now El Cid is first in line to get the keys to this kingdom."

"Last week, I overheard Dr. Whitaker say he wasn't ready to retire," Winnie said. We all turned and looked at her.

"What? When was that?" Madeline asked.

"Well, he and Evelyn Greyson were talking, and…"

"Evelyn! She's the most unsupportive Nursing director ever!" Bev chimed in. "His right-hand gal…yeah, right if that's all she is."

"Come on, Bev. You know the Divine Miss Evelyn has made a second career of unrequited love. She is his protector. She's not romantically involved with him," I said.

Bev shrugged and raised an eyebrow in reply.

"Anyway," Winnie went on, "he told Evelyn he planned to stay on as chief indefinitely. El Cid was at the labor and delivery desk, and I know he heard the conversation."

"Wow. No wonder El Cid was smoking!" Bev exclaimed. "He's redecorated and remodeled the chief's office ten times over in his mind."

"What do you think changed Dr. Whitaker's mind?" Winnie asked. "The buzz at the perinatal conference was he would retire next year."

Without thinking, I added, "I heard he'd planned a six-month sailing trip after his retirement and had already made most of the arrangements." The group turned and looked at me, a few mouths hanging slightly open.

I shrugged sheepishly. "Heard it at the in-laws'."

Bev grinned at me. "Blue blood confidential."

I put my hands up in a sign of surrender, and we both started laughing.

"Now," Madeline announced to the group, "we need to figure out who will wind up as king or queen of this department and how it will affect us. Even though he's vice chair, El Cid isn't guaranteed the promotion."

The group was silent. We all knew midwifery was often on unsteady ground without strong physician support.

"Madeline, do we need to think about that right now? Dr. Whitaker isn't even buried yet," Winnie asked incredulously.

Bev nodded her head. "She has to, Winnie. You know that El Cid would like to see the midwives subservient to him."

"You're right about that. He often tries to ridicule us at rounds," Winnie responded.

"What he really wants is for us to be gone from Creighton," Bev pointed out. "What about Sanjay Patel or Fran Raymond becoming chair?"

"What about your John?" I asked.

Bev was married to Dr. John Armstrong, the chief of Maternal-Fetal Medicine. John was tall, always impeccably groomed, dressed out of a Brooks Brothers catalog, and had a reassuring, calm demeanor.

"John would never give up his clinical and research time for more administrative duties. He's very happy running his division," Bev replied.

"I think Fran Raymond is too young for the trustees' taste," Madeline said. "Also, sad to say, I'm not sure being a woman helps her cause with them. Sanjay also seems like a bit of a long shot. We all know he's a great clinician and very experienced, but politically the trustees are likely to turn to Dr. Cydson. He's an original member of the old boys' club."

"Not all the trustees are old boys," I piped up.

Bev smiled at me and nodded. "Will's grandmother *is* a powerful force on the board."

"Well, for now, let's keep our ears open," Madeline directed, letting her gaze go from face to face down the table. Then she laid down the critical question. "What is our consensus? Whom would we like as chief?"

"Sanjay," Winnie said.

We all agreed enthusiastically, and there was an immediate sense of solidarity in the room that lasted until Bev pointed out the obvious. "Too bad we don't get to vote."

Madeline looked thoughtful. "You can be sure I'll let the powers that be know how we feel. Oh, and one quick reminder. Please explain to all your students that if they push the red code button found in every patient room and operating suite in this hospital a cardiac arrest team will appear in minutes–and they will *not* be very happy if it's a false alarm. Last week a respiratory tech trainee pushed it by mistake and his patient was startled by the emergency response."

We all chuckled. Learning hospital protocols and procedures could be overwhelming. Finally, the group sat in silence for a moment.

Madeline turned to me. "Are you okay, Maeve?"

"Will is barely able to function," I sighed. "The police have been going through all of his supplies."

"Well, everyone knows he didn't do it," she reassured me.

"What motive would he have?" Winnie asked.

"Very PD James, Winnie," Madeline said.

"Brits are the best detectives," Winnie answered with a wry smile.

"But it did happen at an event he was catering," I said.

"Sweet baby Jesus in the manger, get a grip, woman. Will is blameless. And we are here for you," Bev said.

Winnie patted my back. "Whatever we can do to help, Maeve. We are your family."

"That's right," Madeline said. "Anything you need, you just let us know."

"Thank you," I said.

This is how it was in every clinical setting I had ever worked. Hospital people took care of their own. It indeed was a second family, and once again, I realized how lucky I was to have this community.

I could sense the meeting was over, so I announced to the group, "I brought some cookies. I thought we needed a little treat." Dead silence immediately filled the room.

"How did you find the time to cook?" Winnie finally asked as I pushed a container into the middle of the table.

"I couldn't sleep. I was up early." Again no one spoke or reached for a cookie. I blinked in amazement. "Hello? My friends? My support group? My family?"

"I'd love to try one." Bev gamely reached into the plastic container. She bit into the cookie. "Ohhhh," was all she said as most of it dropped down the front of her scrubs in the form of raw cookie dough. It was very, very underbaked.

"Maeve, do you ever taste these before you bring them in?" Madeline asked.

"They looked fine," I objected. "Plus, I tried some new tricks this time."

"Not working," Madeline said.

"At least they're not hockey pucks, Maeve," Winnie offered as she placed the cookie she'd taken on the table in front of her, untasted. "Maybe it's your oven." Everyone looked at her.

"She lives with a chef, Winnie," Madeline pointed out.

Bev wiped the front of her scrub top where the dough had fallen. "Maybe the timer was off."

"It could be from shock," Winnie said. "You know, after the wedding fiasco."

I shook my head. "I'll never get this right."

"You're just stressed, Maeve. Even the best bakers have off days. Watch *The Great British Baking Show*. They are amazing bakers, and even they have huge flops," Bev pointed out.

"How about just using the recipe on the wrapper that the chocolate bits come in? It's easy and foolproof," Winnie said.

"That's what I used, Winnie," I mumbled

"Oh, dear." She frowned.

"That's the way the cookie crumbles…or doesn't," Madeline said.

Everyone started laughing. Even I had to chime in as I dumped the cookies into the nearest trash bin.

"Such a waste of eggs and chocolate," Winnie said.

"Shush," Bev said.

Madeline stood up. "Okay, battle stations, everyone. Time to work."

CHAPTER FIVE

Miscarriage occurs in approximately ten to twenty percent of all pregnancies.

    As I scanned the morning schedule at the prenatal office, I saw a text from Meg. *Meet me for lunch @ deli.*
    I texted back, *Bring lunch here. Can't leave. Too many patients.*
    She replied, *Tuna on rye coming up.*
    I quickly looked over my list of patients. Kara Cook and her husband, Garrett, were first. Kara was thirty-six years old. She'd had a miscarriage six months ago at eight weeks gestation. Now Kara was nine weeks pregnant and had started spotting last night. She was so worried that she had already called the triage nurses with questions three times this morning. I took a deep breath and knocked on the door to her exam room.
    "Good morning, Kara and Garrett. Kara, I heard you were spotting. Tell me what's going on."
    Kara was about five feet six inches tall, with very short brown hair. There were dark circles under her eyes. A former Marine turned electrician, Garrett had his well-muscled arm around her shoulders. He looked serious and concerned.
    "Well, last night, I went to the bathroom and had a few spots of blood, but no cramping," Kara began. "I called the on-call line, and the nurse told me if the bleeding wasn't heavy and I had no pain, I could wait to have an ultrasound this morning. Do you think everything is okay?"
    "What color was the spotting?" I asked.
    "Pink."
    "Did you have recent intercourse?"
    "No. Why do you ask?"

"Sometimes you can have spotting from your cervix after intercourse, which is harmless."

"Do you think the baby is okay?"

"Kara, many pregnancies have spotting early on. I know that you are very worried because of your prior loss. It's too early for me to hear the heartbeat with the fetal heart doppler, so I am going to have you get an ultrasound, and then we can talk."

A tear escaped down Kara's cheek.

"I know this is stressful," I said to her gently. "Let's see what the ultrasound shows."

"Okay, Maeve," Kara said.

Garrett took her hand, and I watched them walk toward the ultrasound suite. I said a quick prayer that this was not another miscarriage for them.

Next up was Macey Cunningham, a nineteen-year-old with a history of opioid use during her pregnancy. She lived with her chronically unemployed, thirty-two-year-old boyfriend, Tim, although there was no sign of him today. As I walked into the exam room, she immediately said, "I'm tired. I want to have this baby today."

"Let's see how you're doing," I said and proceeded to examine her. Then I picked up her chart.

"Macey, you're thirty-eight weeks. The baby sounds great and is growing well, and your blood pressure is good. How is the baby's activity?"

"She never stops moving!"

"Fetal activity is a healthy sign. How are you feeling?"

"Terrible. I told you I want this baby out today."

"Why do you feel terrible?" I asked her.

"I'm too big. I have heartburn. I want a C-section now."

"Macey, let's take one thing at a time. You look well. You have gained twenty-two pounds, which is right on target for you. Are you trying small, frequent meals for the—"

"I'm tired of this!" Macey snapped.

"I know, it does get tiring," I replied as calmly as I could.

"How would you know? You don't have any kids, do you?"

Take another breath. Keep going. I met Macey's eyes. "Women get fatigued at the end of pregnancy. Is Tim helping you out?"

"No, he never does. He does buy takeout for dinner, though."

"Has he found a job?"

"Not yet."

"That must be difficult."

"You think?" Macey sneered.

"Have you used any drugs lately, Macey?"

"*No*."

I so wanted that to be true. "You are doing very well. I am going to send a drug screen on your urine sample. Is that okay with you?"

"I told you I'm not using," Macey said, looking at her feet.

"Remember our contract," I reminded her. "Because of your history, you agreed to be tested." Macey continued to stare at the floor. "Have you been seeing Faye, the OB social worker?"

"No, I don't need to. I'm fine. The drug test will be fine."

"Macey, I want to help you get ready for motherhood. A negative drug test will show everyone your commitment."

"Do you have any kids?" she asked again.

I swallowed hard. "No, I don't." *But I was so longing to be pregnant this month.*

"Well, then, why should I listen to you?"

I didn't want to go through any explanations with Macey. Male obstetricians care for women. Cardiac surgeons don't need to have cardiac surgery to care for their patients. I reminded myself that I would not let her get to me.

"Macey, I am trying to provide the best care possible for you and your baby."

"Ha! Then give me a C-section."

Once more, I went over the signs and symptoms of labor. I repeated to her that there was no indication to intervene in her pregnancy at this time. Finally, Macey agreed to the drug testing and stomped out of the exam room.

As I went to check the appointment tracking on my desk monitor, Jayda, the ambulatory obstetrics RN, stopped me with a look of sadness on her face. "Bad news for Kara. The ultrasound showed no fetal heart activity. The fetus stopped growing two weeks ago."

"Oh, no. Bring them to my office."

Kara was sobbing, just heartbroken. Garrett was blinking back tears but held himself in control and supported her.

"Why does this keep happening, Maeve? Was it something I did?" Kara asked.

"Kara, in most cases, early miscarriages happen because the embryo has a chromosomal abnormality. There is nothing you did to cause this. Nothing."

Kara started to sob silently. I held her hand and waited until she dried her eyes and looked up. "I'm so sorry, Kara and Garrett. Do you feel ready to talk about your options, or do you want to think about it overnight?"

"I just want this over," Kara insisted. "I remember the treatments you told us about from the last time. I want a D&C. I want the same as last time, and I want to be asleep. And please make sure they examine the baby to see if they can find out what went wrong?"

"Yes, we can arrange to have everything looked at by the pathologist," I assured her. "Let me call the scheduler and book a date for the surgery. I will have you sign the consents and have your blood work done today."

"I want this done as soon as possible, Maeve," Kara said. By sheer luck, there was a cancelation for early the next morning.

"Kara, remember. Nothing to eat or drink after midnight. You need to be in the pre-op area at five-thirty tomorrow morning."

"Who will do the D&C?" Garrett asked. A dilatation and curettage, or D&C, is a surgical procedure where the cervix is dilated so that a curette can remove tissue inside the uterus.

"Dr. Sofia Krebs. She is very experienced and extremely compassionate. You will meet her before the procedure. I think you will be happy with her."

"Okay," Kara said.

"I'll see you for a follow-up in a few weeks, and I'd like you to have a consultation with Dr. Beth Chisholm, one of the reproductive endocrinologists," I said.

"Why?" Garrett asked.

"Well, Garrett, I want to make sure we cover all the bases, and I think it would be helpful to get an expert opinion. Usually, we wait until a woman has had three miscarriages before a consultation, but Kara is thirty-six, and I don't want to waste valuable time." *My own ticking biological clock was also always on my mind.*

"That makes sense. Thanks, Maeve," he replied.

When I finally finished the paperwork and handed them written instructions, I hugged them both. Then I went to the main desk where Jayda was waiting for me.

"Next up is a gestational carrier named Elaine Colton," she told me. "She may have ruptured her membranes, and she's due tomorrow. You're seeing her for Dr. Lewin."

This was a new phenomenon we were seeing more frequently. Couples hired a woman, referred to as a gestational carrier, to have a baby for them. Eggs from the woman of the couple or donor eggs were used. Then pregnancy was achieved by using in-vitro fertilization and implanting the fertilized egg in the carrier.

I knocked on the exam room door. I saw Elaine, a thirty-six-year-old with long, dark hair and a pale complexion, on entering. Her face still showed some evidence of long-ago bouts of acne. She was dressed in bright fuchsia sweats and white Golden Goose sneakers. Next to her, a forty-something guy out of the pages of *GQ*, clad in Armani and with an earbud in his ear, was madly texting on his iPhone. He did not look up as Jayda and I entered.

"Hello, Elaine. I'm Maeve, one of the midwives. I'm seeing you for Dr. Lewin."

"Is Dr. Lewin ill?" blurted out the startled male model, I mean companion.

"Dr. Lewin is in the operating room," I told him, trying to be reassuring.

"Oh," he said, recovering his composure as well as his death grip on the iPhone.

I put out my hand. "I'm Maeve, and you are?"

"James Rostoni, one of the fathers. Austin is also in the OR in Boston, but he can be here as soon as we need him. And the videographer is on the way."

"Is Austin in the medical field?" I inquired. Elaine giggled.

"Yes," James confirmed. "He is a reconstructive surgeon in Boston."

I quickly realized that "Austin" was Dr. Austin Hedgewood, Boston's preeminent cosmetic plastic surgeon. He was a regular in the society pages and a generous contributor to many charity fundraisers. At fifty, he was tall, had a deeply tanned complexion, and was handsome in a way that led to rumors that he partook of his own wares.

"This child is Austin's and yours?" I inquired.

"Correct."

"Well, very nice to meet you." He gave me a quick nod as he began texting again. "How are you feeling, Elaine?"

"I'm fine, thank you. I think my water broke, but I'm not positive. You'd think I'd know by now."

"Sometimes it can be hard to tell. That's why we always want you to come in and be checked." I took a quick look at the chart and saw that this was baby number four for her. "Elaine, how were your other labors?"

"Well, the first two were my own, and I had them when I was fifteen and seventeen. I didn't know much then, but I don't remember having any problems. The last one was Austin and James's first baby. I had an epidermal. That labor was fine, about six hours."

"That's epidural, Elaine," James corrected.

"I meant epidural," Elaine said.

"I see he was born two years ago," I noted, still going through her record.

"We want our children to be close in age," James said.

"I see, and is this pregnancy using the same egg donor?"

"Yes. She's twenty-three and a Yale graduate. She's tall, blonde, and was a field hockey athlete."

Elaine lowered her eyes.

Well, between the egg donor's genes and Austin and James, this should be a designer baby. With Elaine as a proven gestational carrier, what more could they ask for? "First, let me check the baby's heartbeat." I picked up the doppler and held it to Elaine's abdomen. A rhythmic beat filled the room. "The baby sounds great," I said.

"Let me record it, please." James held his phone over Elaine's abdomen.

"Do you know what you're having?" I asked.

"This is Greer," James said. "His older brother is Lydon."

"James, would you please wait outside while I examine Elaine," I requested as I gave a slight nod toward the door.

"Please let me know the results immediately."

"Absolutely." I smiled as he closed the door. "Elaine, I'm going to check for amniotic fluid, and then I'll do a few tests. I'll explain everything as we go."

"That's fine," she replied.

I looked for signs of amniotic fluid and didn't see anything unusual. "Your cervix looks a bit open," I told her. "But I don't see any pooling of fluid in your vagina. Now let me do a few tests." I touched some nitrazine paper to her cervix, but it did not change color. This was a negative result.

"I'll just take a look under the microscope, but so far, everything looks fine," I let her know. When I was done, I looked up from the microscope. "All the tests for ruptured membranes are negative. Are you having any cramping?"

"Yes, on and off. I had contractions last night for about an hour."

"Okay, I'll do a quick exam of your cervix, Elaine."

She relaxed, and I completed the pelvic exam. Then I turned to Jayda. "You can let James know that Elaine hasn't ruptured her membranes, so Austin doesn't have to rush down from Boston."

Jayda nodded and left the exam room. "Call me if you need me," she said as she left.

"Elaine, you haven't ruptured your membranes, but your cervix is about two to three centimeters dilated."

"I feel so silly coming in to be checked."

"Elaine, you did exactly the right thing. It can be hard to tell if you ruptured your membranes, especially at the end of pregnancy. Remember, this is your fourth baby, so things can happen quickly. Here, let me help you sit up." I helped Elaine to an upright position and adjusted the table so she would be comfortable. "How has the pregnancy been?" I asked.

"Fine. Austin and James are wonderful people, and I have no blood connection to the babies, which makes it easier. James is a bit shy around new people, but they are both kind and wonderful parents."

"Well, that does sound nice," I agreed.

"It is a great situation for all of us."

"Is the postpartum time difficult?" I decided to probe a little further.

"Not really," she answered. "I'll supply breast milk for about six months."

"You are a huge part of the family," I acknowledged.

"They make me very welcome. Plus, it's great to watch the baby grow into a little person."

"What about your own children?"

She perked up considerably. "My oldest is in college. I'm so proud of her. She's going to be a lawyer," Elaine said, beaming. "My youngest is in the Navy and loves that life."

"Is it going to be hard to leave after you have the baby?"

"Well, they want three kids, so I'll be around for a few years." She picked up her Louis Vuitton purse. She noticed me looking at the tote and smiled.

"It's a gift from Austin and James. They gave it to me after Lydon was born."

I smiled back at her. "It's been very nice to meet you, Elaine. Remember to call with any signs of labor or if the baby's activity is decreased. I'll send Dr. Lewin an email about our visit."

"Thanks, Maeve. Nice to meet you."

Jayda entered the room again as Elaine left and raised an eyebrow. "I heard from the labor and delivery nurses that the baby gets handed straight to the fathers, and they rent out a postpartum room so that they have total access for bonding. On top of that, they have nannies and housekeepers, so I guess they plan to have perfect silver spoon kids."

"Money talks," I agreed. "But Elaine also told me they are wonderful, loving parents. She seems very happy with the arrangement." *It's a brave new world. This is the world of obstetrics today, with both new frontiers and old problems.*

CHAPTER SIX

Prenatal care aims to provide excellent care for women and their unborn children through education, surveillance, lab testing, and constant assessment.

I finished the morning session as Meg arrived.

"Cookies for the office and not made by Maeve," she trilled as she hugged Jayda and handed her a box of goodies.

Jayda peeked into the box and then fixed me with a sweet smile. "I'm not a traitor, Maeve, but these cookies do look delicious."

"Yup, eat those fabulous cookies," I laughed.

Today Meg was dressed in an ivory St. John knit, complemented by a black leather purse with a gold chain strap and three-inch black heels. As always, she looked smashing. She unpacked the tuna on dark rye, chips, lemonade, and more chocolate chunk cookies. Meg could eat all of this and never gain an ounce.

"If I ate like this every day, I'd never be able to zip my jeans again," I said.

"Come on, Maeve. You were a Division I rower in college. You look great and are always walking, biking, or rowing that weird boat of yours. All I do is an occasional spin class and a little yoga now and then," Meg said.

"It's called a shell," I reminded her.

"Whatever. It's strange looking. Remember that Aidan, our baby brother, and I take after Dad's side of the family. They're all tall and skinny." She closed the door and glanced around the office. "You really need to update the decor here, Maeve."

The midwife group had chosen primary-colored wall quilts on pale cream walls for our office. "Meg, I've told you a million times, we have to choose from the Creighton Memorial Design Committee's selections."

"Well, they need to come into this century. This must be from the Early Ugly Collection. Boring, boring, boring, but oh, so tasteful." She paused for a second before plunging ahead. "What's the word about the late Dr. Whitaker's department?"

"El Cid will be in charge for the time being."

"No surprise there. Do you think he will be named chief?"

I shrugged. "It's too early to tell. I hope not."

"Is Evelyn wearing widow's weeds?"

"No, although she does seem very sad. She's marching on and keeping a stiff upper lip," I said.

"I wonder if she will cozy up to El Cid now?"

"She seems to love power, so she might. However, she was unusually devoted to Dr. Whitaker. Who knows?"

"Listen up," Meg said, turning conspiratorial. "I have some hot-off-the-press gossip. It seems that the lovely Mrs. Whitaker has been stepping out on the good doctor."

"What?"

"Yep. My very trustworthy source says that Audrey Whitaker and James Zabalon—yes, *that* James Zabalon—are having a torrid affair. They were seen exiting XXI Back Bay, the ever-so-posh uptown hotel, in mutual embrace."

"They could have been at a function."

"At eleven in the morning?"

"A breakfast meeting?"

"Seriously, Maeve."

"Are you sure?" James Zabalon owned five Lexus dealerships in Boston and the surrounding suburbs. He was well known throughout the metro area because of an unending string of commercials starring himself.

"I'm working on my sources. If Mrs. Whitaker decides to exit Langford, the manse might be for sale."

"Real estate rules," I sighed.

"It's always about the Benjamins." This sounded like one of those scenarios you just couldn't make up, but I still had my misgivings. The chief of OB's wife with James Zabalon? Really?

"And there's more. Gwen Pellman, the interior designer at Zabalon's manse, said three weeks ago, Mrs. Whitaker was seen leaving after an afternoon delight at his estate."

"Wait, how could she know what they were doing there?"

"Well," Meg was practically purring now. "It seems that Mrs. Whitaker's signature, gold knot earring was found on the king-size bed coverlet in the primary suite. Gwen noticed it when she checked the color against the silk swatch that she brought for the new window treatments."

"Many women wear gold knot earrings," I pointed out.

"Not ones with her initials carved into the knot."

"Oh."

"Now that's profound, Maeve."

"But why would she cheat on Dr. Whitaker?" I wondered.

"Well, for one thing, I heard he was very controlling. She couldn't even change her hairstyle without his permission."

"Come on."

"Yes, and he hounded her about her weight," she added.

"How could he complain about her weight?" I protested. "She looks like she's never had a slice of bacon, not to mention four children."

"He kept a tight rein on both her and the kids. They went to the schools he selected and only dated people he deemed acceptable," Meg said.

"Seriously?" I asked incredulously.

"He even had to have the final say on the house decor."

"Well, I guess you never know what goes on inside a marriage."

"Just full of sage wisdom today, aren't you, Maeve."

My phone began to vibrate. "Hey, Will's calling. Hold on." I picked up my cell phone. "Hi, honey."

"Hi, Maeve." I could hear the tension in his voice.

"What's wrong?"

"The police have called in one of the wait staff for further questioning."

"Why?" I asked as Meg motioned for me to put the call on speakerphone. "Meg is here, Will. You're on speaker."

"Hi, Meg," he said.

"Hi, Will."

He went on. "Apparently, Dr. Whitaker did die from an acute allergic reaction to peanuts."

"The autopsy results are back?" Meg asked.

"The early allergy testing is back," he explained. "The police are keeping it under wraps for now."

"What do they think happened?" I asked.

"Well, we knew about his and Charlotte's severe allergy to nuts, so we were scrupulous about safeguarding the food and drink. The menu was nut-free. It appears that somehow peanuts were added to his champagne."

"Wait," I interjected. "Dr. Whitaker and Charlotte both had nut allergies?"

"Yes. We went over that fact many times with Mrs. Whitaker when we were in the planning stages."

"Do the police think it was intentional?" I asked.

"Who knows? They're not saying."

"Could it be possible that he was murdered at his daughter's wedding?"

"I don't know, Maeve. But if he was, someone used A Thyme for All Seasons to accomplish the act."

"This cannot be happening." Will was silent on the other end.

"Peanuts? Wouldn't he have seen them?" Meg asked.

"They think peanut oil was used. It would only take a very tiny amount because his allergy was so severe."

"That's awful," I said.

"Also, his EpiPen was defective," Will said.

"I'd been wondering about that. Did they find it?" I asked.

"They found part of it. The mechanism looks faulty. They found a partial serial number, and they are checking to see if it was part of a recall."

"There *was* a recall of EpiPens not that long ago. I had to write new prescriptions for some of our patients to replace their defective ones," I said. "Surely Dr. Whitaker would have checked his EpiPen against the recall list."

"Something went very wrong then," Will said.

"Who was called in by the police?" Meg asked.

"Kevin Reardon."

I almost dropped the phone. "Oh, no! Not Kevin!"

"Pete Reardon's grandson?" Meg asked, turning to me. Before I could explain, Will continued.

"Yes, and it turns out he's an old beau of Charlotte's. The relationship ended after Dr. Whitaker let it be known he did not have the proper social standing." He was silent for a moment. "There was much ill will between them. He knew about Dr. Whitaker's peanut allergy, and they think he might have tampered with his champagne."

That didn't sound right to me. "How would Kevin know which flute to lace with the oil? And how could he even get it to Dr. Whitaker?" I asked.

"There was a small tray for the head table," Will explained. "I had originally assigned Kevin to serve the back tables, but because it was a special toast and we needed to present the champagne on time, Kevin ended up with the tray for Dr. and Mrs. Whitaker and Charlotte and Brooks."

"So he had opportunity," I said.

"He did. The police seem to be suggesting he added peanut oil to the champagne, but I told them it was already poured when the wait staff picked the trays up."

"How could he add it without being seen?" Meg asked.

"I don't know," Will said. "I didn't even know he used to date Charlotte. He never said anything about it to me. I certainly didn't want to cause any ill feelings on Charlotte's wedding day. If I had known about their prior relationship, I would have told him to sit this event out and join us for the next one. But that aside, I just can't believe he would try to harm anyone."

"Will, I feel terrible," I put in. "I was the one who encouraged you to hire Kevin."

"I hate to rush off, honey, but please stop worrying about that. I interviewed him and made up my mind. I need to run now, but I wanted to fill you in on what's been happening."

I sighed heavily into the phone.

"No guilt about Kevin, please," Will continued. "I don't think he had anything to do with this affair, even though I honestly don't know how this happened. Hopefully, it turns out to be a giant mistake. Got to run now. Bye, honey. Bye, Meg."

"Bye," I replied. "Love you."

"Bye, Will," Meg said as he hung up. Then she looked directly at me with eyes of steel. "Please tell me that you did not ask Will to hire one of the Reardon clan because of Dad's funeral."

"Meg, wait. Before you start on me…"

"Maeve, that is ancient history."

I thought back to my childhood when my dad helped Pete Reardon get his funeral home up and running, working on weekends and nights. *My dad was my hero. Always working for a better life for us. Always helping a friend.*

"Meg, remember when Dad died—we were all still teenagers— and he had no life insurance. Seriously, I don't know how Mom coped. Mr. Reardon provided the funeral for free because Mom didn't have the money. It meant so much to her."

"Maeve, it was a very nice gesture. But we don't owe the Reardon family into perpetuity."

"It was a huge deal back then," I reminded her. "Kevin is Mr. Reardon's grandson. Mom told me several weeks ago that he was looking for temporary work, and I knew Will needed help. I thought it was a win-win. I didn't know he had any connection to the Whitakers."

"You're a better man than I am, Gunga Din."

I sighed and took a bite of a cookie. It was delicious.

"Tell me, why bake when you can buy that?" Meg asked me.

I stuck my tongue out at her.

"That's a lovely look for you, Maeve. Very professional."

I decided to ignore her. "Poor Kevin. He must be so upset."

"Poor Kevin? He might be a murderer, Maeve! In case you have forgotten so quickly, Dr. Whitaker's flute had peanut oil in it, and Kevin served him."

"Will said the champagne was already poured," I pointed out.

"Yeah, but the peanut oil had to get into the flute," Meg retorted. "Who else had access? Kevin put the flute at Dr. Whitaker's table setting."

"But why hurt Dr. Whitaker? And why kill him at his daughter's wedding? There had to be easier venues, right? Did he want to ruin Charlotte's day?"

"That sounds like a severe case of revenge."

Pressing ahead, I posed the next obvious question. "If Kevin was so unhinged, why not go right to the source and kill Charlotte?"

"You mean if he couldn't have her, why should anyone?" We were both silent for a few minutes. Then Meg pointed out, "It also could have been Mrs. Whitaker."

"What?" I almost dropped my cookie in surprise.

"Well, isn't it just too convenient?" Meg mused. "With Dr. Whitaker out of the way, she is both wealthy and free."

"You think she would commit murder at her own daughter's wedding?"

Meg nodded. "It's possible."

"Possible," I agreed, "but highly unlikely. She would have to truly hate her daughter to do that on her wedding day."

"People can convince themselves of nearly anything when it suits their needs. You have to admit she would have the perfect alibi."

"Then there is the defective EpiPen," I pointed out. "We used to poke fun at Dr. Whitaker's obsession with detail, but I can't believe that checking his EpiPen serial numbers wouldn't have been at the top of his list."

"As Alice would say," Meg agreed, "Curiouser and curiouser."

"I have to start my afternoon session," I announced. "Thanks for lunch and the fabulous cookie. I'll see you later. Oh, and call Mom."

Meg grimaced as she applied Chanel's iconic Pirate lipstick and began gathering her bag. "This will be a hectic week."

I glanced at my computer calendar. "Hey, a notice just came announcing that Dr. Whitaker's memorial service is Friday at ten a.m."

"Friday? Okay. I'll rearrange my schedule because I'm not missing that show. It will be the biggest ticket in town."

"A little respect, Meg?"

"What? I want to see the flowers, the fashions, and hear the adoring eulogies."

"Meg, really?"

"Come on, Maeve. Funerals bring out the best cast of characters. Plus, we can check out how people react. Maybe we'll spot the real murderer."

"You have been watching too much *Law and Order*."

"Ha. I'll see you there," she said, turning with a wave over her shoulder. "Remember, we also have a family dinner at Olivia and Patrick's this weekend."

And with that, she was off in a cloud of Chanel No. 5.

I sat at my desk in a funk. *First Will, now Kevin. What have I done? Would Will be blamed? Would his business recover? Is Kevin capable of murder?* I looked out the window, down the lawn to the sea. Usually, it calmed me, but today it had no effect. Jayda picked that moment to walk into the office with a frown on her face. "What?" I asked.

"I sent Macey's urine toxicology screen STAT. It's positive for opioids."

"Perfect," I said. "Just perfect."

CHAPTER SEVEN

Linea nigra (or "black Line" in Latin) is a dark vertical line that appears on the abdomen in many pregnancies.

Late that afternoon, I drove up to our charming carriage house, named Primrose Cottage. *Didn't every house have a name?*

Even after three years, the sight of it still took my breath away. It was set back on Seal Cove Way with a stone arch entryway and a drive that meandered through sweeping gardens of hydrangeas, daylilies, and beach roses. Seen up close, the three-bedroom stone dwelling with a small but lovely ocean view was the embodiment of charm.

About a quarter-mile farther down the drive, Will's grandmother lived in Seacrest, a six-thousand-square-foot, gray shingled and turreted Nantucket Colonial directly overlooking the ocean. On his twenty-fifth birthday, she had deeded Will the carriage house, tastefully remodeled and furnished. I often thought that she secretly loved that he did not join the family business but instead took a risk and followed his passion.

The carriage house and two acres of land were legally separated from the main house and had total privacy. But the best part, and the one I secretly felt luckiest about, was that Grandmother Kensington's devoted legion of gardeners maintained the grounds.

I pulled up to the house and saw Will's red pickup sitting in the driveway. As I opened the door, Fenway, always faithful, was there to greet me.

"Hey, Fen, is your daddy home?" I picked her up. She immediately began to lick my face and neck.

"Fenway, please stop licking. Don't you ever get tired of it?" Fenway looked at me with soulful eyes and then tentatively reached out her tongue to my neck.

"Oh, go ahead," I said, giving in.

As Fenway wiggled with pleasure, I was suddenly aware that my husband was standing in the kitchen, patiently waiting for me to notice his presence.

"Hey, honey, I just stopped to grab a folder I brought home last night. I put some pasta seafood salad in the fridge for your lunch tomorrow."

I put Fenway down. "Thank you so much, Will."

"Come. Sit. Taste. You've been working hard," he said, kissing my cheek. He took a beautiful bowl of shells, shrimp, peas, and small slices of peppers, both yellow and red, out of the fridge. The mixture was lightly seasoned with olive oil, basil, and lemon juice. Will put a small scoop on a spoon for me. "It's a new recipe we're trying."

I took a bite. "It's magnificent."

"I think it needs a bit more basil, but it's almost there."

"Will it go on the summer menu?"

"Maybe. I'll ask the staff to taste it and get their reviews."

"Will you be home late tonight?" I asked him. I knew he was catering an event at the Norberg Library, about twenty miles away.

"Not too late," he sighed. "It's a buffet and should wrap up by 9 p.m."

"Are you worried?" I asked, holding his hands.

"You know me so well. And yes. After the wedding nightmare, I just want everything to go perfectly."

"How can it not be fabulous? You've got this," I assured him.

He smiled and kissed my cheek. "I'll give you a call on my way home."

"I'm going to take Mom out for her beloved fish and chips."

His big brown eyes registered concern. "Will you be alright?"

"Oh, you know Mom. I'll hear all the news about Hanville. She'll tell me who is having babies, who died, whose kids are—"

"You know what I mean. Will you be okay hearing about who's expecting?"

I looked at him. "I'll be fine, honey. Don't worry."

He leaned down and gently kissed me. "You are my North Star, Maeve."

"And you're mine."

"Are you going to book an appointment for us with Dr. Chisholm?"

I had put off calling for an appointment with the reproductive fertility specialist for months. I kept hoping that I would not be a fertility patient, but time and my mother's persistent questions had brought me to face reality. "Yes. Yes, I am."

"We'll do this together, love," Will said.

"I know, honey." I smiled back as best I could.

"I'm off to the races," Will said as he kissed me goodbye.

"Bye, Will. Love you."

"Love you, too."

I looked at Fenway, perched by my feet and looking at me expectantly. "All right, Fenway. But I can't let you get too chubby. I have to protect that back of yours."

Dachshunds are prone to disc herniation because of their long backs and short legs. Avoiding pressure on a dachshund's back and keeping their weight in check helped to prevent this complication. I put three shells and a shrimp in her dish. "Now be good."

I changed into jeans and a tired but well-loved blue, shawl-collared sweater and went to pick up Mom. The Hanville Grove Senior Residence where my mother lived had served as a munition factory during World War II and later became a candy warehouse. After filling those purposes, the building had been transformed into a living complex that, owing to its location, had its share of quirks as a home for seniors. Rent was on a sliding scale tied to each resident's income. Planned gardens surrounded its eight floors of red brick with inviting patios that gave the residents scenic views of Hanville Bay. Scenic, that is, if you overlooked the notorious Lincoln Expressway, or the more commonly invoked "Distressway," as locals called it. Overhead, planes going to and from Boston's Logan Airport provided a periodic sonic backdrop for the senior citizens' conversations.

But even with these minor inconveniences, the Hanville Grove was well appreciated by those who called it home. Repurposing the old industrial building resulted in relatively spacious one- and two-bedroom apartments, each with a small balcony. The entire compound was immaculately kept and affiliated with the neighboring upscale Hanville Grove Assisted Living Center and Nursing Home, thus providing continuity of care for the residents whose needs increased. Well, at least it did for the wealthy residents.

I pressed the entry buzzer. As I looked through the glass door, I saw my mother animatedly talking with the group I had come to think of as "the ladies of the lobby." The closest one got up and held the door open for me.

"Hi, Mom. Hello, everyone."

Mary Margaret Callahan O'Reilly was my mother. Widowed young, she had been disabled with arthritis and severe asthma since her fifties. You could say she was a survivor, but she was more a force of nature, like a tsunami.

"Hello, Maeve." Ethel, a vibrant ninety-year-old, beamed at me. "You're looking great."

"I'm praying for you," whispered Gaby, short for Gabrielle, a large-boned woman originally from Jamaica.

Oh, great, I thought. *Now I'm on the baby prayer list.*

Mom was in her wheelchair, decked out in her gold charm necklace and new pink paisley scarf over a rose sequined top. She was the oldest of fourteen children and loved family, friends, animals, the oppressed, all things Irish, St. Jude, the Red Sox, and a good party, or time, as she called it. She had the gift of gab and loved nothing better than to be heading out anywhere with one of her progeny. With evident pride, she said, "I told the girls that Will is catering our 'Hello, Summer' luncheon."

"I know, Mom, and he's thrilled."

"He's a wonderful chef, my Will," she said, and the entire group of ladies nodded in agreement.

I got behind her wheelchair and started moving her toward the door. "Bye, girls," she said, waving to the group.

"See you later."

"Bye, Mary," Ethel replied. "Have a nice dinner with Maeve."

As we drove out of the parking lot, Mom said, "Maeve, I need to stop at the 7-Eleven to get some Scratchers."

"Mom, please don't. You never win. The lottery is just a waste of money."

"Don't tell me what to spend my money on, Maeve. I do win. I won one hundred dollars once."

I didn't remind her that it was five years and hundreds of two-dollar tickets ago. "I just don't want you to—"

"Maeve, I have been a widow since I was fifty-one. I have been using a walker and a wheelchair since I was fifty-three. I gave up my house, and I can't drive. I will not give up this little bit of fun."

"Sorry I said anything, Mom."

"Besides, as the commercial says, you can't win if you don't play," she added with a satisfied grin.

I parked in front of the convenience store and got the tickets. For a while, all was quiet while Mom scratched away.

"Darn lottery," she finally said. "I think they're skimping on the prizes. Well, maybe next week."

I knew when to hold my tongue. "Where should we go to eat, Mom?" I asked.

"Let's go to Finnegan's on the corner," she decided. I wasn't surprised. We always went to Finnegan's. Over dinners of haddock and chips, we discussed the family.

"First of all, tell me how you and Will are, Maeve."

"Oh, Mom." Tears formed in my eyes.

Mom reached across the small table and stroked my hands. "Maeve. Will is blameless. You will see. Somebody wanted that doctor to die. Now, you just hang in there. You and Will are so strong, and I'm praying to St. Jude."

Hm, St. Jude, the patron saint of hopeless cases. Okay. I quickly changed the subject.

"Are Patrick and the girls coming to visit tomorrow?" I asked. Patrick had been married to the always quirky Olivia, a graphic designer, for the past eight years. They had four charming little girls.

"Yes," she replied, not entirely concealing an edge of concern. "The older girls have no school and Olivia has a project due at noon, so Patrick will have the kids in the morning, and then he's off to the station. He's so busy with the Whitaker mess. I know he'll solve the case, but I worry that he works too hard."

"What do you have planned?" I asked.

"I thought we could go to the park. It will be fun."

"It sounds like a great idea," I agreed. "What about Aidan and Sebi?"

Aidan was the baby of the family. He and his husband Sebastian, or Sebi, lived about twenty minutes away in Boxwood with their beautiful daughter, Chloe. Sebi was an architect/builder who had designed and built their home in their favorite style, old Victorian, but with every modern convenience. Aidan had been an elementary school teacher and now had a successful career writing a series of children's books.

"He and Sebastian and Chloe are going to a friend's house in Ogunquit for the weekend," she replied. "Oh, did I tell you that they are taking me to see *Hello, Dolly!* on Broadway?" Mom was suddenly beaming.

"That's wonderful! You will love that!"

"I can't wait. I just love Bette Midler. She is divine and looks amazing. This will be the third time I've seen her perform but first time on Broadway." She stopped and gave a little sigh. "Bette Midler and Broadway. It's just a dream ticket."

Once again, I thought about the fantastic transformation Mom had made. There was weeping and gnashing of teeth the day Aidan came out. Now it was Broadway shows with him and the beloved son-in-law. "You love Sebastian," I said with a smile.

"I do, Maeve. Patrick and Aidan are my boys, and I love them both, but with them, it's sports, sports, and more sports. I love sports, too, but I also read the Arts section of the *New York Times* first thing every Sunday. And Sebastian loves musicals, plays, and ballet. He is a blessing to me. We go to great shows while Aidan minds little Chloe. Then the next night, I get to babysit her so that they can go on a dinner date. It's perfect."

A miracle in my own time, I thought to myself.

I ate my haddock and smiled. There was no subject Mom feared to weigh in on, ever. And as usual, when we were finished with our meal, Mom insisted on treating me and left a generous tip.

On the way back to her apartment, Mom decided we should stop at Bargain Alley. By the time she was done, the car was filled with bubbles, books, crayons, candy, puzzles, and assorted stuffed animals. "Mom, I think this load will hold the girls for a few hours," I said. I was also pretty sure Olivia would just toss everything out when the girls returned home.

"I hope so. I just want them to have a few treats. Olivia won't let them have a sweet, and all their toys must be made of wood. But when they come to Grandma's, they get spoiled," she said, smiling. "Besides, Patrick doesn't mind."

I knew better than to weigh in on her logic.

We pulled into Mom's lot and parked the car. I helped Mom into her chair and loaded some of the packages onto her lap and some into the basket attached to the back of the chair. The lobby was bustling with residents coming and going. Mom quickly joined a group of women in the sitting area.

"Be right back, Mom," I told her. "I'll get everything put away."

I placed her haul onto one of the handy carts the residents used for transporting groceries to their apartments. I knew Mom would love telling her friends about her outing in great detail, so I slowly unpacked and then returned to get her.

"I like your sweater, Maeve," Gaby said when I returned to the lobby. She wore a red plaid cotton mid-thigh skirt and a lemon yellow blouse with a large bow.

"Did you get it at Macy's?" asked Dorothy, a woman in her eighties dressed in a hot pink sweater with padded shoulders and a basket of kittens on the front. Magenta sweatpants, black patent sandals, and too much makeup completed her look.

Hmm, I thought. *If these fashion advisers like my look, I might need a new wardrobe.*

By the time I got Mom upstairs and settled in her electric reclining chair and made her a cup of tea, she had her TV tuned to the security camera channel. It gave a twenty-four hour view of the lobby to any resident who wanted to watch. "Look." Mom pointed to the screen. "There's Gloria and Annie coming back from the casino trip."

"Mom, why watch that instead of TV?" I asked, even though I knew the answer.

"I love it, Maeve. I get to see everyone. It makes me feel so connected to the entire community."

"But you can't talk to them," I pointed out.

"You can see who went on what trips, whose kids come by for a visit, and who gets taken out by ambulance. And you can see if anyone comes into the building that shouldn't be here. It's a perfect system."

It's also a cheap senior security force, I thought. "I'm going to take off, Mom," I told her.

"Goodbye, Maeve. Love you. Thanks for dinner."

"Mom, you paid."

"Oh, stop." She waved her hand to quiet me. "I love seeing you. Please say hello to Meg when you see her and tell her to bring my grandson Henry by. Stop worrying about Will. He will be fine. I'm praying for him. I'm praying for both of you."

Hm, no questions about a possible pregnancy tonight. She must be worried about Will's future. I smiled and kissed her goodbye. On the way out of the lobby, I stopped and waved goodbye to the camera.

CHAPTER EIGHT

Quickening refers to the first fetal movements felt by the mother.

      For the next few days, sleep did not come easy. Dreams of my father, Kevin, and Will woke me every few hours. In one, Will fell off a cliff. In another, my father was in a terrible car crash, and Kevin Reardon was driving the car.
      On Thursday morning, I took Fenway for a long walk on the beach and then stopped in to see Grand, Will's grandmother, for a cup of tea, per her invitation.
      "Good morning, Grand," I called out, waving as I came through the door.
      "Hello, Maeve. I see you brought your lovely pup. Nora will have a nice, juicy bone for you, Fenway." Nora was Grand's live-in cook and companion of many years. "Nora, dear. Look who's here."
      "Hello, Maeve, and hello to you, too, little Fenway," Nora said as she scooped up the dachshund. "You come along with me, mighty mouse." Fenway squealed with joy and began licking Nora's face furiously as they went off.
      "Come and have some tea, Maeve."
      Tea was served in delicate bone china cups and saucers on the veranda, set on a snowy white, embroidered linen tablecloth. Matching napkins lay beside the china plates. Just some of the many family heirlooms in daily use around the place. Earl Grey tea, freshly squeezed orange juice, fruit salad, blueberry scones, and home-baked corn muffins with Trappist Preserves orange marmalade were set out on vintage, white wicker. Dozens of dark purple lilacs in crystal pitchers adorned the enclosed veranda overlooking Langford harbor. I smiled with contentment. Now *this* was tea.

I took a bite of a blueberry scone. It was delicious! Nora was, indeed, an excellent baker.

Grand settled back in her chair and met my gaze. "Is Will exhausted?" she inquired, with just a hint of concern.

"He's doing alright," I said.

Grand smiled. "I am so proud of him, following his passion. That takes a strong backbone in this family."

I silently wondered if Grand had some unfulfilled dreams. Women of her age tended to, as they had not had a wide choice of occupations.

"The police will get to the bottom of this vile business, Maeve. I know it's difficult but try to think good thoughts and carry on."

Grand would have made a good midwife.

"Now tell me about the latest news from the hospital," Grand said. Grand was a trustee of Creighton Memorial. She loved to hear tales of internal politics, although she always seemed to know more than I did.

"Well, as you know, El Cid…I mean, Dr. Cydson has been named acting chair," I began.

I saw a slight smirk on her face. "He is a very ambitious man," she allowed.

"Clinically, he is excellent," I countered.

"Yes, but leadership takes vision and integrity. What about Dr. Patel?"

"He's wonderful!" I blurted out. Sanjay Patel had been with Creighton Memorial since finishing his fellowship in Boston. He was highly competent, charming, and outgoing, and the clear choice of the nursing and midwifery staff. On top of that, his wife, Dr. Betty Li, was a phenomenal vascular surgeon. If he ever decided to leave, we would lose both.

"Yes, that's what I hear, too." She seemed lost in thought for a moment but then said, "How is the midwifery practice doing?"

"Very well," I told her. "We have the volume to add another midwife."

"I hear the *Langford Times* is going to start a new column called *Ask the Midwife*."

"It's going to start next month," I agreed. "We're all very excited about it. We'll address a different topic each week and answer questions."

"I am so happy to hear that the practice is thriving. Women need a say in their reproductive care. I was opposed to midwives in the past, but, luckily, I was outvoted. Since the practice began at Creighton, I have seen all the wonderful care and personal touches you offer. Now tell me about your family."

I was going through the list when Nora came bustling back, still carrying a delighted Fenway. "Come now, Mrs. K. It's time for your weekly hair appointment. Oscar is waiting to drive you." Oscar was Grand's live-in house manager and Nora's husband. She handed Fenway over to me. "Goodbye, Maeve. And you, too, little miss. Oh, and Maeve, Fenway might not need dinner tonight."

Grand gave me a big smile and a hug. "Goodbye, Maeve. Remember, chin up and keep the faith."

I had to smile. "Goodbye, Grand. Thank you for tea."

On Friday morning, I stumbled bleary-eyed out of bed at seven. Will had already left for work, but I hardly remembered him kissing me goodbye.

After a long and very hot shower, I still felt barely alive as I struggled to prepare myself for the day ahead. Funerals were so draining, especially when murder was involved. Twice I sat on the overstuffed lounge chair in our bedroom and tried to do a ten-minute meditation, but I couldn't go longer than two minutes.

I tried to tame my hair but then gave up and went with the default high ponytail. It was not the look I was going for, but it would have to do.

"Goodbye, Fenway." I patted her long brown back. "See you later." She looked at me, huffed, and turned away to sleep on her favorite pillow. Even my dog disapproved of my fashion sense.

Surprisingly, Dunkin's drive-thru was empty as I pulled up to the window and ordered a large hot coffee, heavy on the cream and sugar. Then I drove and sipped, hoping the caffeine would kick in soon. My head was swimming.

In order for most of the Creighton staff to attend Dr. Whitaker's memorial service, moonlighters from other hospitals had been hired to care for the patients for the day. No expense had been spared for this send off. The weather was cloudy and overcast, almost as if the skies were mourning Dr. Whitaker's passing. Of course, the weather would again comply with the script.

St. Andrew's parking lot was filled. This time the colors were subdued, with black Mercedes, BMWs, and Lexuses being the order of the day.

Six large limos were just turning into the circle in front of the church as I entered the side door. I slid into a back pew beside Meg, Madeline, and Winnie as once again there was a full house. Bev and John were in the pew directly in front of us. On the altar, I saw two giant gold vases of white calla lilies flanking a massive oil painting of Dr. Whitaker. There was a golden urn in the center of the altar.

"In the nick of time," Meg said.

Meg was in a black Armani linen suit with a smattering of gold. Madeline and Bev both wore black silk pantsuits. Winnie wore a black kimono-style jacket over a knit skirt with a white-and-black polka-dot scarf. And I was in my standard summer funeral garb, a fitted black gabardine jacket and knife-pleated skirt. I had added my gold locket and a lily of the valley pin Will had given me as a slight upgrade. Together, we were the Women in Black. Maybe we couldn't fight evil extraterrestrials, but we could slay East Coast funerals.

Growing up in a large Irish-Catholic family led to many 'death dates,' as Meg referred to them. I had a similar black wool jacket and skirt suitable for mourning in colder weather. I was always ready to view the dead at a moment's notice and in any season.

I picked up and read the engraved, cream-colored heavyweight card from the pew: *Memorial Service for L. Harrison Whitaker, MD*.

I quickly scanned down and saw that Simon Peters, Chad Whitaker, and Dr. Cydson were doing readings or giving tributes. I realized without surprise that there were no women speakers on the program. Apparently, only men were allowed to speak on such a solemn occasion. I turned the card over. On the back was Robert Frost's poem, "The Road Not Taken."

Just then, the choir began to sing as Mrs. Whitaker entered the church on the arm of Chad, her oldest son. She was in a black linen Ralph Lauren coat dress adorned with large white buttons. Her head and face were covered by a large black brimmed hat and oversized sunglasses, and she clutched a white linen handkerchief trimmed with lace in her hand.

"Where are the veil and the pillbox? She'll let Jackie O down," whispered Meg.

The two other Whitaker boys filed in along with their glamorous wives. They were followed by three grandsons clad in white linen shorts and navy blazers and two granddaughters in navy smocked dresses with white berets. They were the quintessential picture of an upper-crust New England family at their somber best. Finally, Charlotte walked down the aisle, looking ghostly pale in a black Dior suit and oversized tortoiseshell sunglasses with her hair immaculate in a tight twist. Brooks held her by the arm and waist. Assorted friends and relatives followed her.

Simon Peters, the CEO of Creighton Memorial, went to the pulpit. After a very long moment of silence, he began. "On behalf of Mrs. Whitaker and the family, I welcome you to the memorial service for Dr. Livingston Harrison Whitaker. He was a gifted physician, a loving husband, and a devoted father. Dr. Whitaker came to Creighton Memorial as a young physician, just out of his fellowship."

Knowing that Simon loved an audience, and especially a captive one, I figured he would go on forever, and so I tuned out and took time to study the crowd. Evelyn Greyson was sitting on the right side of the aisle, her standard navy suit now changed to black. She sat ramrod straight and nodded in agreement with Simon, steadily holding back tears. She truly had worshipped Dr. Whitaker.

Dr. Cydson and the other senior physicians were sitting in the front pews opposite the Whitaker family. An overflow crowd was standing on the lawn listening to speakers that had been set up. The massive wooden doors had been left open.

The program proceeded along, and I soon realized that Reverend Mathers had already read the gospel and probably blessed everyone yet again. The final stanza of "Abide with Me" ended as El Cid made his way to the podium. He was dressed in a navy suit and red power tie.

"Trying to look presidential," Madeline said quietly.

"Smarmy little man," Meg sniffed.

"Quiet!" Winnie hissed.

"Dr. Harrison Whitaker was my mentor. I thought the world of him," Cydson began and then stopped.

"Oh, no, he's going to cry," I said.

"I...I...I shall do everything to continue his legacy and..." He began to sob heavily. Chad Whitaker rushed over, but Cydson waved him off. "I...I...," he started but again burst into tears. Chad took his arm and helped him to his seat.

Dr. Patel came up and finished reading El Cid's remarks, which were as expected. Then we all rose to sing "Jerusalem," Dr. Whitaker's favorite hymn.

The end of the service was awkward and felt abrupt. There was a sense of leaving without the beloved, accompanied as always by the feeling of uncertainty about the future. The family filed out as we all stood. Charlotte was visibly crying and shaking. Mrs. Whitaker's face was stony and pale. Evelyn Greyson marched down the aisle in her usual rigid posture, looking straight ahead. If she cried, it would not be in public.

Outside, the Whitaker family climbed into the waiting limos and headed to the reception. Dr. Whitaker's ashes would later be scattered on the bay in a private family ceremony.

As we reached the lawn, the sun broke out as if on cue.

"The family invites everyone to The Country Club for refreshments," Madeline said.

"Isn't that a bit macabre, going back to the scene of the crime?" Meg mused.

"We have to put in an appearance," I pointed out.

"And I want to see the decorations, I mean the family," Winnie said.

"Are you still upset about not getting a wedding centerpiece?" Madeline asked.

"Hush, Madeline," Winnie responded.

"Maeve, drive with me," Meg said.

I waved to Madeline and Winnie. "I'll see you there."

"I hate funerals," Meg grumbled on the way to the car.

"I thought you wanted to come."

"No, I wanted to see the family, but this is very depressing."

"Is any funeral pleasant?"

"I mean the platitudes and all the pomp. Really." Meg blew a kiss across the parking lot to one of her real estate agent cronies. "Tell people what you think of them when they're alive.

As Mom always says, 'Don't bring me flowers when I'm dead. I won't be able to see them.'"

"Funerals are for the living, Meg."

"Obviously."

"The family *was* well turned out," I observed, trying to steer Meg away from her thoughts.

"Well, they have the money as well as plenty of caretakers. They only had to get dressed."

"They did seem devastated," I pointed out.

"Maeve, these people can cry on cue. Everything about them is for public display."

"What's got into you?"

"Maybe it's just too many funerals," she sighed. "Or maybe it's because this was a murder, and Kevin may or may not be innocent. It just got under my skin."

"Do you want to skip the reception?" I offered.

"Not on your life." She pushed the starter, and her Jaguar roared to life. "I'll drop you back here afterward to pick up your car."

"Perfect."

The Country Club decor was subdued but elegant. Starched white linen tablecloths covered all the serving and guest tables. White orchids in antique, white-and-blue porcelain vases lined the grand foyer. Around the ballroom, each table held a silver vase containing calla lilies. At the front of the room, two large tables displayed numerous silver-framed photos of Dr. Whitaker and his family, as well as many of his academic awards.

The buffet table was set to one side with gleaming silver trays over warming pans. Will had not been asked to cater. The Country Club kitchen and wait staff were handling the brunch.

"Well, this is appetizing—burnt bacon, overdone scrambled eggs or egg product, canned fruit cocktail, toasted white bread, and coffee that looks like mud. Typical generic catered food, lousy and not enough," Meg said.

"Quiet," I whispered. "Let's go through the receiving line."

Dr. Whitaker's elegant urn was placed on a front table with a remembrance book to sign. The entire Whitaker clan flanked the west side of the ballroom. Lined up, they looked like a small army. Meg and I made our way through the line shaking hands and offering condolences. In return, all the children and extended family warmly thanked us for coming in a display of impeccable manners.

Mrs. Whitaker was the last in line, and I paused as I came up to her. Up close, she was a beauty. She had a glowing complexion, lustrous dark brown hair, and amazing violet eyes that caused me to stare a moment too long. She smiled and waited for me to introduce myself.

"I'm Maeve Kensington, one of the midwives. I'm so sorry for your loss."

"Will's wife," she stammered in surprise, momentarily forgetting her trademark poise. Then Mrs. Whitaker's posture stiffened as she paused and composed herself. "Thank you for coming."

She suddenly took my hand to shake, and I heard a gentle ringing. Looking down, I noticed a large gold charm bracelet on her right wrist. "What a beautiful bracelet," I said.

"Harrison gave me a charm for the birth of each of our children and also when we traveled. It is very, very dear to me." She fingered a gold stork with a pink bundle as she said this. "This one was for Charlotte's birth," she said in a half-whisper.

"How special. It's lovely," I said.

Her eyes narrowed and then quickly moved on to the next person in line. I moved along as well. I had the distinct feeling that Mrs. Whitaker held Will liable for her husband's demise.

CHAPTER NINE

At approximately twelve weeks of pregnancy, the uterus has enlarged enough to be palpated above the pubic symphysis.

Meg was standing on the veranda, which overlooked Oyster Cove. "Well, he was planted in grand fashion," she declared.

"Waked and baked, but not planted," I pointed out.

Meg smiled at me. Our funeral humor was weak, but it never got old. At least not to us.

"Mrs. Whitaker is beautiful," I mentioned. "She looks so young."

"You mean well-kept," Meg retorted. "And remember, she's never had to work a day in her life."

"I think she holds Will responsible."

"Ridiculous," Meg said.

"Still, I do feel sorry for her. Losing her husband that way."

"It's all for show. I'm telling you she is having an affair," Meg said.

I realized I had to cajole Meg out of this mood. "Hungry?" I asked.

"Not really, but let's at least get coffee and mingle."

The buffet was dismal. I got a cup of coffee heavy with cream and sugar and the least-burnt piece of toast I could find. Meg and I sat with Winnie and Madeline to watch the receiving line make its slow progress. Winnie had filled a plate and was happily eating. Madeline had coffee.

"This cannot hold a candle to Will's catering, Maeve," Madeline declared. "I love coffee, but even I can't drink this."

Winnie gave the three of us a scolding look. "I've had worse. Plus, it would be rude not to eat."

"I don't often have an appetite after a funeral, Winnie," Meg said.

"Funerals help me remember I'm alive, so I treat myself," Winnie replied, taking a big bite of fruit cocktail.

"Well, enjoy too much of this food, and you might be treating yourself to a few Tums tonight," Madeline said with a bit of a smirk.

"Look at the text from Bev." Madeline held up her phone: *Is this food? Seriously sad.*

I looked up to see Bev rolling her eyes while taking in the buffet table.

Then we all watched Evelyn Greyson navigate the receiving line. She hugged each family member but was especially solicitous to Charlotte. Evelyn patted Charlotte's back and wiped away tears as she spoke to her. She must have said something very loving about Dr. Whitaker because Charlotte smiled and hugged her. Next, Evelyn came to Mrs. Whitaker, and they hugged and chatted for a few minutes. She was very close to the family. Reaching the end of the line, Evelyn turned, and her gaze fell on us.

"Hello, girls," she greeted us as she walked toward our group.

I felt Madeline stiffen beside me. "Hello, Evelyn," I answered on behalf of our table. "It was a lovely service."

"Yes, it was. Dr. Whitaker has gone to his final, well-deserved rest."

Turning to Meg, I said, "This is my sister, Meg."

"It's very nice to meet you, Meg," Evelyn responded. "Yes, I see the family resemblance. Maeve has your height but is fuller than you. Well, I must greet the rest of the staff. Dr. Whitaker would want that." She turned away abruptly and departed.

All eyes at the table turned toward me. I could feel my cheeks flushing. Fuller? What a witch!

"You know, I kind of like old Evelyn," Meg said, and she and Madeline broke into uncontrolled laughter.

"She's a foolish woman," Winnie clucked. "A trouble starter."

"Sorry, Maeve," Madeline finally got out. "But she always knows just how to undercut someone. She is the master of digs. The original mean girl."

"Well," I said, "I think I've paid about as many respects as I can in one day. Let's go, Meg."

"Before you do," Meg pointed out, "you better go say hello to Will's family, or you will be the aloof fuller daughter-in-law."

"I'll be right back," I sighed while throwing a glare at her. Then I went over to greet the Kensingtons.

"*Cin cin.*" Meg raised her coffee cup.

Lydia and William were at a table chatting with their country club friends. I felt uncomfortably underdressed as Lydia looked me up and down before saying hello. But then again, I always felt frumpy in front of her. Lydia was dressed in a black tweed Chanel suit with telltale interlocking *C*s on the buttons and a long rope of Chanel pearls. Her hair was freshly done, and her makeup was flawless. Blood-red fingernails completed the look. *She looks fabulous if you like a Cruella de Vil vibe.*

"Hello, Lydia," I greeted her. "It was a lovely funeral." She gave a ghost of a smile but did not reply and continued speaking to the woman on her left. "Well, I won't keep you. I just wanted to say hello."

She nodded slightly in my direction as if to dismiss me.

William Jr. was engrossed in a spirited conversation, probably with another CEO. He gave me a distracted wave.

As I turned to leave, I heard one of Lydia's friends say, sotto voce, "Will's wife. Mary or Molly, is it?"

"Is she the midwife?" another asked.

"Did she have to go to school for that?" added the first.

I tuned them out and quickly walked back to our table. "We're leaving now," I said to Meg. "Right. Now."

"The Stepford wives get you down?" Meg inquired sweetly.

"I have a sudden headache," I said.

"Remember, they were all born on third base and think they hit a triple. What they need is some fine Irish blood in them," Meg observed.

"What?" I asked incredulously.

"They need an open bar, large deli platters, and everyone telling stories about the deceased, including the good, the bad, and the ugly. Everyone reliving old times and someone a little tipsy singing, 'Danny Boy.' That's the way to do a proper sendoff," she declared.

"Please invite me to one," Winnie pleaded.

"Me, too," Madeline said.

"Meg. Now," I ordered.

We said our goodbyes and headed to the parking lot. Small groups of people were beginning to leave.

"Let's hit Dunks on the way," Meg said, referring to our favorite, Dunkin' Donuts. "I need a decent coffee and a bagel." When we got our order, we drove to the bayside parking lot. It was our usual heart-to-heart meeting place, and we sipped our coffee while looking out at the bay and the ocean beyond.

"Okay," Meg said. "Let's review the facts."

"What facts?" I asked.

"Come on, Maeve. You know we are going to do this."

"Do what?"

"Has Will's family completely zapped your brain? We are going to figure out who murdered Dr. Whitaker," she said with resolve. "We can do this, and we must keep Will from any harm. You know how this town works. Just one bad review can shut you down, never mind a death at an event you catered."

"Maybe Patrick and the police force will solve this soon," I said.

"Maeve, I know where all the bodies are buried in this town. I can get the dirt. You can cover the medical angle. And we have the most to lose."

"We?"

"Family, Maeve. We stick together. We fight together. You know we are doing this."

After a moment, I found my determination and replied, "Yes, we are."

"Thank goodness you're back. I thought I was going to have to shake some sense into you."

"Ha!" I replied.

"And I know you feel guilty about Kevin. I want this entire Reardon payback deal to end with our generation."

"So, where do we begin?" I asked.

"First, there is the faulty EpiPen. Can you research that?"

I saluted. "Yes, ma'am."

Meg grimaced. "Come on, Maeve. We must play to our strengths. You check out hospital-related issues and let me concentrate on town issues."

"What do you suggest?"

"Follow the money. It's always about the money. Who benefits from his death? Mrs. Whitaker clearly should be a suspect."

"Especially if she is having an affair," I agreed. "Just remember, though, that we do not have definitive proof of that."

"Pretty darn close," she answered. "Now, what about Dr. Cydson? With Whitaker gone, he stands to be chief."

"He does. Interestingly, Dr. Whitaker had planned a post-retirement sailing trip, but one of the midwives heard him say recently that he had decided to stay on at Creighton indefinitely, which would have kept El Cid as the second fiddle."

"Why did his plans change so suddenly?" asked Meg.

"No idea. So, next we turn to revenge and Kevin Reardon," I said.

"Ah, yes," Meg said. "The proposed jealous suitor. Do you think he's capable of murder? Especially at Charlotte's wedding?"

"We at least need to investigate him."

"You check out EpiPens, and I will check out Kevin's background. Does Evelyn gain more power now that Dr. Whitaker is gone?"

"Well, she may move up in the administration ranks a little, but nothing to murder for. Plus, she was his biggest fan."

"As they say, keep your friends close and your enemies closer."

"Seriously, Meg?"

"At this point, we can't exclude anyone with something to gain by Dr. Whitaker's death," she pointed out.

"Do you think Patrick might be helpful at all?"

"You know Pat. I love him, but he will not tolerate us meddling in police business. He may be protective of us. You know, the oldest Irish son carries the family when the father dies. But that doesn't extend to letting us onto his police turf."

"Come to think of it, he did come on a bit strong to any guys we brought home."

"You think? He practically Mirandized them before every date," Meg said.

"Maybe Sunday, at dinner, we can gently pick his brain."

"Very gently," Meg cautioned.

We drove back to St. Andrew's, and I got out.

"I can't believe Aidan and Sebi conveniently picked this weekend to go away and miss our family dinner," Meg said from the open driver's window. "Do not be late." And with that, she drove off.

CHAPTER TEN

The weeks of pregnancy are counted from the first day of the last menstrual period and not from the date of conception.

Sunday afternoon found us *en famille* at Patrick and Olivia's tidy Cape-style house in West Langford. While East and West Langford are the same town, East Langford encompassed the ocean and bay, while West Langford had the huge town forest with its miles of walking trails and Eagle's Nest Pond. Patrick and Olivia's home bordered conservation land, so the setting was peaceful and home to deer, fox, and many species of birds.

As Mom, Will, and I pulled into the driveway, I said, "Now, Mom, let's try to keep this upbeat."

"I'm always in a good mood," she informed me.

"I know you are, Mom. I just want this to be a mellow day," I said.

"Mellow day? What does that even mean, Maeve? You make it sound like I need a tranquilizer."

Maybe it's just the rest of us that do. "Okay, Mom. Please just forget I said anything."

Her glare told me my remark would be analyzed and dissected at a later time.

Will gave me a half-smile as he helped Mom to the front entrance where Patrick was waiting and holding the twins. "Welcome. Come on in," he said.

"Hello, you lovely girls!" Will grabbed Cassie and Becca's feet, which gave them giggles.

Penelope and Abigail, ages four and six, came racing down the hallway looking for their hugs. Buttercup, their large poodle mix, bounded up behind them. Will scooped the girls up one at a time. Not wanting to be left out, Buttercup nearly knocked Will over with a single leap.

I kissed the girls first and then Pat. I hugged Buttercup while Mom made a huge fuss over Pat and the girls.

Meg was already sitting at the kitchen island drinking a large glass of cabernet sauvignon. She greeted me with a raised eyebrow. "GPS on the fritz?"

"We had to pick up Mom," I said as I put her bags on the table. Toys and candy were peeking out the top.

Just then, Olivia came in from the patio, dressed in an ankle-length, bleached cotton dress and wearing no makeup. Her waist-length, curly brown hair was bordering on a dreadlock style. She was only five feet tall and petite, so the shapeless shift seemed to swallow her. Olivia changed her style frequently. A few months ago, she was the epitome of a cool, hipster mom. Her daily uniform had consisted of black leggings, fitted tee shirts and an ever-present baseball cap with an opening for her long ponytail. She had often color-coordinated her lipstick, nail polish, and crossbody bag.

"Hello, everyone. Welcome to our loving home," she said. "Hello, Mother O'Reilly." She went over and hugged Mom.

Mom gave Olivia a light peck on the cheek but then touched her hair while she hugged her with a look of puzzlement on her face. "Do you ever go to a hairdresser, Olivia? They can do wonders."

"Speaking of hairdressers," Meg stepped in, "I just sold that cute cottage-style home across the street from the Clam Shell Salon. A lovely couple from Boston bought it. He's taking over the music department at Langford High, and she's a pediatric dentist."

"Is she joining Dr. Peters and Dr. Elliot?" Mom asked. Drs. Peters and Elliot were Langford's long-established and beloved dentists.

"She is. The town is growing, and I bet Doc Peters is getting ready to cut back to part-time." Meg and I exchanged looks, and we each took a long sip of wine. Meg had scored a brilliant deflection.

"Dinner is almost ready," Olivia said. "Will, could you please whip up the salad dressing?"

"Love to," Will said.

We moved out to the patio where Meg's son Henry, short for Hendrick, was shooting hoops on the half basketball court Patrick had built.

"Hey, Henry," I called out.

"Hi, Aunt Maeve. Hello, Gram." He came over to hug and kiss us all. When he went back to the court, Penelope and Abigail joined him. He was very patient with them, and they adored playing with their older cousin.

Olivia set out cheese and crackers and went back into the house while we all sipped our drinks and relaxed. The sky was cloudless, and it was a perfect seventy-five degrees with a light breeze. "Come out and join us, Olivia," Mom said.

"In a minute, Mother O'Reilly. I just need to put a few finishing touches on dinner."

"So Pat," Meg began, "since we're alone, we were wondering how things are going?"

"We know you must be so busy," I said.

"The police department in Langford is so thorough and professional," Meg added while kicking my leg under the table.

"Absolutely," I said. "What a great force." *Okay, that was weak, and Patrick would not fall for flattery.*

"Maeve and Meg, you know this is police business," Pat said.

"Pat, come on. We were there. Just fill us in on the latest," Meg said.

Pat looked us both over and smiled. "While the kids are occupied, I will tell you the latest. It's not privileged information, and everyone will know by tomorrow morning. Ava Martinez, the Whitakers' long-term housekeeper, is coming in for questioning tomorrow."

"What?" Will said, joining us. "I thought Kevin Reardon was the prime suspect."

"Loved Helen Mirren in that show," Meg murmured.

"Ava isn't a suspect. Just a person of interest. Mrs. Whitaker said that she was fired recently after a disagreement. We are interviewing anyone who may have had a grudge."

"I wonder if she knows about the affair," Meg mused.

Patrick looked genuinely puzzled. "What affair?"

"The lovely Mrs. Whitaker and that lounge lizard Zabalon."

"Are you sure, Meg?" Patrick asked.

"I have many sources saying they were doing the horizontal mambo."

"Is that a new dance?" Mom asked.

"A very old one," Meg said.

"I want those sources," Pat said.

Meg shook her head. "Sworn to secrecy."

"This is better than *NCIS*," Mom said, beaming.

Meg pushed ahead. "Don't the police always look at who would benefit from the crime?"

"My guess would be Mrs. Whitaker and the kids," I offered.

"Or Dr. Theodore Cydson, better known as El Cid," Meg pointed out.

"Maybe it was a crime of revenge," Mom said.

"Why would you say that, Mom?" I asked.

"Well, people may say they forgive, but they never forget. Maybe one of Dr. Whitaker's surgeries went wrong. Maybe a mother or baby was hurt."

"But if that was the case," I said, "why not just sue for malpractice?"

"Maybe they did, and they didn't win in court."

"That is an avenue I hadn't even thought about," I allowed. "I should check his malpractice cases."

"Perhaps we should check out the lovely Mrs. Whitaker. Informally, I mean," Meg added.

"Mrs. Whitaker might have an affair, but she wouldn't leave Dr. Whitaker," Mom said.

"Why not?" I asked.

"They are the king and queen of Langford. Why give up that prestige? Why rock the boat?"

"Exactly," Meg declared. "Just kill him off, and avoid all the bad press."

Patrick cut into our conversation. "Meg and Maeve, listen to me. Leave this to the detectives. This is not a game. Someone was murdered, and the killer is still out there."

We both gave Patrick guilty looks.

"We know, Pat," Meg finally said. "It's just that sometimes civilians can get access to things that the police can't. Remember Will's catering future may hang in the balance."

"I wonder how long the affair has been going on," Mom wondered aloud.

"Mom, we don't even know if there is an affair. Please don't repeat it," I begged.

"Loose lips sink ships," Meg added. "But there is an affair. Do you think Ava was fed up with the Whitakers and decided to take action?"

"She will be interviewed tomorrow, Meg." Patrick crossed his arms. "Please leave this alone."

Meg and I silently sipped on while studying the bird feeder in the yard.

"I know one thing for sure," Mom said. "None of the Reardons are murderers. Impossible."

"Oprah has spoken," Meg whispered.

"It's time for dinner, dear. Enough shop talk," Olivia said as she bustled onto the deck, carrying a stack of dinner plates. We all went back into the kitchen and helped bring the rest of the dinner out. The large patio table was quickly covered with three-cheese lasagna, stuffed shells, a large green salad, garlic bread, sausages, and a bowl of extra sauce.

"Olivia, this looks wonderful. You must have cooked for days," Mom said. When everyone was seated, she added, "Henry, will you please say grace?"

"Dear God, thank you for this food, and thank you so much for this family," Henry intoned, solemnly but quickly and hungrily.

Mom beamed at him. "Perfect."

The food was passed around. I noticed that Olivia had what appeared to be raw bark on her plate.

"What is that, dear?" Mom asked.

"Mother O'Reilly, I have decided to eat only raw food. It helps to purify one's body."

"You mean uncooked food?"

"Actually, anything in its natural state."

"Well, that sounds fool—"

"Pass the salad, Mom," I said, cutting her off. "It looks so delicious."

"This is fabulous, Olivia," Meg said. "Just like Deluca's." Olivia beamed, and we all dug in.

Mom gave me *the look*, but thankfully, she kept eating.

"Girls, let me help you with your plates. Would you like some lasagna?" Will asked.

"We love zanya," Penelope said.

I looked around. The family was seated around the large teak table under a red-and-white, striped umbrella. Sarah and Becca were in their highchairs with their bowls of pasta, some of which went in their mouths, but most wound up on the ground. Everyone was thoroughly enjoying the meal, including Olivia, who was eating leaves or branches or something. I took a sip of wine and smiled at the scene. It was my crazy, wonderful family. Well, all of them except for Aidan, Sebi, and Chloe.

"Henry, what's up for the summer?" Patrick asked.

"Well, Uncle Pat, I hope to go to wrestling camp and then work for Uncle Will."

"If I still have a business by then," Will said softly to me.

"I'm going to wrestle like Henry when I get big." Abigail flexed her little biceps.

"Me, too." Penelope copied her sister.

"I'll teach you some moves," Henry offered.

Meg let out a sigh. I knew she wanted Henry to play a country club sport like golf, tennis, or lacrosse. Anything but wrestling.

Olivia came bustling out of the kitchen with hazelnut coffee and homemade strawberry cheesecake. She was a Martha Stewart clone. Sipping coffee, I thought about how well the visit was going. There had been no incidents to speak of, and so far, all was well.

After everyone was done, Mom, Meg, Olivia, and I stayed at the table while the guys played hide-and-seek with the kids in the yard.

"How was the spa, Olivia?" Meg asked.

"It was so healing. My inner self feels renewed. One gets such a sense of peace that lasts for weeks."

I was about to add my own observation when I felt Meg again kick me under the table.

"It is wonderful to have a little time to yourself, dear," Mom said.

"Yes, it is. And I learned about the raw diet while I was at the spa."

"Don't you worry about diseases, Olivia?" Mom asked. "Is the food washed? Lila in my building got very ill with sanorella or something from eating a salad dressing with raw egg. You need to be very careful."

"Mother O'Reilly, I think you mean salmonella. That would never happen to me. My diet is approved by Desi, my yogi. It has many health benefits."

"A dogi? A jogi? Is that a chef?"

I stood up. "Mom, we need to get going. It's getting late."

"Will! Henry! It's time to wrap things up," Meg called.

"Can we help clean up, Olivia?" I asked. She always said no, but I always asked.

"Oh, no, Maeve. But thanks so much for asking. I enjoy the ritual of cleansing and restoring my kitchen."

Meg shot me a look, daring me to laugh.

We did the many rounds of goodbye kisses and hugs, and then we were finally settled in the car.

"Raw food—I just don't understand it. Why have a stove? That girl is odd, bless her," Mom observed. "But at least she cooks for Patrick and the girls. Patrick is a—"

"Saint," Will and I said in unison.

CHAPTER ELEVEN

A normal fetal heart rate usually ranges from 120 to 160 beats per minute.

"Hello, Val!" I called out as I arrived on the labor floor.
"Good morning, Maeve. How are you?"
"I'm great. Are we busy?"
"It's not too bad. A few patients are in early labor, and one woman just delivered. Dr. Cydson has a cesarean section at seven-thirty, and we have two inductions coming in at eight."
"I'll be out in a jiff," I called from the locker room door. I changed into scrubs and went out to the labor board.

El Cid went down the list of women, summarizing each one's progress and relishing his new role. Evelyn stood immediately behind him.

"In room one, we have Ms. Rivers, a primigravida. She is a patient of Dr. Whitney. She has had an uncomplicated prenatal course. Last night, she came in at two centimeters dilatation with ruptured membranes and is now four centimeters and asking for an epidural. Anesthesia has been called. The baby looks fine, about seven pounds. She should progress nicely. Room two is Ms. Parsons from the midwifery practice. She delivered at five a.m. Baby and mom are doing well. She can be transferred to the postpartum unit after shift change."

He droned on, but I listened with only one ear as I was assigned to triage today. I would be seeing all the patients sent in for labor evaluation, blood pressure, incision checks, or emergency treatment. When he was finally done, I went off and made myself a cup of lemon tea with honey. Next, I went to see Angie, the triage RN of the day.

"Hi, Angie," I greeted her. She was a small, sturdy thirty-eight-year-old whose parents had emigrated from Cape

Verde. She was a Boston native but now commuted from southern New Hampshire. Angie and her husband, Mike, had a massive house with a pool, two pugs they loved dearly, and they were fervent Disney World addicts.

"We're good right now," Angie informed me. "Go do some charting or get something to eat. I'll beep you if we get any action."

"Thanks, Angie. I'll go in the back to make a phone call."

I walked to the midwifery call room. It was used to catch a few winks during downtimes on a long shift. It had been sparsely furnished when it was assigned to us, but Winnie had insisted on adding chintz pillows, floral mugs for all of us, thick, buttery fleece throws, and a few Jonathan Green prints. I settled onto the bed and took my datebook out. I needed to make a reproductive endocrinology appointment for Will and me.

Infertility. I even hated the sound of the word. And why do people feel so entitled to ask couples without kids the most intimate questions? Have you been trying long? Are you relaxing? Is it you or Will? What doctors have you consulted? Have you tried IVF? Do you have irregular periods? Are you trying at the right time? And why do they feel like they always have the perfect advice? Go on a vacation. Stop drinking tea. Drink herbal tea. Think good thoughts. Relax. Try acupuncture. Try to adopt, and you'll get pregnant. Try yoga.

Here goes. I tapped the number out on my phone. *I hate this.*

A cheerful voice picked up on the first ring. "Welcome to Creighton Memorial Reproductive Associates. How can we help you today?"

"Hi, I'm Maeve Kensington. I would like to schedule a consultation with Dr. Beth Chisholm."

"Hello, Maeve. I'll be happy to help you with that. We are currently booking in October. Dr. Chisholm is very busy."

"October will be fine." I quickly realized it would give us a few more months to get pregnant. Maybe we wouldn't even need the appointment.

"Do you have a Creighton Memorial patient ID number?"

"Yes, I am an employee."

"Oh, wait a minute. That makes a huge difference. Employees get preference. We can see you tomorrow at two p.m."

"Tomorrow? That soon?" I nearly squeaked. I quickly scanned my schedule to make sure I was available. Will had already given me his schedule, so I knew he was free.

"Yes, I always save a few openings a month for employees or VIPs."

Just great. "Uh, okay. Should I bring anything?"

"Just a photo ID. I'll email you a health history form that you and your partner need to print, fill out, and bring to the initial consultation."

"Thanks."

"We look forward to seeing you. Goodbye."

I stared at the phone. *Did I just make that appointment? Yes, I am going to officially become a fertility patient. In a perfect world, I would already be pregnant.* I had to let go of the hopeful thoughts, though, as I was a few days from getting my period and already had cramps.

My beeper started vibrating at my waist. Angie was calling me to triage. I got off the bed and went back down the hall.

"Hi, Maeve. One of the private practices is sending in a forty-year-old. She's thirty-six weeks with no fetal heartbeat. The practice did an ultrasound, but they want us to repeat it."

"First pregnancy?"

"No, it's her fourth, but she has had three miscarriages. This pregnancy is the result of four IVF cycles."

I took a deep breath, and a few different thoughts went through my mind. *A definitive diagnosis would be needed. This woman could be facing an unspeakable tragedy. I need to give her my best.*

"Is Faye available?" I inquired. Our obstetrical social worker, Faye, was wonderful with patients and knew every resource available.

"Already paged her."

I heard the Labor and Delivery buzzer. An Asian couple walked up to the admitting desk, where they were directed toward us. The man was grasping the woman's elbow as if to hold her up. They both looked as if they were walking in a fog.

"Come right in." Angie quickly had the woman in a gown, vital signs taken, and sitting in a labor bed. "Maeve is our midwife today," she explained. "She and Dr. Patel are going to do an ultrasound."

"Hello, Mr. and Mrs. Lee," I said after checking their names on the computer. "Tell me about today."

"Please call us Maya and Phillip," the man said.

Maya took a shaky breath and began, "I know I felt the baby move last night before we went to bed. I was up a few times to use the bathroom, and I think I felt him during the night, but I was so tired that I'm not sure. This morning we overslept and were both rushing to get to work on time. After eating my muffin at work, I realized that I hadn't felt him move. I called the office, and they told us to come right in. They couldn't find his heartbeat." She could barely finish her last sentence.

"Maybe their equipment was faulty," Phillip soothed.

The door opened, and Dr. Patel appeared. "Good morning. I'm Dr. Sanjay Patel."

"This is Maya and Phillip Lee," I said.

Dr. Patel moved to the sink to wash his hands and said, "Maeve and I will do an ultrasound exam." His eyes met mine, and I picked up the ultrasound wand and swept it over Maya's abdomen. I saw a thirty-six week fetus, but there was no fetal heart movement.

"Does he have a heartbeat?" Maya asked.

I slowly shook my head.

"Mr. and Mrs. Lee, I'm very sorry. There is no fetal heart activity. It appears that your son has died in utero," Dr. Patel said.

Maya sobbed as she grabbed at Phillip. He put his arms around her while his eyes filled with tears, and I gently patted Phillip on the back. Maya looked wildly around and then slowly moaned, "Nooooo." She buried her head in Phillip's chest.

Telling a pregnant woman that her term baby was dead, which I was thankful didn't happen often, was a moment of the most profound sorrow. It was unnatural to get so close to the end of a pregnancy and not deliver a live baby. It was unnatural to go through labor and not have a live baby. It was unnatural for your breasts to contain milk for a baby that didn't exist. It was unnatural to leave the maternity unit without a baby. It was agonizing to go home and disassemble a nursery. It was one of the cruelest blows a woman and her partner could suffer. I never forgot those patients. A piece of my heart stayed with them always.

"We'll give you some privacy. Then we will come back and discuss the plan of care," Dr. Patel said. "We are so very sorry."

Outside the room, Sanjay, Angie, and I just looked at one another. We had no answers. But we also knew that no answer would ever heal the Lees' hearts. To get so close to having a baby, especially to thirty-six weeks, only to experience an intrauterine fetal death.

"Maeve, after you examine her, why don't you discuss induction of labor. Is Faye aware?"

"On her way," Angie said.

"I knew you two would cover all the bases," Sanjay said as he gave a sad smile. "Maeve, I'll leave her care in your hands. I don't know anyone whom I'd rather have handle this." And with that, he went back to his other duties.

I knocked softly and then re-entered the room. The couple was staring off into space. They were numb with shock. Maya was still sobbing silently.

"I am going to examine you now, Maya. I will be as gentle as possible," I said to her.

"Was it my fault? How could this happen?" Maya sniffled.

"Maya, it was nothing you did, nothing at all," I said, trying to be as reassuring as possible. "We don't have any answers yet, but I promise you that nothing you did caused this to happen."

"We hoped for a baby for so long. Phillip and I didn't marry until we were thirty-five. We were so blessed to find each other, and then came all the miscarriages. We got so far this time. We even bought a crib and a few baby clothes." She began crying again. Through tears, she said, "I wouldn't let anyone give me a baby shower because I was too worried, but I wanted a place for him to sleep."

Phillip held her tightly. I waited until she calmed down and then prepared to examine her.

"Maya, take a slow, deep breath. If anything hurts, tell me."

Maya shut her eyes, and I began the exam.

"Maya, your cervix is closed. We will need to give you some medications to get your cervix ready, and then tomorrow, we will induce labor. Anesthesia will be available to make you as comfortable as possible, and someone will explain what is happening every step of the way. The nursing staff is excellent, and one of the midwives will be readily available."

"I want to be knocked out," Maya insisted. "I don't want to see anything. I don't want to feel anything."

"Maya, this is a terrible loss. Let's take it one step at a time. We'll do our best for you. You'll have medication and anesthesia. I'm also going to have Faye, a social worker, come in to meet with you and Phillip to discuss some issues. Have you called your family?"

"I shut off the cell phone," Phillip said.

"They are welcome to visit," I assured them.

"We want to be alone for now," Phillip insisted.

"I understand. I'll be back in a bit. Please use the call button if you need anything. Can I get you something to drink or eat?" Maya did not respond, but Phillip shook his head.

Angie had three other patients for me to assess, so I had to move on. You learn to compartmentalize early in this business. Soul-crushing situations had to be placed in the back of your mind so that you could continue with the day. The sadness did not leave but had to be put away for another time. I knew I needed to attend to other women, and I would debrief later with my colleagues. It was how we coped.

"Go ahead and evaluate the patient in room two. She delivered four days ago and now has a headache and elevated blood pressure," Angie said. "I'll introduce Faye to the Lees. We also have a possible rupture of membranes at term and a multipara seven weeks pregnant who can't keep any food down and had hyperemesis in her last pregnancy. She's going to need IV hydration."

"Aye aye, captain!"

Angie smiled. "Buckle up. It's gonna be a crazy morning."

About an hour later, as I was finishing some charting at the desk computer, Faye approached me. "So sad about the Lees. Such a lovely couple, too."

"Yes, they are," I agreed.

"She's a history prof at Boston University, and he's an investment banker. They so desperately want kids. This was their fourth cycle of IVF with her sister's egg."

I mentally counted. "That means she's had four IVF cycles and three miscarriages. Such a long, grueling road, and now this. I'll have her stay overnight on the GYN unit and be induced in the morning."

"I'm trying to talk her into seeing the baby and allowing me to take a photo," Faye said. "She is very resistant right now, but we know from experience they'll want the photos later."

"Does the baby have a name?" I asked.

"Phillip George, after her dad and Phillip." We shared a sad look.

"I'll stop back and see her tomorrow," I finally said. "Winnie will be with her on labor and delivery. She'll be great with them. She's so mothering and calm. Who was following her?"

"Dr. Eve Martin," Faye said. "But she's on vacation this week. She will be shocked when she hears."

"You're right," I agreed. "I'll call her when she gets back."

"Not that it will help, but I hope we get some answers tomorrow," Faye said.

"No matter what the answer, death is death," I said with a sigh. "And grief is grief. But sometimes having answers, even with a lousy outcome, helps."

"Spoken like a therapist," she said.

When my shift was finally over, I was exhausted. But I decided to stop by for a quick dinner with Meg and Henry since Will had gone to the Red Sox game with Aidan. I pulled into Meg's circular driveway, my tires crunching over the crushed-shell surface, and parked behind the navy Jaguar and the black Mercedes SUV. Getting out of my Jeep, I followed a rose-covered trellis around the house to an expansive back deck overlooking a magnificent view of the bay and the ocean beyond. The house had been built on a high ridge to take full advantage of the surroundings.

The sun was low in the sky, the vista went on forever, and the fragrance of the Rosa rugosa was intoxicating. I saw Henry paddling his kayak in the bay while Meg sat in her white Adirondack chair with a pitcher of wine coolers beside her. Brady, Henry's black Lab, met me at the gate.

"Hello, beautiful boy," I said, rubbing his head.

Meg was in a black bandeau suit with matching chiffon sarong and, of course, looked flawless. Her nails were a brilliant flaming red, probably OPI—"Madam President," I'd guess. Her hair was pulled back through an opening in her scarlet beach visor, and her skin glowed.

"Hi, Maeve. Take a load off," Meg said, pointing to a chair.

"Fuller sister reporting for duty." I poured myself a wine cooler but added from a bottle of Perrier to dilute it a bit more.

"Shelley is making burgers, corn, and salad per Henry's request."

Shelley had been Meg's nanny and then became her house manager. She was from a prominent Portuguese family of fishermen. Meg had helped Shelley and her husband close on a beautiful home in West Langford and provided all "the extras" for their two children, including piano lessons, hockey camps, and theater groups during their school years. She also assisted mightily with their college tuition. She made sure Artie, her ex, used his connections to book Shelley and her family top accommodations for their semiannual vacations. Working for Meg was a great gig.

"Sounds wonderful." I put my feet up on the wicker ottoman and took a long sip.

"Let's have a little debrief before Henry joins us," Meg said.

"Well, it'll be short," I replied. "I've got nothing."

"Hmmm. I hear that the Whitaker housekeeper, Ava Martinez, was blackmailing both Mrs. Whitaker and Dr. Whitaker to keep the affair quiet."

"How did you hear this?" I asked.

"Shelley has connections. She says that's the word on the street."

"Interesting," I said. "Maybe they stopped paying her and then fired her. Perhaps Ava wanted to get back at them for being let go. You know, to be blackballed by the Whitakers around these parts is tough."

"I can only imagine." My heart fell as I thought of Will and his catering company.

"I'm sure Ava saw all and knew all," Meg observed. "All the details will eventually come out. They always do."

"Hey, Henry!" I called out, signaling an end to our theorizing. He walked through the white arched gate from the beach, glowing with that special light of youth as he stepped onto the patio.

"Hi, Aunt Maeve. I'll hug you after I change. How soon till dinner, Mom?"

"Five minutes, honey."

"I'll be back in a flash." He went in to change with Brady trotting closely behind.

"He's simply the best, Meg," I said.

"I know. He's a gem. I just wish he would pick a more mature sport than wrestling."

"More mature or more country club?" I needled.

"Don't start! I just don't want him to get hurt. Plus, wrestlers get all those awful skin infections. And their ears!"

"Well, there are ways to avoid all that. He really loves wrestling, Meg."

"I know, and I keep trying to wrap my head around that."

"What does Artie say?" I asked.

"He's all for wrestling, but you know he's a hugely successful venture capitalist and he's away so much he never sees Henry's matches. It's typical of Artie, with his constant 'my son, the athlete.' But he can't quite make the time to see him compete."

We sat in silence. Although Meg had been divorced for two years, a marriage is never truly finished when children are involved. Artie loved Henry, and I believed he still loved Meg, but he was a total workaholic. Sadly, for him, closing deals had come before time with his family.

"Are Will's bookings off?" Meg quietly inquired.

"The Chambers' anniversary party, the Langford Tennis Club reception, and the Seaside Art Gallery artist meet and greet all canceled, and there are no new bookings," I said with a sigh.

"Give it time," Meg said. "Those events are all closely tied to the Whitakers. I talk him up all the time to my clients."

"I know you do. And thanks so much for that."

"Maeve, we need proof of Mrs. Whitaker's relationship with James Zabalon."

"How can we get that?" I asked.

"First off, I can check out the hotel. I have many contacts there—it's where I put my high rollers when they come to town to buy a multimillion-dollar summer 'cottage' on the water. I'll find out how many rendezvous they had and whether they use aliases."

"Go to it, Hercule," I urged her.

Just then, Shelley came onto the deck and announced, "Dinner time!"

"To be continued." Meg stood.

It was a wonderful evening. The setting sun, the hamburgers and corn, and listening to Henry explain how wrestling is scored, all combined to pull me out of my worries. I still had no idea how a wrestling match was decided, but I loved his excitement. I shut my eyes and listened, and by degrees, my anxiety and the day's sadness drained away.

CHAPTER TWELVE

A fetus can hear by eighteen weeks of gestation.

I woke up with a slight headache after a fitful night. Will had already left for the morning to visit an oyster farm on Cape Cod. Our appointment at the reproductive endocrinology office was at two p.m.

I was still anxious about our upcoming appointment with the fertility specialist, Dr. Chisholm. I had wanted children for as long as I could remember. I had always envisioned myself as a mother. I wanted to be pregnant. I wanted to breastfeed. I wanted that strong mother-child connection. I wanted pregnancy to be spontaneous. However, Will and I had been married for three years and had been trying to conceive for two years without success. And at thirty-four, I wasn't getting any younger.

Will was excited to finally be moving on in the process, which was typical of him. He always dealt with problems head-on and believed that the only way forward was to identify the cause and find a solution.

I had the day off, so I took Fenway to the beach in the morning. Even though it was chilly and windy, Fenway was overjoyed as always to be near the ocean. No matter the weather, this was her favorite place. Her tail was wagging non-stop, and she was ready to explore every weed and blade of beach grass. And she was very proud of her ability to dig in the sand.

The parking lot was nearly deserted since most people were either at work or chased away by the weather. The few people walking on the beach had parked by the closest access point, so I decided to park down at the far end of the lot. Fenway liked her space.

I had only gone a short way on the beach when I came to the closed concession stand. I was surprised to see a white Lexus parked in the small space behind the building. I quickly saw that Mrs. Whitaker and James Zabalon were sitting in his car, talking with the windows down. They didn't notice Fenway or me, so I slipped to the side of the large stand and listened.

"We need to be careful," Mrs. Whitaker said.

"Why? He's dead," Zabalon scoffed.

"You're so callous," she retorted. "I just don't want anything to go awry with the will."

"Nothing will go wrong. No one knows about us."

"What about Ava?"

She's talking about the housekeeper.

"You fired her, right?" he asked. "She'll be too afraid to say anything."

"Yes, but the police called her in for questioning."

Zabalon barked out a laugh.

"She knows about us," Mrs. Whitaker said.

"Who cares? People are gonna think what they want," Zabalon pointed out, "but they won't know for sure."

"You don't know what Ava will say."

"Ava won't talk. She wants to protect her husband and her kid. She doesn't want the police in her business."

What is that about? Why is Ava worried about her husband and child? Is the husband ill? Are they in danger?

"Are you sure?" Mrs. Whitaker sounded very stressed.

"Yup." Zabalon flicked his cigar ashes out the window. "That memorial service was boring, but we got through it. Let some time pass. Everything will be fine."

I wanted to hear more, but Fenway began to strain at the leash. All I needed was for her to start barking. I picked her up and walked quickly toward the sea wall, careful not to be seen.

So they were seeing each other. But could they have planned to kill Dr. Whitaker? Could they have done it at Charlotte's wedding? But how crazy was that? I must fill Meg in.

Later at home, I changed into a long, moss green skirt and a pale green, embroidered fitted jacket. There were no guidelines for what to wear to your fertility appointment.

At the doctor's office, I arrived to find Will sitting in the waiting room reading *Sports Illustrated*. I saw copies of *O*, *Vogue*, *Vanity Fair,* and *People* displayed in neat rows on one side of the chocolate-and-rose-colored room. Will looked crisp in a tweed sport coat and khakis with a white, open-necked linen shirt.

"Hi, beautiful," he said as I walked in.

"How are you?" I kissed him on the cheek.

"Okay." He smiled, but I could see a weariness in his eyes. Before I had a chance to question him, though, our names were called by a tall, friendly-looking woman.

"Hello, Mr. and Mrs. Kensington. I am Adeline Bennington, the nurse practitioner here."

"Please call us Maeve and Will," Will said.

"Nice to meet you. I know this is your first visit. I'll start by taking Maeve's vital signs, and then I'll get a medical history from both of you. After that, you will have a consultation with Dr. Chisholm. I did go over the forms you submitted, and I put that information in your record."

Adeline took my blood pressure and pulse, which amazingly were not elevated. Will and I sat side by side in upholstered wingback chairs, and she sat across from us with a tablet computer.

"Maeve, I'll start with you. Let's start by reviewing your history. Are your menstrual cycles regular?"

"Every twenty-eight days," I answered.

"How old were you when they started?"

"Thirteen."

"Have you ever been pregnant?"

"No."

"How long have you been trying to achieve pregnancy?"

"Two years."

"How often do the two of you have intercourse?"

"Have you ever had a sexually transmitted disease?"

"Have you ever had any pelvic surgeries?"

I began to answer the intimate questions about our life mechanically. *This is what I didn't want, someone in our bedroom examining every aspect of our personal lives.* Adeline went on to ask about my medical, surgical, and family history. From a professional point of view, I was very impressed with her thoroughness. From a personal point of view, I felt turned inside out.

Finally, it was Will's turn. "Will, have you initiated any other pregnancies?" Adeline asked.

"No."

"Have you ever had erectile dysfunction?"

"No."

I tuned out for the rest of his interrogation, or rather, history. *Maybe if I don't listen, this appointment won't be real.*

Adeline entered all the information into her computer. "Maeve and Will, is there anything you would like to add?"

We both laughed. "I think you covered everything," I replied.

Adeline smiled. "I know it seems intrusive, but it helps to form your plan of care.

"Dr. Chisholm will order some initial tests, and then you can make a follow-up appointment to review the results and schedule any needed procedures."

We nodded and turned to look at each other while she left to brief Dr. Chisholm. "What's up, honey?" I asked, stroking Will's hair.

"I'll tell you later. There's something strange about the Whitaker affair."

Dr. Chisholm appeared at the door and invited us into her office. She had very short wavy black hair, accentuating her high cheekbones and tawny skin. Her office had a superb view of Langford harbor, and the beautifully framed pictures demonstrated an evident love of travel. Photos of London, Rome, and Australia were prominently displayed on her shelves.

"Hello, Maeve. You and I met briefly at the OB/GYN annual breakfast. Will, I'm Beth Chisholm. So nice to meet you," she said, shaking our hands and motioning us to high backed, black lacquered wooden chairs in front of her desk. She sat down and asked for more information about a few items in our histories and then said, "I would like to do a physical exam on you today, Maeve, and then chat with you both about a plan."

I smiled and went into the pale rose-colored exam room to change. *I am not a fertility patient,* I found myself thinking as

I undressed. *We just need more time.* Infertility just wounded my soul. I hated even to read articles about it. Nothing else in my life gave me such pause.

Dr. Chisholm was very gentle, exceedingly professional, and spoke softly while performing my exam. Even with that, it was a blur. I felt as if I was having an out-of-body experience. I did not speak but instead practiced taking slow, calming breaths. I somehow got dressed and joined Will and Dr. Chisholm in her office when it was over.

"Now comes the data gathering for the both of you. Maeve, I would like to draw some blood today for the standard endocrine workup. I'll check your ovarian function, thyroid levels, endocrine labs, and a standard blood panel. Will, testing for men is relatively straightforward. Adeline will give you the slips and instructions for a semen analysis. I'll have you make a follow-up appointment to discuss the results."

"Sounds great." Will shook Dr. Chisholm's hand. "Thanks so much for fitting us in. I'm happy to get this process started."

Dr. Chisholm gave him a warm smile. I shook her hand with a smile plastered on my face and said nothing. I was numb.

We left her office, and as we waited for Adeline to make up the lab slips, Will asked, "Are you all right, Maeve?"

"Great!" *Was that high-pitched squeak my voice?*

I went with Adeline into the lab. But before she introduced me to the lab tech for the blood draw, she turned and said, "Maeve, I know that you can look up these results on the computer. But trust me, it's best to wait for your next appointment to get them. Then you can discuss the results with Dr. Chisholm."

I nodded. *What does that mean? Is she assuming something is wrong with me? Does she know something I don't know? Wow! Paranoia patrol! Slow down—breathe.*

Finally, I finished the blood work and tried to push the entire visit from my consciousness. I knew I could look at the results, but I told myself I would resist the temptation. *There is nothing in this process that I have any control over. Just keep a positive outlook.*

I found Will in the waiting room, and together we headed back to the parking lot. As we sat in Will's car, I asked, "What's going on with the investigation?"

"The detectives called me today, and it was all very curious. The glass that Dr. Whitaker drank from was meant for Charlotte."

"How could they tell?"

"The planning for the wedding was extreme. Mrs. Whitaker said that all the champagne glassware had to have pearls in the stem."

"It was lovely, and I am sure it was very costly."

"The flutes were handmade. All the pearls were white except for Charlotte's. Her champagne glass had a pale-pink pearl."

"What?"

"Yes," Will said. "Mrs. Whitaker insisted that Charlotte's flute had to have a pink pearl. But somehow, hers was switched. Kevin Reardon picked up that tray at the last minute. The server he was helping says that he forgot to tell him about the pink pearl."

"Do the detectives think someone was trying to kill Charlotte?"

"Who knows?"

"Maybe someone wanted to get back at Dr. Whitaker by killing her," I mused, starting to get lost in possibilities.

"This whole thing just gets crazier and crazier."

"I still can't believe Kevin is guilty," I insisted. "His family was so good to mine. Christmas gifts, Easter dinners, and Thanksgiving turkeys were always dropped off without fanfare. I know those were from his grandparents, but it's hard to believe a murderer would come from that family."

"Maeve, let the cards play out. I just hope Kevin has nothing to do with this mess."

We both leaned back in our seats and stared out the window. Will took my hand. "Honey," he said, "I know this appointment was very hard for you, but I feel that we are starting down the right road."

I smiled at him.

"You know," he went on, looking out the window, "I had many expectations and restrictions placed on me at an early age. You and I will raise our kids in a loving home, where they are free to pick their activities, their friends, their careers. You will be such a wonderful mother."

I squeezed his hand gently. "We're finally making a plan."

"Yes, we are. I love you so much, Maeve."

"I love you, too," I said, kissing him.

"Look at the time," he said at last. "I need to run, but I'll see you tonight."

"Wait a minute, what's for dinner? Don't think I'm going through this day without a great dinner waiting for me!" I teased.

"Well, my love, since you mentioned it, I've planned for you to have a very nice Cobb salad with a new molasses bread I'm trying."

"Mmmm. My favorite. See you at six-thirty then," I said as I got out of the car. I waved goodbye and went toward my Jeep. I decided to stop off at Langford Library. For a small-town library, it was a magnificent structure. A repurposed Catholic church, it had been renovated ten years ago to become the town's new library. Sparing no expense, in the Langford tradition, the design was a brilliant pairing of old and new.

The gray stone walls and thick wooden doors opened to reveal a circulation area brightly illuminated by a combination of recessed lighting and skylights. There was a delightful and spacious children's area in a side wing with colorful rugs and floor cushions. Upstairs, a state-of-the-art computer area was always bustling. Nooks and crannies along the walls provided spaces for patrons to study, read, or just relax. There were meeting rooms that any group in town could reserve on the lower level and a gallery that showcased a rotating selection of work by local artists. There was also a boutique movie theater, home to enthusiasts who held weekly showings of independent and foreign films. A small café served coffee, tea, and light fare on afternoons and weekends. Outside, a perennial garden flourished, nurtured by the town's gardening aficionados. As soon as the refurbishing was complete, the Langford Library immediately became the town's community center.

Swati, the attractive, raven-haired librarian, greeted me as I stepped to the circulation desk. She had a pair of crutches propped beside her.

"Hey, Maeve, we have some holds for you," she said, turning to the shelves behind the desk.

"Thanks, Swati. What happened?" I asked, motioning to the crutches.

"I sprained my ankle playing soccer with the kids," she admitted. "That will teach me."

"I'm so sorry. Sometimes sprains hurt worse than fractures."

"It's not too bad," she said with a shrug. "I'm taking Advil."

"Remember to take it with food. Can you keep your ankle elevated?"

"More or less. I have a small stool back here that I try to use as much as I can."

I nodded at the DVD shelves. "I'm going to browse the films—I'll be right back."

I always had a feeling of delightful anticipation when entering the library—the feeling some women have when entering a jewelry store, a sense of wondering what gems awaited. Sometimes a new book by a favorite author arrived unexpectedly, and sometimes I found a book I never knew I wanted to read until I browsed a few pages. This time I picked up a few interesting-looking foreign films and headed back to pick up my books. Swati saw me and began to get her crutches to walk over to the hold shelf.

"Stay where you are, Swati, and keep your foot up. Let me get my holds."

"Thanks, Maeve." She smiled, sitting down, and putting her injured foot back up on the stool.

I walked over to the hold shelf behind the circulation desk and found my name. I was picking out my books when I accidentally knocked a few neighboring books to the floor. "Oops, sorry. I'll put these back."

Swati laughed. "I've done that so many times before."

The books that fell were a collection of children's titles. Picking them up, I saw the tag naming the patron: *Greyson, E.* Evelyn Greyson, the older, caustic Creighton Memorial Obstetric Nursing director? But, no, it must be another patron with the same surname, a younger one who had young children.

I picked up the books and returned them to the shelf, but the odd coincidence lingered with me for a moment. When I came around to the front of the desk, Swati looked at my stack of books and saw a copy of Kathryn Harkup's *A is for Arsenic: The Poisons of Agatha Christie.*

"That looks interesting, Maeve. Planning on killing anyone?"

I suddenly imagined myself as a stealthy murderess and chuckled. "No, I just love how Agatha created such suspense with poisons. I can't wait to read it. Feel better, Swati."

My cell phone rang as I got into my car. "Hi, Mom."

"Hey, Maeve. I'm off to bingo, but I wanted to remind you to bring the Whitaker wedding pictures the next time you come. I am dying to see them. There were only a few in the newspaper."

"I can send them to your phone."

"You know I don't like to look at pictures on the phone. They're too small. I want to see them in print."

"Already ordered them. I'll swing by to pick them up and then bring them to you. Have you heard from anyone?"

"From Patrick and Aidan, of course. They call me every day like clockwork."

I also called daily, but that was just expected from a daughter.

"Meg called," she went on. "You know, she needs to let Henry be…"

I put Mom on speaker, tuned out, and watched the scenery as I drove home.

CHAPTER THIRTEEN

The third trimester of pregnancy is from twenty-eight weeks until the baby's birth.

I arrived at Creighton Memorial early the following day and met Bev in what was officially "The Davis Family Dining Room" or, as the staff called it, the cafeteria.

It could easily have been mistaken for an upscale restaurant. Dark mahogany beams, clusters of round oak tables, and very comfortable padded leather chairs were scattered across a spacious dining room that overlooked the harbor. The head chef had been recruited from New York City. She changed the menu seasonally and used local ingredients as much as possible. On offer for breakfast were an omelet station, a fresh-pressed juice bar, and an assortment of cereals, rolls, waffles, and yogurt parfaits. The coffee station rivaled Starbucks. Employees ate free while patients and visitors were given a generous discount. Locals would frequently stop in for a meal even if they didn't have a medical appointment.

Bev looked tired as she sipped her tea.

"Tough night?" I asked.

"I stopped in to see the Lees. Their IUFD was so sad." IUFD was the term used for an intrauterine fetal demise.

"How are they holding up?" I asked.

"Grieving but accepting. Just trying to hang on."

"Any idea what happened?"

"The baby had a very short cord that was wrapped tightly around his legs and neck. It was a cord accident."

"Oh, no."

"Yeah, just awful. Winnie said he was a beautiful baby. They are strong and coping, but that doesn't make it any easier," she said with a sigh.

I sighed too. "Winnie is wonderful."

"She shines in tough situations," Bev agreed. We sat in silence for a moment, lost in our thoughts.

"Hey, guess who came into the Emergency Department last night?" Bev asked. "Charlotte Whitaker."

"Why?" I asked.

"She was assaulted while leaving Miss Bloomfield's School."

"What? Assaulted?"

"Physically, not sexually. She was walloped on the back of the head. She is on bereavement leave from the school but went there last evening to get some of her things. She was locking up when it happened."

"How is she?"

"I heard she needed ten stitches but had a negative CT scan and is improving. She was shaken, but there were no major injuries. She is resting now and under tight guard, I might add."

"Sounds like she is in danger," I said.

"Looks like the entire family irritated someone," Bev added.

I looked down at my uneaten breakfast.

"How are you and Will doing?" Bev asked.

I gave her a weak smile. "Okay."

"John and I are here for you, Maeve. Anything you need. And when things settle down, we need to set a beach cookout date."

"Absolutely," I agreed.

"Well, I'm exhausted and heading home. Hope you have a good one." As she began to walk away, she stopped and hugged me and reiterated, "Anything," into my ear.

"Thanks, Bev."

What is going on with the Whitaker family? And how could this be happening in my tiny town, USA?

As I sat watching the staff come and go, Will called. "Hi, Maeve. I hope I caught you before you started seeing patients."

"I'm having coffee. Did you hear about the Charlotte Whitaker assault?"

"Ella told me when I got in. The story is all over town." Ella was Will's newly hired second-in-command.

"What's going on, Will?"

"I don't know, Maeve. People are speculating that it's somehow connected to her father's death. Anyway, it's unbelievable."

I could tell Will wanted to say something else. "What is it, honey?" I asked.

"Maeve, I need to take out another business loan."

Will already had a hefty business loan and had planned on making a sizable early payment after the Whitaker wedding. "Can you afford that, Will?"

He was silent for a moment. Then he answered carefully, "I don't have a choice, Maeve. Mrs. Whitaker has not paid her balance. I need that money, but how can I push her when her husband was murdered at an event I catered? And now she must be distraught about her daughter."

"She owes you that money, Will. You provided the services."

"And maybe the murderer," Will said.

"Kevin?" I gasped.

"I didn't say Kevin, but someone tampered with the champagne."

We were both silent. The new loan would put added stress on both of us.

"Maeve, I wanted to let you know about the new loan, but now I have to run. I have an early appointment with the Langford Historical Society. They want to discuss a brunch using local produce and some recipes from the eighteen-hundreds, which is great for the company. Remember, we're having dinner at stately Wayne Manor this week."

"Now that you mention it, your father *is* a bit like Batman."

I realized that Will had hung up abruptly. I didn't get a chance to add that his father was like Batman gone to the dark side.

The new loan would be daunting. The old loan was already daunting enough. I knew that Will could make his business a success, but this murder needed to be solved quickly, and Mrs. Whitaker needed to pay her bill.

I sat contemplating all the news since there was still twenty minutes before my shift started. Looking up, I was surprised to see Meg approaching my table. As usual, she was impeccably dressed in a navy crepe wrap dress. "What are you doing here?" I asked.

"Had my annual mammogram. I was hoping I would catch you before work."

"Did you hear about Charlotte?" I asked her.

"I know everything about the assault."

I filled her in about the pearls in the flute stems.

Meg looked incredulous. "Who would even think of that? For one toast? Who would notice the pearl? Even for me, that's over the top. Charlotte certainly was their pampered princess. How is she doing?"

"Bruised and tired but recovering." I brought her up to speed on the conversation I'd overheard between Mrs. Whitaker and James Zabalon.

"You are a wealth of information today. Why didn't you tell me this sooner?" Meg asked.

"Ah, work, stress, worries. I just forgot," I said.

"Weak excuses, but at least I was right about the affair," she added triumphantly. "Now, I just want all the details."

"We also need to find out who attacked Charlotte," I said.

"Agreed. Either Charlotte was the intended poisoning victim, or someone has a vendetta against all the Whitakers. Something crazy is going on here. I just feel it."

"What, with your Spidey sense?" I teased.

We were silent for a moment. The cafeteria was filling up. Even though it was busy, one never heard the clatter of dishes or silverware that was the staple of most hospital cafeterias. The dining room was a true oasis in a busy medical center.

Suddenly, my more immediate problem came back to me. "Meg, Will and I are having dinner at the Kensington manse this week, and I am freaking out."

"Delightful. Well, I have Xanax," she offered.

"No, no Xanax. But I need outfit suggestions, please."

"Oh silly, silly girl. You really should consider better living through chemistry, especially with that crew. But all right—wear your black silk slacks and a black shell. Carry that pink gauze wrap and wear your pearls. Keep it simple and stellar. You know that Lydia and Eloise, her mini-me, will be coiffed and dressed to the max. So you go in there with your shoulders back and your head held high. Use your height."

"What about conversation?" I asked.

"Keep it light. Whenever possible, pretend you are deaf. And smile, smile, smile. Focus on them. Remember, they are narcissists and not interested in you."

"Yes, ma'am," I said with resignation.

"It won't be terrible, Maeve. Well, okay, it might be. But you are the daughter-in-law. They must include you to see their son. Use your power," Meg urged.

"For good, right?"

"Funny woman," Meg said.

"Come on, I'll walk you to the elevator," I said.

"I have to go show some lookie-loos a few properties. It will be a colossal waste of time, but I am doing it as a favor to a mortgage broker who refers a lot of business to me. Have a good day, and I'll see you at Mom's for breakfast tomorrow."

I gave her a quick hug, and off she went. I set out for the conference room on the second floor. It was my turn to give a lecture on prenatal genetic testing to the medical students. This was a treat for me as I enjoyed teaching, and it was great for medical students to learn early that midwives were their colleagues.

The morning went by quickly, and I stopped by Madeline's office after I finished. "Did you hear about Charlotte Whitaker?" I asked.

"Scary stuff," Madeline replied. "By the way, our badges no longer work to enter the Pavilion. It seems they are keeping her well protected."

The Pavilion was the floor for VIP patients. "I guess they are," I agreed.

"Why would someone want to kill the Whitakers?" Madeline wondered.

"I don't know," I replied. "It makes no sense to me either."

"By the way, how's Will doing?" Madeline asked.

"He's still getting a few cancelations a week. The Creighton Hospital Women's Club just decided he didn't need to cater their afternoon high tea party."

"Ridiculous! They're a bunch of lemmings. Hang tough, Maeve. It will get better."

"I sure hope so. Well, I'm off to triage."

"Be sure to grab some lunch before you go. You know how triage can be," Madeline reminded me.

"Will do," I replied as I left the office.

Just keep going. One foot in front of the other. Keep moving. Meg and I will get to the bottom of this...quickly.

CHAPTER FOURTEEN

Gestational diabetes is a condition in which a woman without prior diabetes develops high blood sugar levels during pregnancy. Women are usually tested for gestational diabetes around twenty-eight weeks.

"Hi, Mom," I said, stepping into her apartment at the senior center the following day.

Mom was dressed in a bright teal, sequined top with black polyester slacks. Her hair was done, her makeup was on, and she wore four rings. As usual, she was ready to step out.

"Hi, Maeve. Don't you look nice. I like your outfit."

"Thanks, Mom. I got it at Marshall's." I was wearing a lilac embroidered tunic over white crops.

"Well, you look good," Mom observed. "We should stop at Marshall's the next time we go to lunch."

"It's a plan. And here are the wedding photos," I said, handing the packet over. "I'm starving. Do you have any muffins?"

"How about some date nut loaf and cream cheese? The kettle is on."

"Sounds great," I answered. "I'll get everything ready."

Mom was already leafing through the pictures from the wedding. "Oh, look at Mrs. Whitaker! What a dress! She looks like the sister of the bride, not the mother."

I knew I was in for a blow-by-blow critique by the self-elected queen of the fashion police. Joan Rivers, take a seat.

"Hello!" Meg came through the door laden with flowers, blueberry scones, and a large espresso from Starbucks.

"You know I always have date nut loaf for you, Meg," Mom complained.

"Well, hello to you too, Mom. Yes, I know. But I wanted a scone today."

"Okay, women," I called out from the kitchen alcove. "Come on. Tea is ready."

"I want to look at all the photos first," Mom said.

"Later, Mom. Let's eat."

I brought out the tea and bread, and we all settled in. Mom's date nut bread was always cut into thick slices with crispy walnuts peeking out. Topped with cream cheese, the taste always took me back to childhood.

"Poor Charlotte," Mom said in between bites.

"There's more to it," I said, and I told her about the pearl in the stemware.

"What a foolish waste of money," Mom said.

"But someone switched the glasses if Charlotte was the intended target," I said.

"That's the big mystery," Meg concluded.

"I wonder," Mom asked, "how many people knew she had a pink pearl in the stem of her glass?"

"Will knew, some of the catering staff knew, her family knew, and probably her girlfriends," I replied.

"That's a lot of potential suspects," Mom mused.

"Do you want to hear the latest on Mrs. Whitaker?" Meg asked.

I leaned forward in my seat. "Share with the class, Meg."

"Well, for starters, she's getting ready to put the manse on the market."

"What!" Mom exclaimed.

"She will be marrying the car king," Meg added.

"No way!" Now it was my turn to be surprised. "So soon?"

"I hear within the next few months," Meg confided.

Mom put her mug down. "Amazing. And her poor husband barely in the grave."

"That house will sell for a fortune," I observed.

"Conservatively, I'd say about four point six million," Meg agreed.

Mom was suddenly quizzical. "Who did you hear all this from?"

"The real estate agent group. They have their antennae out all the time, especially when a juicy property might be involved."

"Very interesting." I nodded. "I wonder what the Whitaker kids will say."

Mom frowned. "I feel so bad for them, first losing their father, and now their mother getting married so fast."

We all chewed and silently sipped our tea for a few minutes. Then I asked, "Any family news?"

"Olivia's going off to some New Age conference next weekend," Meg said.

"Where?"

"Some ashram in Western Mass."

"What's an assram?" Mom asked.

"Assram? No, it's ashram," Meg laughed, unable to stop herself.

I shot her a look. "Stop it, Meg. It's a type of spiritual center, Mom."

"No kidding. I never heard of an assram before. Olivia is always searching for something, but she doesn't realize what she has right here at home."

As usual, Mom was right.

"When are you going away with Aidan and Sebi?" I asked.

"In September, and I can't wait." Mom was beaming.

We talked and laughed for two hours. Finally, I got up from my chair and cleaned the kitchen.

"Well, I need to get going. There's dinner at the Kensington's tomorrow, and you both know I can't wait for that. But today, I want to take Fenway for a walk and start knitting a new watch cap for Will for next winter. Hope you enjoy the wedding photos, Mom."

We hugged and said our goodbyes. Goodbyes are always a huge event in our family. When you lose a parent in your early years, you never take goodbyes for granted because you just never know.

Out in the hallway, the elevator came, and we stepped inside. Meg turned to me as the doors closed. "I didn't want to ask in front of Mom, but how did the appointment go?"

"Fine. It was just preliminary testing."

"Any answers yet?"

"You mean is it him or me?" I glared at Meg.

"No, fool. I meant any answers with solutions."

"No. Not yet," I said in a quiet voice.

The elevator opened onto the waiting area, which, amazingly, was empty. We waved goodbye to Mom as we passed the camera, and I walked Meg to her car.

"I didn't mean to be so touchy," I started.

Meg held up her hand. "You know, Maeve, I hated pregnancy. I love Henry, but I hated being pregnant. There was the hideous clothing, the heartburn, the hemorrhoids, ugh. But listen to me. If you need me, well, you can use my uterus. I would be your surrogate. But only once. I'm not a broodmare. And if we could, I'd like to do this in the winter. Who wants to be knocked up in the summer? So that's my offer. Think about it. And listen to me about tomorrow night. Just be you. Kick butt, take names, and remember our motto, *Illegitimi non carborundum.*"

Don't let the bastards grind you down. We'd discovered it in the lyrics of the "10,000 Men of Harvard" song when Artie was in college, and it had been ours ever since.

Meg laughed. Then she looked at me for a long minute. "What else is wrong?"

"Nothing."

"Maeve, come on. This is me asking."

"Oh, Meg. Mrs. Whitaker has not paid Will yet, and his loan payment is due. He's talking about taking out another loan."

"What? She needs to pay up right now."

"He feels like he can't push her."

"He has to, Maeve. Business is business."

I was silent.

"When is his payment due?" Meg asked.

"The end of the month."

"I can cover it and—"

"Absolutely not, Meg. I appreciate the offer, but Will would never accept it. You are the only person I am sharing this with."

"Gee, have enough stress?"

I sighed deeply.

"We'll figure this out, Maeve. I've got your back."

And with that, she hugged me and then swept into her navy Jag and zoomed off. I found myself staring at her taillights with my mouth open. *Sarcastic, haughty, queen witch, and then two unbelievable offers. That is the conundrum that is Meg. Sisters are the best. They're just the best, through thick and thin.* I shook my head and smiled as I drove off to pick up Fenway and walk the beach.

CHAPTER FIFTEEN

The umbilical cord usually has two arteries, which carry blood that contains waste from the baby to the placenta. It has one vein that carries oxygen and nutrients back to the baby.

As Will and I pulled into his family's front gate, thoughts of the help arriving at Buckingham Palace floated through my mind. *Of course, they would have had to enter through the back door.*

A long, winding private drive led through massive elm trees up to Fairview, the Kensington's red-brick Tudor mansion. The estate encompassed five acres overlooking the Atlantic. It took five full-time gardeners to keep the lawns and plantings in showcase arboretum condition.

Will parked beside the Tuscan fountain in front of the main entrance. As we walked up to the front door, he took my hand and smiled. He was dressed in a navy blazer with a pale blue shirt and khakis. I was dressed as Meg suggested, and hopefully, I looked chic and confident.

"It will be fine, Maeve," Will said, squeezing my hand.

"They are so not the Walton clan," I replied, frowning.

"Remember, honey, it's just a little dysfunctional family dinner."

"Yes, I know. This won't hurt a bit," I smiled.

The Kensington's longtime family butler, Roberts, opened the massive front door adorned with a bronze lion head knocker. "Good evening, Mr. and Mrs. Kensington."

"Roberts, it's so good to see you. How is your family?"

"Excellent, Will. Thank you for asking. Drinks are being served in the lower rose garden."

What mansion is complete without both an upper and lower rose garden?

On the way to the conservatory, Will and I walked through the ornate black-and-white marble foyer, complete with a magnificent display of peonies and a sweeping bridal staircase. Every room we passed was suitable for commemoration in *Architectural Digest*, the financial baron issue. Finally, we stepped onto an extensive piazza with more fountains and a small staircase leading down to a circular stone patio surrounded by every color and size of hydrangeas. I could picture entire flower clubs weeping with joy over this display.

William and Lydia were seated in intricately hand-forged wrought-iron chairs with white linen seats and backs. William was dressed in a navy blazer over an open collared, pink-and-blue-striped shirt and Nantucket red slacks. His belt was embroidered with lobsters. Lydia was sixtyish, five feet two, petite, and toned. Call it very well preserved. She was a vision, of sorts, in cream silk slacks and a cream, sleeveless silk top complemented by her large silver David Yurman bracelet. Two beautifully behaved *Cavalier King Charles spaniels,* Duchess, and Jackson, made the scene a tableau worthy of F. Scott Fitzgerald's talents.

Will's sister, Eloise, looking poised and petite, wore an ivory crocheted eyelet shift and sat beside her husband, Taylor, who, in his navy blazer, was a walking Vineyard Vines commercial. Teddy, the youngest brother, also wore a navy blazer with a crisp white shirt and navy-and-white seersucker shorts. Did this family always dress like they were preparing for a photo op? Perhaps paparazzi were lurking in the shrubbery. Did I miss the text that all women were to dress in off-white? All I could think of was the song that went, "One of these things is not like the other; one of these things just doesn't belong." *Easy breaths, in and out, just like I tell my patients.*

"Good evening, Will. Hello, Maeve," William said.
Hands were shaken and backs slapped all around.
"You look adorable, Maeve," Eloise said.
Adorable? I'm not a child. But I smiled broadly.
I saw Lydia look me over from head to toe, and I felt as out of place as Gulliver with the Lilliputians. Somehow my black outfit seemed classic at home, and it was what Meg advised. *Meg could pull off any look. Here, I felt like Johnny Cash in drag.*

"What can I get you to drink?" William asked.

"I'll have bourbon and ginger ale, please," I said.

"Knob Creek or Maker's Mark?"

"Maker's Mark, please." I wanted to tell him to make it a double.

"Can't convert you to Knob Creek, Maeve?"

I smiled. William asked me this every time the subject of bourbon came up, and I never changed my order. *There are serious control issues on both sides.*

"I'll have a Manhattan, Dad," Will said.

"Sit and let's have a chat before dinner," Lydia said.

Will and I settled onto the overstuffed white linen love seat.

"How are you feeling, Maeve?" Lydia inquired.

"Uh, fine."

"Those night shifts must be very tough. I don't know how you do it."

"Well, you never get used to it, but it comes with the territory."

"Yes," Lydia said, "I suppose it does. My friend Pauline's daughter, Greta, is an OB/GYN. She has a lovely office in Boston."

Wait for it.

"I know some women prefer midwives, but I just can't imagine going to one. Well, each to her own, I suppose," she said with a smile.

My pulse didn't even rise because we had been down this road so many times before. Instead, I took a big swallow of bourbon.

"Will, how is the business going?" William interrupted.

"We've had a bit of a slowdown after the Whitaker fiasco," Will said.

"Yes, that was very unfortunate," his father agreed. "What's the latest with the investigation?"

"I assume you know about the attack on Charlotte. It appears that she may have been the true target."

"Are they still suspecting that Irish boy?" his father inquired.

Oh, great. Let's just put out the old "No Irish Need Apply" signs while we're at it.

Before Will could answer, his father continued, "Don't you vet your employees, Will?"

Will swallowed hard and said, "Kevin has been a very strong member of my team." I saw his jaw tighten.

I jumped in, trying to deflect attention from Will with a tried-and-true gambit. "I heard that the Whitakers' housekeeper was fired because she may know something about Mrs. Whitaker's, um, extracurricular activities."

"Ridiculous!" Lydia exploded. "I've heard those rumors. I play mahjong with Audrey. She was always faithful to Harrison."

Oops. Looks like I touched a nerve.

"Well, someone appears to have a vendetta against the Whitakers," I pointed out. Silence filled the room as everyone stared down at their glasses.

"Terrible tragedy," William finally said. "I hope your business pulls through, Will. Small enterprises are difficult, and people have long memories regarding tainted food."

Will looked at me, and I could see him silently willing me not to respond. Another stellar evening at the in-laws was well underway.

Luckily, Roberts appeared at that moment. "Dinner is served," he announced. Will squeezed my hand as we filed into the conservatory for dinner and took our assigned seats at the table.

Snowy white linen napkins were folded beside the pink-and-white Meissen china. Green hydrangeas and white peonies in cut-glass vases adorned the wrought-iron and glass table. Dinner was a choice of salmon or beef filet along with veggie skewers complemented by long-grain rice, tomato with mozzarella and basil salad, and pan-fried cornbread.

Meals at the Kensington manor were always a study in stark contrast. They provided lousy conversation with powerful jabs to the ego but compensated with excellent food.

Lydia and Eloise passed on the rice and the cornbread. Heaven forbid an unwanted carbohydrate would pass their lips and offend their carefully controlled diets. But that didn't stop Lydia from examining my full plate. She smiled and said, "Is there enough for you, dear?"

I felt a blush creep up my cheeks. "It's wonderful. Thanks so much." I smiled back, though a touch more grimly. I felt Will's hand put pressure on my knee.

"Before we begin," William said, "let's raise a toast to Taylor."

I glanced around the table. Was it my imagination, or did everyone except Will and I seem to know what the toast was about?

"Taylor will be offered a partnership in the firm on Monday. He has surpassed all the partners' expectations." Holding his goblet up, William added, "To a wonderful future."

We all raised our glasses in response and echoed his words.

"Congratulations, that's wonderful." Will shook Taylor's hand.

Lydia smiled like the Cheshire cat.

"Save a place at the table for me," Teddy said.

"No worries, Teddy," William answered breezily. "You concentrate on your studies in New Haven, and you will find there is always a place for family." He paused, then added, staring fixedly at Will, "Well, interested family, anyway."

Now it was my turn. I lightly tugged on Will's blazer sleeve.

The meal continued with small talk about boating, summer plans, and updates on Langford friends. When everyone was finished, Eloise piped up, "Taylor and I have another announcement." All eyes again focused on Eloise and Taylor.

Taylor stood up with a big grin on his face. "Eloise and I are expecting our first child early next year."

"Taylor, Eloise, that's great." Will hugged his brother-in-law.

"I'm so very happy for you," I added.

"I am thrilled," Lydia joined in, throwing air kisses.

"Perfect timing." William grinned rather smugly.

"I am going layette shopping tomorrow." Lydia was positively beaming.

William laughed. "Of course, you are."

"You look wonderful, Eloise. How has your pregnancy been so far?" I asked.

I should have realized. She has been drinking seltzer water all night instead of wine.

"I feel wonderful. I'm ten weeks according to Dr. Whitaker. Oh, except that now it's Dr. Cydson. But Dr. Whitaker said just a few weeks ago that everything was progressing as expected." She paused for a beat. "Maeve, I feel safer, or rather, more comfortable with a physician."

"Every woman should choose the provider she wants," I said, smiling thinly.

"We are so blessed." Eloise smiled and added, "Now it's time for you and Will to have a baby."

Will and I smiled back broadly. I had to keep reminding myself *I will not cry. I will not cry.*

"Yes, it's about time for you two," Lydia said.

I felt tears pricking at my eyes.

"What's for dessert, Mother?" Will broke the fixation on me.

"Strawberry shortcake, of course. It's your father's favorite. Let's move to the veranda and get comfortable. We have so much more to talk about."

"Maeve and I have early wake-up calls," Will put in, "so we will take some to go."

"All right," Lydia agreed. "Then you and I will go talk about nursery furniture, Eloise. Lydia put her arm around Eloise, and they headed back to the veranda.

Will and I said our goodbyes, and we headed to the car. As we buckled up, he asked, "Was it worse than a sprained ankle?"

"Yes, definitely worse."

"Worse than a migraine?"

"Much worse."

"Worse than a root canal?"

"Not quite that bad."

"Okay, then. We'll score it a win." He grinned, then quickly added, "Only kidding, Maeve. I'm sorry."

"It was fine. Okay, not fine. And it has been worse."

"They never disappoint, do they? Don't let them get you down."

I squeezed his hand. "Will, do you ever wish…"
"What?"

"That you went into the family business?"
"Not for one day. Not even for one minute."
"Okay, then," I said. "We'll keep on going…"
I stopped there, and then we both laughed and said in unison, "Second star to the right and straight on to morning."

CHAPTER SIXTEEN

All eggs carry X (female) chromosomes. Sperm have either an X (female) or Y (male) chromosome. Gender is decided by the sperm that fertilizes the egg.

On Monday morning, I grabbed a large, iced coffee and headed straight to the midwifery office. I planned to meet Alec, the med student assigned to shadow me for the day before the patients arrived. We had a full schedule, and I wanted him to have a positive experience. Jayda was waiting for me as I came through the door.

"Hi, Jayda," I said. "How are you doing today?"

"Fine, Maeve. And you?"

"Doing well. How are Patrice and Gus?" Patrice and Gus were Jayda's twins.

"They're great. Looking forward to starting high school next year."

"Wow," I said, shaking my head in disbelief. "That went by fast."

"No kidding," she replied. "I can hardly believe it's been that long since they first started school." She pulled out her phone to show me some recent photos.

"Are they going to Langford High?" I asked.

"Yes, and I hope that it's a good fit for them. It has wonderful music and drama departments, plus every sport a kid could want. You know, it's so well-funded that it's practically a private school masquerading as a public school. Some people in town send their kids to private school, but I don't know why. The public schools are why we live here even though we could get a bigger house in another town."

"I've heard that the schools in town are superb. And just think, you won't have to downsize when the time comes. That's a good thing."

Jayda laughed. "That's if the property taxes don't drive us out first."

Looking at the schedule, I began to plan the day. This was important because, as much as I loved teaching students, I knew I had to move along to get all the patients seen. Plus, I never forgot that the very nature of obstetrics always meant there was a surprise or two lurking in every schedule.

"Hi, Maeve," Alec said as he walked into my office. He was about five feet ten inches tall and slim with wiry black hair and large brown eyes.

"Hi, Alec. Are you ready for a busy morning?"

"I am," he shot back.

"I'll have you look over the schedule in a minute. Jayda has written prep notes on every patient."

"Prep notes?" He looked at me questioningly.

"Prep notes include gravity, parity, number of weeks gestation, any major issues, plus what we need to do today."

Sounds great," Alec said, looking over the schedule.

"You're at the end of your third year of med school, right? Do you know what you'll be specializing in?"

"I'm attracted to cardiology, pediatric cardiology in particular," he explained.

"Well, best of luck," I told him. "I can't wait to hear where you match."

"Thanks, Maeve."

I looked down at the list. "So our first patient of the day is Carmen Novak. She is a primigravida ten-and-a-half weeks pregnant. I know that you watched Madeline do a physical before. Do you want to watch me, or do you want to do the exam?"

"I'd like to do it," Alec said, with more than a touch of eagerness.

"Perfect. I'll let you take her history, and then I'll be with you for the physical exam. It will be a great learning experience, especially since you are thinking of pediatric cardiology. Remember, parents like these and their children may eventually be your patients."

"I never thought of that," he replied.

"Hearing a fetal heart at ten weeks can be difficult, and we may need to get an ultrasound, but we will try with the fetal doppler first."

He nodded.

"Let's go meet Carmen and her partner, Ben."

After brief introductions, I left Alec to take the history. Carmen and Ben were very willing to have a medical student participate in their care. When Alec was finished, he would call me in for the physical. I appreciated the break because I was still reeling a bit from the latest Kensington dinner. The baby news would dominate every Kensington gathering. And, worse yet, now I would have endless pregnancy events to attend since Lydia was no doubt already planning any number of baby showers.

Did I need to be reminded of infertility at every turn? I shook my head at myself. *Get a grip, Maeve. Put the big girl pants on. Eloise deserves to be happy. She has nothing to do with you not being pregnant. Do not go down that dark road. You are surrounded by birth every day.*

"Maeve, are you ready?" Alec was standing at my office door.

"Sorry, Alec. I was just daydreaming. Did you find anything special in Carmen's history?"

"Carmen's sister is a carrier of cystic fibrosis, and Carmen and her partner have never been tested."

"Did you tell her that she could be tested today?"

"No, I thought I would wait for you."

"Fine. Let's go talk with them," I said.

I knocked on the exam room door and opened it after Carmen called us to enter. "Hello, again. Alec will do a physical exam, and we can talk about any questions or concerns you have. He told me that your sister is a carrier for cystic fibrosis," I said, addressing Carmen.

"Yes, she found out when she was pregnant."

"Was her partner tested?"

"He was negative."

"Well, we can test you today. The results take about a week."

"Should I get tested, too?" Ben asked.

I shook my head. "Let's wait for Carmen's results. If she is negative, then there is no reason to test you. Both of you must be carriers to have any issues."

It turned out that Alec was very adept and had good clinical skills. He completed the exam and then looked at me.

"Okay, now let's try to hear this little human," I said as I lowered the table and put a bit of sound-enhancing gel on the end of the doppler for Alec. "Remember, the baby is tiny and moves around, so we may need a few minutes to locate the heartbeat."

At first, nothing but static noise came from the fetal doppler. Then there was the rhythmic beat of a pulse. "Is that it?" Alec asked.

All eyes turned to me. "It sounds slow. Check Carmen's pulse and see if they match."

He picked up Carmen's wrist to find her pulse. "They do," he said, a little dejectedly, realizing that he had found the mother's pulse.

"That's fine," I reassured him. "Keep looking."

I put my hand over his and redirected the doppler down into Carmen's pelvis. We all heard the rapid beat at the same time. "That's it!" cried Alec. Carmen and Ben beamed.

"He, or she, sounds wonderful," I confirmed.

Ben recorded the heartbeat with his cell phone.

"That's amazing." Alec seemed almost as excited as the new parents.

"Alec is going to be a pediatric cardiologist," I said to Carmen and Ben. "This may be the earliest fetal heart he has ever heard."

"It is." Alec beamed.

"We'll let you get dressed, Carmen, and then both of you can join us in the office to talk."

Outside the room, Alec said, "That was great. I saw how you redirected the doppler."

"Alec, you have excellent clinical skills, and you put Carmen and Ben at ease. It can be tough to hear the heartbeat at ten weeks, especially if the mother has extra padding. Carmen is slim, so that makes it easier."

Carmen and Ben rejoined us, and I let Alec take the lead discussing genetic testing, nutrition, exercise, and warning signs.

Then Alec wrapped up the session, and Carmen and Ben left with a host of brochures.

"Okay, Alec, we have two patients waiting and a full schedule, so follow me, and I will let you participate as much as I can."

CHAPTER SEVENTEEN

Preeclampsia is a complication that develops after 20 weeks of pregnancy. Its symptoms include high blood pressure, facial edema, and headaches.

Luckily, there were no surprises for the rest of the day, and one patient even canceled because her toddler was sick.

At the end of the session, Jayda and I reviewed the patients and the lab work. I had let Alec leave early to meet with his classmates. "Thanks so much, Jayda," I said. "I couldn't have done it without you."

"You are welcome. It's always a pleasure to work with you."

My cell vibrated as I walked down the hall, and I instinctively fished it out of my pocket. It was Meg.

"Hi, Maeve," came Meg's familiar voice. "I hope you're ready because I have a scoop."

I stopped walking and paid attention. "Spill."

"Charlotte was attacked with a bat. It was a baseball bat with the Langford High insignia stamped on it."

"Some high school kid attacked Charlotte?"

"Maeve, anyone with access to the high school baseball team's equipment could have attacked Charlotte. But who would you guess is the JV baseball coach at Langford High?"

"Please don't tell me that it's Kevin Reardon," I groaned.

"Okay, then I won't tell you."

"Oh, Meg."

"It's looking bad for Kevin," Meg pointed out. "I heard, when he was a senior in high school, there was a shouting match between him and Dr. Whitaker at the Whitaker home. Police were called, but no charges were filed."

"Something to do with him dating Charlotte?" I asked.

"Who knows? But there was some bad blood."

"How did you find all this out?" I asked.

"Shelley is best friends with the Whitakers' live-in chef."

"Kevin has been out of high school for a long time."

"Kevin was a server at the 'no money spared' wedding of the century featuring his ex-girlfriend. And it sounds like he and Dr. Whitaker had some issues," Meg said.

We both went silent, thinking about this new information.

"Did you find out anything about the EpiPen?" Meg finally asked.

"I'm on my way to the pharmacy right now. I'll let you know if I learn anything."

"Hey, I just had a thought," Meg interjected. "I wonder if Aidan taught Kevin Reardon in high school."

"I'm going to his house tomorrow. I'll ask him."

"Say hello to Aidan and Sebi for me, and please kiss that beautiful niece of ours."

"Of course, Meg."

I put the phone away and started walking again. I headed to the basement where the outpatient pharmacy was located.

Tori, a fortyish pharmacist, came to the window. "Hello, Maeve."

"Hi, Tori. How's little Matthew?" The midwives had delivered Tori's baby two years ago.

"He's wonderful. I never thought I could be so lucky." Tori got out her phone and swiped around until she found what she was looking for. Holding it out, she said, "Here, look at him." She showed me a photo of a sturdy two-year-old with red corkscrew curls and huge dimples.

"He's lovely! Look at that hair!" I exclaimed.

"Thanks, Maeve. We are so happy. He is just the love of our lives. So what can I do for you?"

"I wanted to ask you about the EpiPen recall."

Tori's face clouded over. "What a nightmare. This cannot be over soon enough. We are in full-blown crisis mode."

"What's going on?" I asked her.

"Come inside."

She opened the pharmacy door just enough so that I could squeeze in, and then she shut it tightly behind me.

"Maeve, I am only sharing this with you because you're an OB provider. Please keep this confidential."

"Of course, I will, Tori."

"About six months ago, we were notified that a batch of EpiPens was recalled for faulty plungers. We checked the lot numbers and personally called everyone on the list. We accounted for every single one." She frowned and lowered her head.

I prompted her gently. "Was Dr. Whitaker's current EpiPen on the recall list?"

"Yes. Larry Smith, the head pharmacist, personally exchanged Dr. Whitaker's EpiPen. But now, with Dr. Whitaker's death, Larry has been accused of not being thorough enough. He's on leave as of today."

"Oh, no," I gasped.

"He's been here for thirty years and is excellent. If anything, he is overly obsessive, which is what you want in a pharmacist. I can't imagine him making that mistake." She frowned again and shook her head. "This is awful."

"What do you think happened?"

"I can't imagine. We triple-checked the list. The company wanted the defective ones back and sent us new EpiPens to distribute to those patients affected by the recall. The company didn't want the EpiPens destroyed because they wanted to study the defect. Larry personally packed and sealed the box."

"Who picked up the box?"

"It had to go by registered mail. It was sent out from the Creighton mailroom." Tori shook her head once more. "I don't know what to think, Maeve. It's just unbelievable."

I was shocked. "Did you call the EpiPen company?"

"Yes, and that's the other part I don't understand. We sent back twenty EpiPens, but they said they received nineteen. They said our paperwork also said nineteen were returned."

"Does Larry have a copy of the paperwork?"

"No. It was a packing sheet that the company sent by mail, so it isn't in our computer files. I thought Larry made a copy, but now neither of us can find one."

"So it's Larry's word against theirs?"

"Yes."

"Do the police think the defective EpiPen somehow got to Dr. Whitaker?" I prodded.

"Yes, and they are also saying that Larry might be charged with criminal negligence." Tori looked on the verge of tears. She went on. "It's tearing him up. Larry is a wonderful pharmacist. Sharon, his wife, is in treatment for breast cancer, and he doesn't need this right now. Again, please keep this confidential, although it will all come out soon enough."

I nodded.

"Well," Tori said, pulling herself together, "I need to get Matt from daycare. I've been getting there late because of this mess, and I'm tired of getting fined every day."

"Tori, please call me if I can do anything to help."

"Thanks, Maeve."

I hugged her and left.

What a day. The session had been tiring enough, but now there was all this. My head was swimming as I headed home. I got in my Jeep and pulled the visor down to look in the mirror. *Do I look as tired as I feel?*

Out tumbled a package of red licorice, my favorite treat, and a tiny note. It was a drawing of Fenway and Will surrounded by hearts. Underneath, it read *A little snack from your pack.*

CHAPTER EIGHTEEN

Infertility is defined as the failure to achieve a pregnancy after twelve months or more of regular, unprotected sexual intercourse.

Aidan, Sebastian, and Chloe lived in a beautiful Victorian-style house in Boxford, about twenty minutes west of Langford. It was referred to fondly as the "hydrangea house" because, thanks to Sebi's love of dark blue hydrangeas, rows of the plants lined both sides of the stone walk as well as the front of the house. They made a striking contrast to the building's lemon-colored façade.

I opened the screen door and heard the familiar tune of "The Wheels on the Bus." Aidan, my football star brother, danced in the kitchen with Chloe in his arms. Chloe squealed with delight while Ishmael, their golden retriever, turned in circles and barked.

"Hi, Maeve," Aidan said as he came to a stop.

"Hello, loves." I kissed first Chloe's chubby cheek and then Aidan.

"Look, angel," he said, pointing to me, "it's Auntie Maeve."

Chloe reached out for me, and I took her and held her tight. She was so beautiful, with straight black hair and light brown skin.

"She's getting so big, Aidan."

"I know, growing like a little flower. She'll be seventeen months old on Monday."

"Look, Chloe." I pulled out a tiny pink stuffed octopus.

"Oh, Maeve. Thank you. It will add to her huge collection unless Ishmael claims it first."

"This is for Ishy," I offered, pulling out a large bone.

"He'll love that."

Ishmael grabbed his bone and ran off to the living room.

"Sit, Maeve. I'll make some tea."

I sat down at a handcrafted maple farmhouse table and looked out at the garden. There were peonies, wisteria, roses, and, of course, deep blue hydrangeas everywhere. Birds were at the feeders at the garden's edge, and beyond that, there was a small pond and a blue slate fire pit.

"Aidan, your yard is amazing," I marveled.

"Says the woman with an ocean view," Aidan retorted.

"I know, but I saw what this mound of dirt looked like before you and Sebastian built the house."

"Sebi is the man with a plan. I just rake and dig. We hired Sebi's gang for a lot of the heavy lifting."

"Well, it's a work of art."

Aidan brought out hazelnut coffee and cinnamon bread. I put Chloe in her highchair and kissed her head. She held tightly to my finger.

"You and Sebi are so lucky," I said.

"We know. Gay adoption is not the easiest." Two adoptions fell through before Chloe was finally placed with them.

"Have you seen her birth parents recently?"

"No, we left visiting up to them. They are both in college now, just finishing their first year. They go to different schools, and both are in relationships. We sent Christmas photos, but we'll let them decide about contact. They know we love her and that this was a great decision for all of us."

"It's a happy beginning," I said, smiling.

"Sebi's parents are still coming to terms with the fact that she doesn't have a Cuban first name."

I continued to smile, but I could feel it was getting forced. Aidan reached out and touched my arm.

"Maeve, I know you are going through a lot, but have faith. Babies come in many ways, and they are all little miracles. But I guess you know that."

"I do know," I said with a sigh. "It's just so difficult to go through the process."

"I doubt that delivering babies every day is much help," Aidan said.

"I just wish it would happen naturally."

"Look whom you're talking to, Maeve."

"Oh, Aidan, you know what I mean."

"I know, sweetie. Now come on, have some bread before Chloe eats it all." Chloe was already happily munching away on a tiny piece.

"How's the new book coming?" I asked.

Aidan had taught high school English for a few years, but his passion was writing. In the past five years, his children's books featuring Lawrence the Lion had become bestsellers.

"Well, Lawrence will be getting a new sister this year."

Great, even lions could get pregnant easily.

"That should be fun. I can see why kids love your books, Aidan."

"I've been lucky."

"You've been lucky, but you are also hardworking and an excellent writer," I pointed out. We sat together comfortably watching Chloe. "I take it that you heard about the Whitaker wedding and the attack on Charlotte," I said.

"Mom keeps me informed."

"I'll bet she does."

"Was it as much of a disaster as she says?" Aidan asked.

"I would say seeing your father die at your wedding had to have been tough on the bride. For the rest of us, it was just surreal—surreal and so sad."

He took that in for a moment before inquiring, "Has Will's business been affected?"

"Well, bookings are down, and Kevin Reardon, one of his wait staff, is under suspicion."

"Kevin Reardon? You mean Kevin of the infamous Reardon clan that the O'Reillys owe their lives to?" He looked thoughtful. "You know, I taught him in high school."

"Did you know him well?" I asked.

"It was my first year of teaching. As I remember, he was a great kid who had a tough break."

"Do tell," I insisted.

"Kevin was an ace pitcher for Langford High School. He had his pick of Division I colleges offering him scholarships. Kevin decided on Duke but then tore his rotator cuff in his first game freshman year. The surgery was successful, but he lost his pitching speed and control, ending his time at Duke. I heard that he ended up back here and went to Adams State but dropped out before graduating."

"Tough break," I muttered.

"Yes, it was," Aidan agreed. "I'm sure he has many 'what if' days."

"Did you know he was dating Charlotte Whitaker in high school?" I asked.

"She went to private school. But I was a prom chaperone, and I remember he introduced me to her."

"I heard there were some issues between Kevin and Dr. Whitaker," I said.

"I never heard anything about that."

"Well, now the police are looking at him for the murder and assault cases," I explained.

"You mean the murder of Dr. Whitaker?"

"Yes," I said, "and they think he may also have tried to harm Charlotte."

"Maybe he did become very bitter. I have not seen him in years. But when I knew him, he was a nice, humble kid. I recently heard that he was helping out with the Langford High baseball team."

I looked directly at him. "Did you know Charlotte was attacked with a bat?"

"Maeve, anyone can get a bat," Aidan scoffed.

"But not necessarily a Langford High bat," I pointed out.

"What? Maeve, I swear Langford has turned into the Wild West. What on earth is going on there?"

I shrugged. "Who knows? But it's looking like either Kevin is the killer and the attacker, or he is being set up."

"This is unbelievable."

"I know." I grimaced. "Aidan, I was wondering, can you ask around about Kevin?"

"Really? If Patrick finds out I am asking questions, there will be hell to pay."

"I just don't want an innocent person to be convicted, and I want Will's business to survive."

"Maeve, take some brotherly advice. Let Pat and the police solve this."

"Could you at least ask, Aidan? Maybe just in casual conversation?"

He smiled wryly at me. "Well, I'm doing a writing workshop on college essays this week at Langford High. The juniors worry about their college applications and acceptances, so I try to make the personal statement a fun experience. Maybe I'll hear something, and if I do, I will let you know."

"That's perfect," I said sincerely.

Aidan sighed. "I really should know better than to get involved, but I will ask," he said with resignation. "You and Meg are a dangerous combo."

I smiled as innocently as I could. Then I nodded toward the highchair. "Look at Chloe." She was leaning to one side of her highchair with her eyes closed.

"I guess it's time for her nap," Aidan said. "Stay, Maeve, and we can talk more."

"I have to go, Aidan, but thanks. Thanks so much." I hugged him hard, then stepped back. "Give my love to Sebi."

"And you to Will," he replied. "Remember, the next family dinner is here."

"You know we wouldn't miss it."

"Love you, Maeve."

"Back at you." I turned to go.

"Bye, Ishmael," I added and gave him an ear scratch on the way out.

At home, I started Googling chocolate chip cookie recipes. I was determined to master just one darn recipe. Just one. Scrolling down, I found various suggestions that all promised cookie nirvana every time. Underbake a bit, use more brown sugar than white, don't overmix, and use prime ingredients. Add a bit of coffee and be sure to add nuts.

By the time I got to the nuts, I had lost the thread of what came before. I leaned back on the couch and closed my eyes. *How could a small recipe mystify me so much?*

As I sat there, my mind wandered back to Dr. Whitaker. *Why did he have a defective EpiPen? He must have known about the recall. And did Kevin have a dark side? Or did Mrs. Whitaker kill Dr. Whitaker because of her affair? Could Ava be so angry with the Whitakers that she would seek revenge? And who but a hospital employee could get their hands on the defective EpiPen? Was El Cid or Evelyn involved?*

I began to get a headache, so I decided to curl up with Fenway to take a nap before dinner. As my eyes started to shut, my cell phone jolted me awake. I picked up my phone and looked at the screen. "Hey, Mom."

"I just wanted to let you know that I loved seeing those wedding photos," Mom gushed.

"That's great," I said, feeling the tug of sleep again.

"You know, I've seen one of the guests around here a lot."

"Who?" I asked, immediately waking up.

"The older woman with that tight French twist."

"Do you mean Evelyn?" Now I was interested.

"I don't know her name. She wore a powder blue suit and is in photos with the bride," Mom confirmed.

"What?" This was getting truly interesting and very curious.

"She goes through the main door to the assisted living center. You can see the entrance to the assisted living center on Channel B. I switch between the channels."

Why would Evelyn be a regular there? She lives alone in a harbor view condo in Langford. I never heard that she had any family in this part of the country.

"I see her a lot, but always on Tuesdays, I think." There was a short pause. "Oh, yes, on Tuesdays. That's it because that's when my groceries get delivered. While I wait for them, I watch both channels."

"Mom, are you sure?"

"I'm old, but I'm not blind, Maeve."

"Sorry, Mom, I didn't mean to doubt you," I backpedaled. "I'm just surprised."

"Well, maybe she moonlights there. I have to go now. I'm off to play bridge with Gaby and the girls. Love you."

"Love you, Mom." Mom clicked off, and I sat still, just holding the phone. Evelyn and the Hanville Grove Assisted Living Center made one very odd combination.

CHAPTER NINETEEN

Premature birth is defined as one that occurs before the thirty-seventh week of pregnancy.

The following day, I found Madeline and Winnie standing outside the midwifery office. "Forgot your keys?" I asked, smiling at them.

"The locks have been changed."

"What?" I gasped. "Why?"

Winnie explained, "Apparently, Dr. Cydson wants the midwives to have lockers only, no office space. Bev has gone to talk with John."

"You're kidding, right?" My disbelief was mounting.

"Also, we are not allowed to teach the medical students any longer or to be on call. The OB residents will deliver our patients if we are not here," Madeline explained. "In short, he's trying to disband the midwifery practice."

"Over my dead body," Winnie said, her face visibly tightening.

I stared at Madeline. "He did this?"

"Yes," she confirmed.

"Where are we supposed to see patients?" I demanded as if it was somehow Madeline's fault.

"In El Cid's old office. The one he used before he was made acting chief. It's all in the note he sent out this morning. You'll see it when you log on to the computer and read your email."

"Let me get over there, and I'll get started on seeing this morning's patients. Are they going to be redirected to his office?"

"Yes, he's thought of everything."

"We'll fight this!"

"You can bet your life on that," Madeline reassured me. "Right now, though, I am waiting for security to open this door so that Winnie and I can remove the midwifery belongings."

At that moment, Evelyn Greyson came bustling around the corner with two large security men. "Good morning, girls," she practically sneered. "Let's make this snappy."

"Make it snappy? Evelyn, these are our offices," Madeline said. She was as exasperated as I've ever seen her.

"*Were*," Evelyn stressed the word, "your offices, dear."

"Evelyn, you're a nurse," I pointed out, although it may have come out a tiny bit sarcastic. "How can you possibly think this is just?"

"Dr. Cydson is streamlining many areas of the department. Your little practice is just one of many. As you know, it's all about dollars and cents these days," Evelyn chirped.

Winnie was not about to let that go by. "We bring a lot of patients and money to Creighton. We allow women to have a choice of providers. Women who give birth at a hospital tend to bring the entire family there for care. That equals more patients for the hospital."

"Well, now you need to do all that in a different office. I'm told this suite has already been promised to the orthopedic department."

"Is Dr. Cydson trying to close our practice?" I asked.

"How paranoid you've become, Maeve. I would have thought you have too much on your plate right now to be worried about the future of the midwifery practice."

She obviously thought that was sufficient to put me in my place because she turned away abruptly. "Madeline, the painters come in thirty minutes. Security will stay with you until you are finished. Please pack quickly." And with that, she strode off down the corridor to the main hospital.

"Pompous nasty woman!" Winnie headed into the office suite.

Madeline and I looked at each other. It took a lot to get Winnie ruffled. "Go ahead and get started with patients, Maeve. We'll take care of this."

I went to see what awaited me.

To save time, I took the stairs up to the third floor and opened the door to El Cid's old office suite. The inside looked like an abandoned strip mall storefront. Bulletin boards were stripped bare, shades were down, and a few old furniture pieces were left behind. Jayda had gotten in ahead of me and was already clearing tables and setting up supplies for the day.

"Where does El Cid get off saying we're supposed to see patients here?" I asked. Jayda just shook her head. "With all my heart, thank you. You've done incredible work already with this mess. I'll go get started in El Cid's office."

As I went into the office, I heard her mutter something unflattering about the acting chief under her breath.

I put my bag on the desk and turned on the computer inside the office. I pulled up the schedule and began to get my bearings. I read the email from El Cid. It managed to be both sickening and shocking at the same time. When I couldn't stand to read anymore, I looked around more closely. El Cid had two exam rooms, an office, and a small waiting area. As hospitals go, it wasn't bad for space.

On the other hand, the décor was hunter green and dark leather. It was all very masculine and austere and chosen from Creighton's "men are in charge here" decor line. There were no magazines or brochures in the waiting room, and all wall hangings had been removed. Faint lines marked the outlines of the frames like outlines of bodies at a crime scene. When El Cid had departed for greener pastures, he'd left scorched earth behind.

In the short time she'd been working, Jayda had stocked supplies, turned on a soft background of easy listening music, refilled the waiting room water cooler, and was ready to greet the first patient. She had even lifted an orchid from someone's office for the table in the waiting room.

"Jayda, it looks great," I said with awed admiration.

"Well, it's better than nothing," she grumbled.

I sipped my coffee and looked at my preps. Caroline Laine was my first patient. She was one week postpartum and was in for a blood pressure check since she'd had elevated blood pressure after her delivery. Jayda had taken her blood pressure, and it was 122/68. That was perfect. This should be a quick visit.

I knocked on the door and walked into the exam room. Caroline was sitting on a chair next to the desk. Tomas, her newborn son, was in a stroller sleeping beside her. I noticed that Caroline looked very pale, with dark circles under her eyes. Her hair was pulled into a messy ponytail, and it looked like it had not been washed or combed in a few days. Her shirt was stained on the collar. *Baby spit-up?*

"Hi, Caroline. How are you doing?" I pulled up a chair to face her and immediately saw tears rolling down her face. "What is it?"

"I'm a failure," she sobbed.

"What's wrong?" I asked, taking hold of her arm.

"I tried and tried to breastfeed, Maeve. Tomas just screams, and nothing I do makes a difference. Yesterday, Dr. Brewster, his pediatrician, said he's lost too much weight and needs to be supplemented with formula."

"That happens sometimes."

"Last night, I gave him formula, and he slept great. But now he is screaming again when I try to breastfeed him. What is wrong with me?" She continued to cry desperately.

"Caroline, there is nothing wrong with you. Tomas looks very content, which means you are taking excellent care of him. Sometimes breastfeeding works well, and sometimes it doesn't. Right now, your baby needs to gain weight, and the formula will help with that. You also need to be kind to yourself. You look very tired. Remember that you had a very long labor, and you're still exhausted."

"But I want to breastfeed him."

"Okay. Then let's decide to do that," I assured her.

"You know, none of my friends or my sisters had any problem breastfeeding."

"Caroline, first remember that this isn't a contest. And all that doesn't mean you won't breastfeed him. It just means you need to go at your own pace. This is a learning process for both of you. Tomas needs to gain weight, and you need rest. Let's formulate a plan, and one of the midwives will call you tomorrow to check in. For now, though, you just rest, supplement with formula, and enjoy Tomas."

We went on to talk about herbal supplementation, the timing of nursing, hydration, help at home, and other measures. I also put her in touch with one of our lactation counselors.

"Thank you, Maeve. It's been such a disappointment so far. But I'll follow the plan and see what happens."

"Remember," I said as she was leaving, "give it time. The midwives are always here for you, Caroline." She looked a bit brighter as she left the office.

Well, that ten-minute brief visit ran to twenty-five minutes, and now I was backed up. But what else was new?

Next up was Aisha Robertson, a forty-year-old who was eleven weeks pregnant. This was her first visit. She was medium height with an athletic build and impeccably dressed. I had ordered an ultrasound because of her age, and it showed an active fetus.

"Nice to meet you, Aisha," I greeted her as I entered the exam room.

"You too, Maeve."

"Well, everything on the ultrasound looks fine. How do you feel?"

"Anxious and overwhelmed but very happy."

"Have you been trying to get pregnant for a while?" I inquired, noticing at the same time that a partner's name was not listed on her chart. She blushed slightly and looked at the floor.

"I thought I couldn't conceive. My periods are irregular, and I thought I was going into menopause. This pregnancy is a complete surprise. The father won't be involved. He doesn't even know."

I waited for her to continue.

"He's someone I see on occasion. He works at a law firm in Manhattan, and we see each other at conferences a few times a year. We meet for early morning runs when we are in the same city. Well, I guess we do more than just jog when we see each other," she said with a wry smile.

"Do you think he would welcome the news?"

"He's married," Aisha said. "I know, it's an old cliché. I don't want to disrupt his life. He has two older children. We were content to see each other when we did with no strings attached." There was another pause, and then she laughed. "I guess this is a big string. But I also always wanted a baby. I'm financially secure. I'm a partner in my firm and own a lovely home here and a vacation home in Maine. I have lots of family and friends in the area, and I know they will be supportive when I tell them."

"That's wonderful, Aisha. But you also might want to think about letting him know."

"I go back and forth about it. I have been discussing it with my therapist."

"Well, keep an open mind. He might want to be involved."

"I know he has rights. I just need to think of all the options."

I proceeded to do the physical exam and ordered blood work. Then I faced her. "Welcome to the practice, Aisha. I see Jayda gave you the emergency contact numbers and a notebook full of material to read."

Aisha smiled again. "Yes, she did. Are you redecorating the office?"

"This is a temporary space for us. There is a bit of reshuffling going on."

"Well, I am so happy to be with the midwives. I think this will be a great experience."

I smiled and walked her to the waiting room. *What else could I say? Who knew what would happen with the midwifery practice?* Then, turning back to the office, I heard a raised voice.

"Where is she? I'm not waiting all day."

Macey was pacing back and forth in front of the exam room door. She was dressed in a gray hoodie with hot pink sweatpants and had no makeup on, unusual for her. Her eyes looked dark and heavy from lack of sleep. I decided a show of professional innocence was the best approach.

"Good morning. Sorry I got a bit backed up." I took her arm and gently guided her back into the room.

Macey glared at me. "I think my water broke."

"When did this happen?" I asked.

"Last night."

"Macey," I said, restraining my impulse to lecture, "remember when we talked about your test coming back positive for Group B strep and that you needed to call as soon as your water broke because you will need antibiotics in labor?"

Many women carried Group B strep in their vaginas. It was only a concern during pregnancy because it could pass to the fetus during labor. Treatment with antibiotics during labor could prevent issues with the baby, but antibiotics needed to be started as soon as possible if a woman ruptured her membranes.

"My cell was broken."

"Okay," I said with a sigh. "Let's see what is going on. I will check and see if you did rupture your membranes."

Macey lay back on the exam table, and I gently palpated her uterus. "Is the baby active?" I asked.

"She never stops moving."

"Her heart rate is one hundred and fifty-six. Nice and strong."

Macey stared at the ceiling and said nothing.

"Any contractions?"

"I can't tell. Everything hurts too much, and she moves too much."

Macey's abdomen felt soft to the touch. I would have to observe her for any contractions.

"Is Tim with you today?"

"No," she sneered.

"Is anyone with you?"

"No."

"I'm going to do a pelvic exam now. I will be as gentle as I can."

Jayda was standing beside Macey as I began the exam. "You'll feel the speculum now," I told her.

I saw a copious amount of amniotic fluid as soon as I placed the speculum in Macey's vagina. I dipped a piece of nitrazine paper in the fluid and watched it turn blue, which indicated her membranes had ruptured.

"You broke your water, Macey. It's time for a baby. First, though, I need to examine your cervix."

A quick check told me what I already suspected. "Your cervix is four centimeters dilated, it's completely effaced, and the baby's head is already a good way down. Are you sure you're not having contractions?"

"Maybe a few," she allowed as she grimaced and grabbed her abdomen. I put my hand on her and felt her rigid uterus.

"Macey, let's get you to the labor floor and get those antibiotics started." I took hold of her arm to help her sit up. "By the way, your last drug test was positive for opioids."

"Did you tell DCF?"

"You know they had to be told. They will be involved in your daughter's care." She pulled away from me and turned her head to the wall. I put my hand on her shoulder and gently rubbed her back. "Macey, let them help you and the baby."

"They'll take her away and put her in foster care, and she'll get all screwed up just like me. I know the drill."

"Faye, the social worker, is going to be involved, and she will do her best to help you and your baby. She'll help you enroll in parenting classes."

"Ooowww!" She clutched at her abdomen again and tears formed at the corners of her eyes.

"Let's get you to labor and delivery. We can talk about this later," I said. "Just remember, we are going to help you, Macey. Jayda, will you take Macey over to the labor unit, please?"

I tried once more to give some needed reassurance. "Bev is the midwife on call today, Macey. I think you will like her."

Macey silently got dressed and gathered her belongings.

"Can I call anyone for you?"

"No."

Jayda appeared with a wheelchair.

"I'm not using that," Macey snarled

"Jayda will walk you over if you don't want a ride. You're going to do fine. I'll stop by when I'm done."

"I just want this to be over." She stalked away with Jayda at her heels.

CHAPTER TWENTY

Melasma, also called the mask of pregnancy, is common. It consists of dark patches on the face. It usually fades after pregnancy.

After the last patient was gone and Jayda had left, I sat back and reviewed the day. I always had a heavy heart when I needed to involve DCF in any patient's care. It started a long road of checks and balances, but the baby's well-being had to come first. Hopefully, Macey could get into a better situation—I would do everything in my power to help her. I completed my notes and refilled some prescriptions. I wanted to leave time to check on Macey before I left.

As I tried to concentrate on the computer, I realized that my right knee kept hitting the back of the desk drawer. Cursing El Cid for leaving us faulty furniture on top of everything else, I got on my hands and knees to see if I could adjust the drawer. I tried pushing it back, but it was stuck and would not budge at all. With mounting frustration, I pulled it partially out and then shoved it back in as hard as I could. Something fell to the floor as the drawer slid shut.

I looked under the desk. On the floor was a small binder that looked like a check ledger. It had *Department of OB/GYN, Creighton Memorial* imprinted in gold letters on the cover. The bank listed was Rockwell Trust. Inside there were four checks and a few months of bank statements. All the checks had been written to something called the PTD Foundation. According to the bank statement, the money appeared to be coming out of the OB/GYN Department and going to the foundation.

What is the PTD Foundation? What does PTD stand for? Preterm deliveries?

I snapped photos with my phone and slid the checkbook and ledger back into a small hollow under the desk drawer. Now the drawer worked, and the checkbook was still hidden.

I need a debriefing with Meg ASAP. I tried her phone, but my call went straight to voicemail. I would try again after I checked on Macey.

As I walked onto the Labor and Delivery Unit, Angie, from triage, greeted me. "Hey, Maeve," she said. "Here for the night?"

"Just checking on a patient."

"Do you mean the delightful Ms. Cunningham?"

"I take it she wasn't cooperative on her admission."

"She did call me a jerk because I started her IV. She actually singled me out as an evil jerk."

I frowned.

Angie laughed. "I've been called worse. She's scared under her hard shell."

"Did anyone join her?" I asked.

"I think she's still alone. Bev will give her TLC, though. And I think Faye has been in to meet her."

"I'm sure that didn't go over well."

"I saw her positive drug test," Angie acknowledged. "Also, her white blood count is up. She may be infected. We started antibiotics, but who knows how long she was ruptured."

"Thanks, Angie." I made my way to labor room six, where I saw Bev rubbing Macey's back.

"That's it, Macey. You are doing so well," Bev said.

"I want the epidural now."

"The anesthesiologist will be here very soon," Bev soothed. She looked up as I walked in. "Hi, Maeve."

"Hi, Bev. Hi, Macey. How's it going?"

Macey looked out the window and did not turn when I addressed her.

Bev answered, "Macey is doing great. She's five centimeters dilated and one hundred percent effaced."

"Why is *she* here?" Macey asked without looking at me.

"I wanted to check on you, Macey, like I said I would," I replied.

"Are you going to call the social worker again?"

"Macey—"

But Macey cut me off. "*Ahhhhh!*" she gasped. Another contraction had started. Bev immediately began helping Macey to breathe through the pain.

I skimmed Macey's fetal monitoring strip and saw that the fetal heart rate was slightly elevated at 170 but otherwise looked okay. Her temperature was 100.8. Elevated fetal heart rates often indicated infection, and given Macey's rising temperature and white blood count, it needed to be watched. Bev would be on top of this and would get a consult if necessary. I decided to give them some space, so I left the room, closed her door, and walked to the labor desk.

"Hey, Maeve." Dr. John Armstrong was the maternal-fetal medicine physician on call today.

"Hi, John," I replied. "Seems like the unit is buzzing."

"As usual." He smiled. "I looked at the OB statistics yesterday, and our census is growing both in numbers and acuity. By the way, Bev gave me an update on Ms. Cunningham."

"Yes, I saw that her white count and fetal heart rate are both up. It looks like she's probably headed toward chorioamnionitis," I said. Chorioamnionitis is an infection in the membranes around the fetus and the amniotic fluid. It develops during labor because bacteria found in the vagina enter the uterus. This can happen when the fetal membranes have been ruptured for a long time.

"We'll watch her carefully. I also hear DCF will be involved."

"She had a positive toxicology screen for opioids. Faye was in to see her already. Macey is going to have to make some hard lifestyle choices."

He nodded and then asked, "How's Will?"

"Hanging in. It's been rough, but he's committed to pulling through."

"Let me know what I can do, Maeve."

I smiled.

"I mean it," he said.

"Thanks, John. I do appreciate it. On another note, I am sure that Bev has filled you in on the latest developments with the midwives."

"She has."

His eyes swept the hall. El Cid was holding court with a group of medical students in front of the labor board. John lowered his voice, "This is a time of transition, Maeve. Remember, there is great support for the midwives. Word is just starting to get out about the changes. Stay strong."

Just then, Sabrina, one of the operating room technicians, approached us.

"Dr. Armstrong, you're needed in OR two," she said.

John nodded and gave me a quick goodbye.

I decided to head to my late afternoon knitting group and call Meg on the way. As I passed the labor board, El Cid called out, "I see your patient was not informed to call when her membranes ruptured even though she was GBS positive."

"That's incorrect, Dr. Cydson. She was told to call as soon as she ruptured."

"Well, apparently she didn't get the message, or she wasn't informed as to how important it was." He turned to the medical students. "Now, because of this communication failure, both mother and baby are in jeopardy. Come, let's tour the NICU."

My palms were sweating, and my face was flushed. That man was determined to undermine the midwives, if not be rid of them entirely. I watched him and his entourage depart and saw Evelyn had arrived on the unit and was dealing with some paperwork at the nurses' station. Now she looked at me with a big smirk on her face.

"You know the midwives take wonderful care of our patients, Evelyn," I pointed out to her.

"Well, apparently not this one," she sneered.

"Patients don't always do what we ask. You know that."

"Perhaps you did not fully explain what could happen."

"Evelyn, why are you not more supportive of the midwives?"

"Maeve, I am the director of Obstetrical Nursing. I am very supportive of all my nurses. However, I also tell them when they have shortcomings."

"Evelyn, this situation is very delicate. This patient has other issues, which may have stopped her from calling us."

"Every situation is unique, Maeve. The challenge is having the knowledge and experience to deal with it to create the best outcome for mother and baby. That's what makes an excellent clinician."

I glared at her.

"Perhaps obstetrics isn't your field, dear," she said.

My mouth opened, but no words came out.

"There are many other areas where nurses are needed. The geriatrics unit, the oncology unit, and the cardiology division are all hiring."

Working past my shock, I tersely replied, "I am a nurse-midwife, Evelyn, and a very good one." She flashed me her Mona Lisa smile again, so I added, "And speaking of geriatrics, I hear that you regularly visit the Hanville Grove Assisted Living Center."

Evelyn's face fell, and her pencil tip snapped on the ledger. She looked stunned but quickly recovered.

"I help the nursing staff update their protocols and provide continuing education on a variety of topics. What business is it of yours, Maeve? Are you spying on me?"

"Spying? Now I would say that's a bit paranoid, Evelyn. Someone just mentioned to me that you are a frequent visitor. I thought perhaps you were looking for a new job. Maybe obstetrical nursing isn't *your* field."

Take that.

Narrowing her eyes, Evelyn spat out a reply. "I'll be staying right here, Maeve. There is much work to be done. You should worry about your position if you keep making errors like the one you've made today." She gathered her folders and marched to the stairwell, walked through the door, and let it slam.

Angie came over to where I was standing. "Wow, Maeve. What did you say to set off the Wicked Witch?"

"She loves to throw the midwives under the bus, and I took the bait. I should have walked away," I said.

"She throws all the nurses under the bus. Evelyn wishes it was 1950, and we were still handmaids, seen and not heard. Come on, don't let her get you down."

"Thanks, Angie. But I need to get out of here." I left the unit and rode the elevator to the lobby in a quiet rage. I needed to get my mind off Creighton, and knitting offered a respite.

CHAPTER TWENTY-ONE

Amniotic fluid acts as a protective liquid for the growing fetus and facilitates the exchange of nutrients between mother and fetus.

My latest knitting project was in a tangle, just like my thoughts. The drop-in hour at A Stitch in Time was just starting when I arrived.

"Maeve, nice to see you." Priscilla was a slim, middle-aged, copper-haired shop owner.

"See if you say that after you see my mess," I replied as I searched through the contents of my knitting bag.

"Have a seat, and let's see the damage." Lilly was the drop-in hour's knitting maven. "It can probably be salvaged."

Taking my seat, I saw seven women of various ages and ethnicities at the table. Believed to have originated in the Middle East about 1500 years ago, knitting is a prized craft in many cultures. I knew a few of the women from previous drop-in hours.

"Maeve's one of the midwives at Creighton," Lilly said.

Numerous hellos and head nods greeted me.

"This is a mess, Maeve," Lilly declared.

I shrugged. "My mind was elsewhere."

"I would have thought midwives were good with stitching," an older knitter said.

"Only vaginas. Not wool," I said, which started them all laughing except for Kate, a woman at the center of the table with a short white bob cut who turned scarlet and quickly looked down. *Oops, TMI.*

"Terrible business with that doctor and his daughter," Lilly said.

"Yes, it is," I agreed but did not elaborate.

"I hear they arrested Kevin Reardon," Lilly said.

"What?" Kate exclaimed. "When did that happen?" Her fists were clenched, and a few of her stitches fell off her needle as she dropped the scarf she was knitting onto the large oak worktable.

"I heard it on the radio about ten minutes ago," Lilly said.

Kevin arrested? I needed to talk to Pat.

"Kevin's a wonderful kid. The Reardons are a terrific family," Kate said.

"The report said his fingerprints were on the bat used in Charlotte Whitaker's attack," Lilly said.

"Of course, his prints would be on the bats. He's the coach," Kate said.

No one spoke.

Kate continued, "Kevin had some issues when he was dating Charlotte. He wasn't good enough for Mummy and Daddy. They had the typical Langford prejudice toward anyone they believed to have even the slightest shade of blue in their collar. You know that la-dee-da elite country club gang who puts down everyone else. He would never be good enough for their family or their fake high society nonsense. The police will probably force poor Kevin into a false confession."

"I don't think the police would force him to confess," I said. I knew Patrick could be counted on to ensure everyone's rights were protected.

"The police in this town do whatever the ruling class wants," Kate complained. "Kevin volunteers at the food pantry and has a lovely new girlfriend. This will destroy his life." She started packing up. "I've got to run. I must see if the Reardons need anything. This is disgusting." She quickly shoved her knitting into her bag and stormed out the door.

"That kid's going to need a good lawyer. The Whitakers own Langford," Lilly said.

"I'm sure the police will follow all the leads and won't rush to judgment," I said.

"We'll see," Lilly said.

I felt sick to my stomach. Kevin was in big trouble. Maybe he was guilty, but I refused to believe it. Patrick also had to know that some people in town believed the police buckled under the Langford social titans.

Lilly put down my work. "Maeve, I think I have your knitting straightened out." The rows all looked even. The tangles were gone.

"Did I zig when I should have zagged?" I asked in amazement.

"Something like that. It looks like you repeated a row three times and then fell off the grid a bit. Your thoughts were elsewhere. But it was all fixable. Here you go. You are on row ten of the pattern."

"Thanks so much, Lilly. I don't think Fenway will be getting this one."

"Fenway?" Lilly asked.

"My puppy. She got my first three blankets because they were not fit for humans, but she loved them."

"Knitting for dogs," Lilly said. "We've all been there." A few of the group nodded in understanding.

"Maeve, did you see I have some new baby alpaca yarn?" Priscilla asked. "It comes in a beautiful plum."

I threw up my hands in pretend horror. "I have so much yarn. I don't need anymore."

"Said every knitter ever," Lilly chimed.

"Well," I said, caving, "just let me look at it."

A few minutes later, I headed to my car carrying four skeins of plum yarn, along with my corrected blanket. Settling in, I decided to try calling Pat before driving home. He picked up on the second ring. "Detective O'Reilly."

"Hi, Patrick. I heard they found Kevin's fingerprints on the bat and that you arrested him. You could have told me."

"Gee, Maeve, I didn't know I reported to you."

"Don't be snarky, Pat."

"Oh, that's right. You weren't at the official briefing because you are not a police officer."

"Isn't Kevin an assistant coach for the high school baseball team?" I pressed.

"Maeve, I know you want the kid to be innocent. He is an assistant coach, but he had motive and opportunity, and his fingerprints are all over the bat. He also served Dr. Whitaker the drink that killed him. He was placed under arrest. His guilt or innocence will be up to a jury. We can't ignore the facts."

"Did he confess?"

"You know I can't discuss that with you."

"I wonder if—"

"Maeve, please stay out of this. I know that you are worried about Will's business. I understand. Please leave it to the professionals. For now, there is too much circumstantial evidence to overlook."

"But does this mean you will stop investigating other suspects?"

"I'm going to hang up now, Maeve."

"Patrick, you do know some people believe the Langford police are in the pocket of the rich citizens?"

"Seriously, Maeve? Rumors?"

"Well, you know that I don't think that."

"I've got to run, Maeve. Love you."

"Love you, too, Pat."

Well, knitting wasn't going to help me relax tonight.

A text from Meg came in: *Meet me @ On the Rocks in 5 minutes*. On the Rocks was a wine and beer pub located across the street from the knitting shop on the harbor.

I got out of my car, walked across, and found a booth in a quiet corner. Then I ordered Guinness for both of us. Sitting there alone, I suddenly felt very weary and rested my head in my hands. *I do not believe that Kevin is guilty. But then again, maybe Patrick is right. After all, he is the expert. But would he keep investigating?* I felt helpless and hopeless.

A familiar voice punctured my gloom. "Double-fisted drinking? Seriously, not a good look, Maeve." Meg slid into the facing seat with a bag from Pacelli's Bakery.

"Where are you coming from?" I asked.

"Realtor meeting. I remembered you go to that crazy knitting group, so I thought this would be a good place to meet." She opened the bag and pulled out two containers of tiramisu, complete with spoons and napkins.

"Sinful but so delicious," she said.

"Tiramisu and Guinness, a winning combination," I said.

"Always eat dessert first," Meg answered.

"Absolutely," I said.

"Look out at the harbor, watch the boats, and enjoy this amazing treat." Meg raised her glass and looked at me. I raised mine.

"*Sláinte.*"

"*Sláinte.*"

"Now, what's got you down?" Meg asked.

"Well, to begin with, a patient of ours didn't call after her membranes ruptured, and now, she's probably infected."

"How is that your fault?" Meg queried.

"El Cid and Evelyn are making it my fault."

"Maeve, come on."

"I know, Meg, but it's difficult when the attending and the supervisor are both blaming you. Since Dr. Whitaker died, El Cid—and maybe Evelyn, too—have been trying to eliminate the midwifery practice. El Cid took our offices away and is diminishing our role in the OB department."

"That's outrageous." Meg raised her voice.

"Well, he has the power, and Evelyn is greasing the wheels."

"You'll have to buck up. Seriously, they are not worth the stress. You know you provide excellent care to your patients."

"But it does make you begin to doubt yourself."

"Knock it off! You're being ridiculous!" Meg snapped. I grimaced and continued to eat my tiramisu. Meg was silent for a moment while we watched the afternoon's last boats come into the harbor. "You need to mobilize," Meg suddenly pointed out. "Get your supporters out in force."

"Madeline is working on it. We all are. But we were caught by surprise. It happened so fast," I said.

"That's how they conquer and destroy. What about asking Will's grandmother for help? She's on the Creighton board."

"The board doesn't usually get involved in departmental business, and I don't want to use family connections. I don't want Grand to feel compromised."

"I get that," Meg said.

I gave her a weak smile. "I also had another winning conversation with Pat. The police seem sure Kevin is the culprit."

"I saw the news."

"But what if he is being framed?"

"Framed by whom?" Meg asked.

"Who knows?"

"How about Mrs. Whitaker?"

"Mrs. Whitaker wouldn't try to kill her own daughter, Meg."

"People will do anything when money is involved."

"Come on. Let's get serious."

Meg shrugged.

"What about Ava?" I offered. "After this, she'll never work in this town again."

"Who knows? Why did she back down? Maybe she is undocumented."

"Why do you say that?" I asked.

"Mrs. Whitaker is holding something over her head. She must have panicked after getting called in by the police, but she held her tongue."

I pondered that for a minute. "Does she have family in town?"

Meg looked thoughtful. "I'll put Shelley on it."

"Oh, and there's something else. I found some weird checks in El Cid's office."

Meg's eyebrows shot up. "What?"

"Here, let me show you." I handed her my phone, and she scrolled through the photos of the checkbook and ledger.

"Where did you find these?" Meg inquired.

"They were hidden under El Cid's desk drawer."

"Hidden?"

"Yes, in a hollow spot under the main drawer."

"And you just happened to find them?"

"His desk drawer was stuck, and they fell out when I tried to fix it."

"Okay, next question. Why were you in his office?"

"I told you, El Cid took away our offices. I had to use his old one."

"He is an evil little man drunk with power," Meg mused.

"So, what do you make of these checks?"

"We need to find out what the PTD Foundation is and where this money is going," Meg mused. "Any idea what PTD stands for?"

"The only thing I can think of is preterm delivery, but I've never heard of any foundation like that at Creighton Memorial. Why do you think he kept these checks hidden?"

"Let me have Artie look into this. He owes me a favor—I found one of his partners a lovely beach house on the Vineyard. Sniffing out illicit financial deals is his specialty. Remember, most of his friends invested with Bernie Madoff, but Artie always said the deal never passed the smell test."

"Smart man. Thanks, Meg."

"I want the right person arrested as much as you do. Plus, I hate bullies, and El Cid is stepping way over the line right now with your practice." She looked thoughtful for a moment. "Do you think Evelyn is helping him?"

"She seemed delighted that we had to move our patients and lose our office space."

"So why is she so evil?" Meg asked.

"I don't know. She does love control, though."

"What a mess," Meg said with a sigh. We both leaned back in the booth.

"Did you find any malpractice claims against Dr. Whitaker?" Meg asked.

"I went through the state medical database. He's had no malpractice cases filed against him."

Again, we sat in silence, watching people come and go through the large window. "Are you and Will coming to Aidan and Sebi's for dinner this week?" Meg finally asked.

"Wouldn't miss it. Chloe is so adorable."

"They are crazy about her. It's kind of cute to see two city slickers turn into suburban dads with such a vengeance."

"It's also nice that all the parents in the neighborhood adore them."

"What's not to love? They're civic-minded, great dads to a beautiful daughter, one's a best-selling children's author, the other a homebuilder and gardener extraordinaire, and let's just get it out there, they are easy on the eyes. I'm sure those suburban moms have the binoculars out on planting day."

"And some of the dads," I added. We both chuckled. "Aidan told me that he asked around at the high school about Kevin Reardon but heard nothing that we didn't already know."

We were both quiet again for a few minutes, each lost in our thoughts. Finally, I asked, "When will you call Artie?"

"Tonight."

"You know he still adores you, Meg."

"We're great friends, although marriage was another issue. Let's just say we are better as friends than spouses."

"I guess."

"I know. Now get home to that adorable husband of yours. Surprise him. Make him dinner. Just, please, no cookies."

I stuck my tongue out at her, and then we left the pub to go our separate ways.

Dinner. Hmmm. I would make something simple but delicious. Will loved seafood. Grilled swordfish and crab cakes from Delaney's with a few ripe tomatoes would fill the bill. I made a quick trip to the market and then headed home.

Fenway was waiting by the door, wagging as I entered the house. "Hi, Fens. Is Dad out?" Then I saw a note on the black-and-white granite countertop that answered my question.

Gone for a run. Back soon.

Love you, me

It also had a drawing of a stick figure running with little hearts trailing behind. *What a goof. My loveable goof.*

I sliced the tomatoes and then made a marinade for the swordfish and popped it into the fridge. Looking, I saw that someone was feeling ignored by the dinner preparations. "Come on, Fenway. I'll get your dinner now."

I put Tony Crown's new album on my phone and sent it through the house's sound system. I loved his cover version of "Fly Like an Eagle." Then I sat down in the sunroom on my favorite blue-and-white-striped chair and put my feet on the ottoman. Thinking about the day's events, I realized that with the new problems El Cid and Evelyn were causing, Kevin Reardon's arrest, and the increasing number of questions with no answers about the Whitaker case, I had some real issues on my plate.

I was worried I was being pulled into a black hole, and I might not be able to climb out.

CHAPTER TWENTY-TWO

Many women experience mild anemia in pregnancy.

    I heard my phone ringing in the kitchen and realized I must have dozed off. I decided to ignore it. I wasn't on call, didn't recognize the ring tone, and deserved a quiet evening with my husband. Just a few more minutes of napping, I thought, as Fenway snored gently in my lap.

    Suddenly, I was startled by pounding on the door. Fenway simultaneously launched out of my lap, barking loudly in intruder defense mode. *What time is it? Where am I?*

    "Maeve! Maeve! Are you here?" a feminine voice outside the front door called. Looking out the window, I saw that it was Nora. She was flushed and had strands of curly, gray hair unraveling from her perpetually neat hairdo. She was as unkempt as I'd ever seen her.

    I quickly opened the door and waved Nora in. "Is it Grand?" I asked, assuming the worst.

    "No, dear," Nora panted out. "There's been an accident. We don't know much, just that Will's been in an accident."

    "Will!" My heart leaped. "Accident? What? How?"

    "I don't know, Maeve. You need to get to Creighton Memorial as soon as possible. Oscar will take you."

    "I can drive myself."

    "Maeve, listen to me. Grab your purse. I will take Fenway to the main house. Oscar is coming to take you now. Don't forget your phone and charger, dear."

    A black BMW pulled rapidly into the driveway and came to a sudden stop. When I came out, Nora was holding Fenway. She looked to make sure I had my purse and phone. As I stood on the porch, she locked the door behind me.

    "Th-thank you, Nora."

"No thanks needed, Maeve. Call us when you know anything. I'm sending prayers."

I ran to the car, and we took off to Creighton. Oscar was silent. I could feel adrenaline pumping through my body, clouding my thoughts but feeding my worst fears.

The drive took about eight minutes but felt like eight hours. I looked at my phone and saw four missed calls. I recognized the number as the Creighton Memorial exchange.

Oscar pulled up to the emergency department entrance. I grabbed the door handle and was halfway out of the car as it came to a stop. "Thank you, Oscar!" I yelled as I ran into the hospital.

I practically ran to the admitting station, where I said in a booming voice, "My husband, Will Kensington, was in an accident. Where is he?"

The admitting clerk, a very tall, sandy-haired man, looked up and said, "Please take a seat, and I'll find out when you can see him."

"I need to see him now. Get the charge nurse."

He stared at me, and I glared back. "Now," I repeated.

He got up and was gone for a few minutes while I paced. An older nurse dressed in scrubs came out. "Mrs. Kensington? Hello, I'm Andy, the nurse manager. Let's go into my office."

"I want to see my husband."

Andy led me to his small office. "I understand you are one of our nurse-midwives," he said.

"Please, call me Maeve. I'm not trying to be difficult, but I need to see my husband."

"Maeve, Will is having a CT scan right now," Andy informed me.

"Why? What happened?" I blurted out as I slumped into the chair facing his desk.

Andy pulled a chair up beside me. "Let me tell you what I know. Will was found unconscious in the bushes along Stetson Point Road. A passing motorist saw his red jogging shorts and pulled over to investigate."

I listened numbly.

"EMTs were called. They stabilized him and brought him in."

A tall, thin, strawberry-blonde woman in rumpled scrubs entered the office.

"Hello. Are you Mrs. Kensington?"

"Yes, I'm Maeve."

"Maeve, I'm Dr. Teresa Darrow, one of the ED attendings. I wanted to update you on Will's condition."

I nodded.

"He has a fractured left shoulder and at least two broken ribs. There's a lot of bruising on his left side. He regained consciousness in the emergency room but has no idea what happened to him. The medical team wants to ensure he doesn't have a subdural hematoma. You can see him as soon as he's back from radiology."

I exhaled loudly, and tears began to flow down my face. "Is he in much pain?"

"We medicated him before he went off to the CT scanner. His shoulder is immobilized, and his ribs are taped. We will evaluate his head and then decide on that shoulder. He may need surgery."

"How did this happen?" I asked.

"Well, if I had to guess, I would say a large car, a van, or maybe a truck brushed him. It appears he was running in the bike lane."

"No one saw anything?"

"I don't know. I'm just guessing, but that's what I believe may have happened based on his injuries."

"Why didn't the driver stop? Was this a hit and run?"

There was a momentary silence in the room. Then Andy said, "Maeve, would you like some coffee or tea?"

"A coffee, please."

"Milk? Sugar?"

"Both, please."

"Coming right up."

Teresa said, "Is there anyone we can call for you? It's going to be a long night."

"No, thanks. I can do that." I looked at my phone, which I had turned to silent. I had twenty new messages.

Andy returned with coffee and some graham crackers. "Maeve," he said, "let me set you up in the family conference room, and you can make your calls while you wait for Will. I promise I will get you as soon as he returns."

I thanked Teresa, and Andy led me to the conference room. It was furnished with two large couches, a small table with chairs, and a small kitchenette. A TV was mounted on the wall and silently tuned to CNN. The table had paper, pens, and a large box of tissues. *Necessary tools of the trade.*

I called Meg, who picked up on the first ring.

"Maeve, where are you?"

"In the emergency department," I told her.

"I'm in the waiting room. I don't see you."

"Have them show you where the family conference room is located."

I had barely hung up when Meg burst into the room. She was dressed in dark navy slacks and a pale blue linen shirt and had pedicure flip-flops on. I saw newly applied bright red polish on her toes and her left hand.

"How is he?" she demanded.

"He's having a head CT scan to check for any bleeding."

"Oh, Maeve." Meg hugged me.

Sobs escaped from my chest.

"Maeve, Will's strong. He will get through this. What can I do for you?"

I looked at her helplessly. I honestly had no idea.

"Who have you called?" Meg asked.

"I don't want to call anyone until I know all the details."

"Maeve, you need to let his parents and Grand know what is happening. Let me call them. Then I'll call Mom and whoever else you can think of."

"Yes, please," I readily agreed. "I can't deal with his family right now."

Meg started writing up a checklist of names and then sat on one of the couches and began placing calls. Her voice was firm as she told everyone she would be back in touch when we had more information.

The door suddenly opened, and Andy motioned me to join him. I looked at Meg, who gave me a silent thumbs-up.

"Now, Maeve," Andy cautioned as we walked down the hall, "Will's a bit banged up."

I nodded. "Remember, he will see your reaction."

I understood. *Get it together, Maeve.*

We entered the bay, and even though I was a healthcare professional, I felt my knees wobble. Andy quickly steadied me and smoothly said, "Will, Maeve's here."

Will's head was bandaged, and his eyes were swollen and bright red. He had a myriad of cuts on his face. His left shoulder and torso were also wrapped. My six-foot-four-inch handsome husband looked like a fragile, broken bird. Andy led me to the chair placed next to Will's stretcher and quietly pulled the curtain to give us some privacy as he left.

"Will," I said as I rubbed his hand.

"Hey, beautiful."

"How are you doing?"

"Been better," he said, trying to manage a smile.

"Knock, knock." The cubicle curtain opened, and Dr. Darrow entered.

"Hi, Maeve. Will, I'm Dr. Teresa Darrow. I met you when you arrived, but you were in a lot of pain and may not remember."

Will tried smiling again. "I remember your voice."

"I'm sure you could easily pick out my N'awlins accent," she said with a smile. "Well, the good news is that the CT is clean. No bleeding was seen."

"That's wonderful," I blurted out.

"How is your pain?"

"I'm doing fine as long as I don't move too much," Will said. "The pain medication helped."

"That's good. I will have Dr. Adam Schofield, the orthopedic surgeon, evaluate your shoulder and ribs. He'll look at your films and discuss the next steps with you."

"Thanks," Will said. "Can I get out of here after that?"

Dr. Darrow frowned and said, "Will, due to your injuries, you will need to stay overnight. Dr. Schofield may also have some recommendations on your mobility."

"I need to get back to work. I own a small business, and I can't be absent for long."

"Right now, you need to rest and recover. What is your business?"

"I own a catering company. I'm a chef."

Before Dr. Darrow could respond, a tall, olive-skinned, middle-aged man with the gait of a former college athlete strode into the room. A much younger man accompanied him. "Dr. Darrow," he said, nodding toward her while brushing back his salt-and-pepper hair. Then he faced Will. "Hello, I'm Dr. Adam Schofield, the orthopedic surgeon on call. This is Dr. Eduardo Garcia, a second-year orthopedic resident. You must be Will Kensington." He smiled at Will.

"Yes, Dr. Schofield. It's nice to meet you. Forgive me for not shaking your hand, but I'm a bit taped up at the moment," Will said. "This is my wife, Maeve."

Dr. Schofield shook my hand. "Nice to meet you both. Sorry, it's under these circumstances. Well, I looked at your X-rays, Will, and it appears that you have a scapula fracture. I'd like to examine you now if I may."

I got up and said, "I'll be back after your exam, Will."
"Okay, honey. See you in a few minutes."

I went back to the family conference room, and Meg held up a finger while talking on the phone. "No, Lydia, for now, it is better to wait for my call. Will is being examined. I will let you know as soon as we have any updates. Maeve is with him at present."

She stuck her tongue out at the phone.

"Yes, wonderful. Bye-bye now. I will call as soon as I can."

She hung up the phone and slammed it on the table.

"Maeve, I take it all back. Will's parents are impossible. They are so pompous. I know it's their son, but they are masters of control. For now, I held them off from conducting a candlelight vigil in the hospital chapel tonight, but I don't know how long that will last."

"Thanks, Meg. I just can't deal with them right now."
"What's the news?"
"Good news. No hematoma. The CT scan was fine. Will has a slight concussion. He also has a fractured shoulder and a few fractured ribs. The orthopedic surgeon is examining him now. He's also very bruised and has a lot of facial cuts."

"He's going to be sore. Will he need surgery on that shoulder?"

"We'll know in a few minutes," I said.
"Does he know what happened?"
"I haven't asked him yet."
"Knock, knock."

The conference room door opened, and my brother came in, followed by Gabe, a relatively new officer.

"Pat? Gabe? What are you doing here?" I asked.

Pat kissed me on the cheek and hugged me. Then he did the same to Meg. "Maeve, we need to speak with Will."

"Why?" I inquired.

"A vehicle may have hit Will."

"Maybe he just tripped and fell."

At that moment, Andy came into the conference room. "Maeve, Dr. Schofield would like to speak with you."

I looked around the room. "I'll be back," I said.

Dr. Schofield and his resident were showing Will his X-rays on a monitor when I entered the ED cubicle.

"Hi, Maeve," Dr. Schofield said. "We are just going over treatment options."

I sat on the chair and touched Will's fingers.

Dr. Schofield continued, "Will, here is the scapula fracture. At this point, I think you can get by without surgery. However, the treatment plan will require immobilization, pain medication, rest, and eventually, physical therapy. Your fractured ribs complicate the picture a bit. They also require immobilization, taping, pain medication, and rest."

I looked at Will. He grinned—sort of. "I know what you're thinking, Maeve. I promise I will follow orders. I want to avoid surgery."

"That will mean time off work, Will," I pointed out, knowing how hard that order would be for him to follow.

"I know that I can't be hands-on, or hand on rather, but I can still supervise."

"Once you feel up to it," I said with some reservation.

"Yes, I know."

Dr. Schofield said, "I'll see you in the morning. I know the neuro staff will need to approve your discharge. We'll go over medications and immobilization after they do. Can you be here in the morning, Maeve? It will be essential for you to understand the plan."

I nodded. "Absolutely."

"Okay, then I'll see you both tomorrow."

"Dr. Schofield, one question. Do you think Will tripped while running?"

"Will doesn't remember what happened. But in my experience, I think that since all the injuries were on your left side, Will, and you said you were running toward the harbor on Stetson Point Road, it seems that something pushed you into the brush."

Will looked puzzled. "I can't remember anything, but I can't imagine anyone from Langford not stopping if they accidentally hit someone."

No one said a word.

"Try to rest, Will. Those bones need to heal. I'll see you in the morning."

After they left, Will looked at me. "What a day."

I touched his face gently. "Pat is here to speak with you."

"Your brother?" he asked. "Why?"

"Well, there is some concern that a car may have hit you."

"I remember leaving the house and running through the town forest. Then I turned onto Stetson Point Road and headed toward the harbor. I always take that route because it's a six-mile loop. Everyone runs in the bike lane there because the ground is so uneven."

"You were running with the traffic?"

"Yes, just on that stretch of road." I was silent and let him continue.

"Where was I on Stetson Point when they found me?" Will asked.

"Right near Witchell Cove."

"There are no houses there and no parking on that side of the bay. I like to run there because I often see ospreys and egrets."

"My Eagle Scout," I said with a chuckle.

Will had built an osprey-nesting platform on the shoreline for his Eagle Scout badge years ago and was credited with helping to restore the osprey population in Langford.

A shadow crossed his face. "I guess I won't be running for a while."

Then, the curtain opened, and Andy ushered Pat and Gabe into Will's bay. "Hi, Will," Pat said. "You've met Gabe. I know you must be exhausted. Just a few questions if you don't mind."

I glared at Pat. I realized he must have insisted that he speak with Will tonight.

"Detective O'Reilly, I'll give you a few minutes," Andy said. "Then Will needs to rest."

Pat and Gabe stood at the end of Will's bed. "How are you feeling? Do you need surgery?" Pat asked.

"They are going to try immobilization and pain meds for now," Will replied.

"Well, that's a relief. But be careful with those pain meds."

"He will be," I said. "But you need to treat acute pain."

Will pressed my fingers tightly. "I am sure Pat sees much addiction in his business," he said. Then he said to Pat, "I will take as few as necessary."

"Will, what do you remember from today?"

"I don't remember much. I was running along my usual route at my usual time and woke up in the emergency department."

Pat walked him through the timeline and his exact route. "Did you see any cars on Stetson Point Road?"

"No," Will said.

"Did you hear anything?"

"Just some Sam Hunt."

"Earbuds. Of course," Pat said.

"Don't you think if a car hit Will by accident, the driver would have called for help?" I asked.

Pat looked down at the floor and then up at us. Finally, he said, "Perhaps it wasn't an accident." Silence filled the room. Will looked stunned.

"What? Who?" I asked.

"I am just raising all the possibilities." Pat shrugged. "We've just had a murder and an assault in this town."

"Will had nothing to do with the murder," I said, standing up to face Pat head-on.

"Maeve, please don't get upset," Will said. "I see where you're going, Pat, but really, who would want to hurt me because of Dr. Whitaker's death?"

"I thought Kevin was supposed to be the guilty party, but he's in custody," I said with a touch of sarcasm. Pat gave me a long stare.

The curtains rustled as Andy returned. "Time's up," he said. "Will, you'll be moved to a room in the observation unit for tonight. If all stays well, you'll be released in the morning."

"Can I stay with him?" I asked.

"There is a recliner in his room," Andy said.

"Maeve, please go get some rest. You'll sleep better at home," Will pointed out.

Pat interjected, "Gabe is going to be outside your room tonight, Will. It's standard procedure until we find out more answers."

"A police guard?" I must have looked shocked.

"Maeve, Will's my brother-in-law," Pat said.

"Pat, I don't think anyone is out to get me," Will put in. "But if that's the standard police routine, it's okay."

Just then, two orderlies entered the room to transport Will.

"I'm going to say goodbye to Meg, and then I'll be back," I said. I kissed Will on the top of his head and saw that some blood was matted into his curls. That's when I realized that we were fortunate his head injury was not worse.

"Okay, honey. I'll see you in a bit," he said to me. He waved as he was wheeled through the door. When he was gone, I turned to Pat and Gabe.

"Seriously," I said to them both, "what is going on?"

"Let's go back to the conference room and talk," Pat said.

CHAPTER TWENTY-THREE

Guidelines for pregnancy weight gain are based on maternal pre-pregnancy body mass index (BMI).

We walked into the conference room and saw Meg getting the finishing touches on a pedicure and manicure. She was sitting on the couch with her feet propped on a small table. "Hello, everyone. This is Jasmine from Pretty Nails."

A small, dark-haired Vietnamese woman of about twenty smiled shyly at us while packing up her supplies.

"Jasmine, this is Patrick, Gabe, and Maeve," Meg added.

Mouth agape, I stared at Meg while Patrick and Gabe didn't react at all.

"Bye, Jasmine, and thank you," Meg said. "See you next week."

"Thank you!" Jasmine said as she left the room.

As the door closed, Pat started chuckling.

"You are unreal, Meg," I burst out.

"What? I was in the middle of my nail appointment when I got the call about Will, and my nails got ruined in my rush here. Jasmine stopped by on her way home. No harm, no foul, and I made it worth her time."

I slumped into a chair and rubbed my eyes.

"Maeve, can I get you tea or something?" Meg asked.

"It's been a long day," Patrick said.

Weary to the bone, I looked up at Patrick. "Do you think someone tried to hurt Will?"

"Whoa, whoa, whoa!" Meg exclaimed. "I need a debriefing, please."

Gabe began, "Will's injuries appear to be consistent with a hit-and-run incident."

"I love when you do police talk," Meg said in a sultry voice.

Gabe blushed to the roots of his buzz cut and suddenly found a lot of interest in the conference room ceiling.

Pat rolled his eyes, but his voice was serious when he turned to me. "That's why I want Gabe to guard him. Something is afoot in this town, and I want Will to be safe."

"Do you think it involves Dr. Whitaker's death?" Meg asked.

"I honestly don't know," Pat said.

"Pat, come on. What else could it be?"

"I don't want to speculate, Meg."

"So, what do we do now?" I asked.

"Take it day by day," Pat said. "First, get some rest. Things always look clearer in the light of day, and we have just begun our investigation. The important thing right now is for Will to heal."

"Amen," Meg said. "Maeve, you are going to stay with Henry and me tonight. Fenway's with Grand. You need rest, and Will needs rest. I'll drive you home in the morning."

I looked at the three of them, feeling numb. "I have to say goodnight to Will."

"I'll walk you up," Gabe said.

"I'll be waiting here, Maeve," Meg said.

I hugged Patrick. "Thanks, Pat."

"We'll get through this, Maeve. We are O'Reillys. It takes more than this to knock us down."

My eyes filled with tears, and I turned to Gabe. "Thanks for staying the night."

"It's my job, ma'am."

"Gimme more of that talk," Meg said.

I quickly rescued Gabe from another awkward blush, and we walked down the hall to the elevator. He pulled up a chair in front of Will's private room and began his surveillance.

I went into the room and sat down next to Will's bed. He grunted softly as he turned toward me, and there were deep lines on his forehead.

"Are you in pain?"

"Just a bit. The nurse came in with pain meds, but I told her I would wait a while."

"Will, this is when you need the pain meds. You need to rest and heal. Trust me. In a few days, you will need fewer meds, but you have been through an ordeal today."

"I just feel like I'm being a wimp."

"Wimp? You are bruised and broken from head to toe!"

"Gee, thanks, Maeve."

"Come on, Will. You know what I mean." I reached over and rang the call bell.

"How can I help you?" a voice from the wall said.

"May Will Kensington please have his pain medication now?"

"I'll tell Laura, his nurse."

"Thank you." I turned and faced Will. "I want you to take your meds on schedule tonight. Remember they take about twenty minutes to kick in, so you want to think about that before they get you up."

"I love having a health professional as a wife," Will remarked.

I kissed him on the lips and began to open his dinner tray. "Oh, look, Will. It's apple juice, broth, and Jell-O. Lemon, perhaps?"

Will sighed. "Delightful."

A twenty-something nurse dressed in bright pink scrubs and red clogs walked briskly into the room. "Talked some sense into him?" she asked me.

"You mean about the meds?"

"Yes, I couldn't convince him to take them before."

She looked at Will's wristband and asked him his name and birthdate. When he gave the correct answer, she dropped the meds from a plastic pouch into his hand.

"Thanks, Laura," Will said. "By the way, this is Maeve, my wife."

"Nice to meet you. I heard you were one of us," she said and smiled. "Will, I am going to give you a stool softener, too."

"A stool softener?" Will asked.

"Yes, you are on opioids and immobile. That's a great setup for constipation. The stool softener will help."

Will sighed again. "The delights of modern medicine."

"Ring if you need me," Laura said. "Call for help before getting up. Between the pain meds and the immobilization, you will be unsteady. You don't want to fall. I'll be back soon," she promised as she exited the room.

"Maeve, I want you to go home and get some rest."

"Meg is insisting I stay with her. Fenway is with Grand. But I'll be back early so we can talk to Dr. Schofield."

"That sounds perfect. I love you, honey. Now get some sleep tonight. Do not stay awake dreaming up conspiracy theories. I was probably hit by a texting teenager who was too scared to stop."

"All right, all right," I said. "Love you, too."

We kissed again. As I left, I said goodnight to Gabe.

I found Meg holding court at the nurses' station and passing out her business cards. When she saw me, she said her goodbyes, and we walked to her car.

"Never miss an opportunity," I observed.

"I'm just trying to help the staff find housing. You know the prices in Langford keep rising. The time to get in the market is now."

I let her ramble on as she drove us home. When we arrived, Henry was already in bed. Meg and I sat down to a lobster mac and cheese casserole left by Shelley. Meg poured some white Zinfandel, and I felt my body start to relax.

CHAPTER TWENTY-FOUR

Advanced maternal age is defined as age thirty-five years or older at the time of delivery.

The decor in Meg's guest room rivaled that of the Ritz. Pale cream wallpaper and a king-sized, walnut sleigh bed enveloped in white, imported linens greeted me. I took my shoes off and sunk my feet into the white Aubusson carpet. I looked over and saw that the antique armoire was open, displaying a selection of La Perla nightgowns, robes, and slippers. There was even a set in a pale lavender color laid out on one of the overstuffed chairs. The attached bath was a study in white Carrara marble. A lavish collection of Chanel toiletries nestled in a silver tray on the counter.

When I was ready for bed, I spent a few minutes at the window, watching the waves lap at the shore. Then I got into bed and put my head back on the soft, silky pillows. *Maybe I'll turn on the TV for a bit or read one of the magazines neatly stacked on the bedside table. Perhaps*, a distant voice suggested, *I should let Meg adopt me.*

Suddenly a voice chimed out, waking me from my reverie. "Good morning, Maeve! Did you sleep well?"

I reluctantly opened one eye, only to see that Meg was standing at the foot of my bed, dressed head to toe in a navy Caroline Rose dress and jacket. Her makeup and hair were flawless as always.

A crisis in the family? Who would notice?

Groggily, I realized that it was my turn to say something. "Yes, I guess I did. What time is it?"

"It's six a.m. I know that you want to get to the hospital early, and I wanted to talk without Henry listening in," Meg said.

I brought myself up to a sitting position, arms wrapped around my knees. Meg handed me a steaming mug of coffee. I took a long sip. "Shoot," I said.

"Maeve, what if someone did try to harm Will? What if it's connected to the murder and Charlotte's assault?"

"First off, why Will?"

"For starters, he employed Kevin."

"But I don't think Kevin is guilty," I replied.

"Someone thinks he did it, and they may be blaming Will."

"Who, though? Someone in the Whitaker family?" Incredulity was beginning to get the better of me.

"Maybe one of the sons."

"Come on. They seem too, um, cultured for murder."

"Oh, like a rich frat boy never killed anyone?" Meg's arched eyebrows wrinkled her forehead, something she usually tried not to do.

I shrugged. *She has a point.*

Meg continued, "What we need to see is who is set to inherit Dr. Whitaker's empire."

"It's not always about money."

"Trust me—it is always about the money even when they *say* it's not about the money."

"But Will is so well-liked in Langford."

"Well, somebody knows something."

"Maybe it was just an accident?" I said, more than a little hopefully.

Meg sighed. "Yes, Pollyanna, that must be it." She paused. "But just give some thought to what I said."

"Okay," I agreed.

"On another note," Meg continued, "Will's parents have arranged for private security for Will. They spoke to Pat last night, and he is happy with the plan. And I hate to say it, but it's for the best. Will needs protection until we know what happened to him."

"Did they think about running any of this by me?" I complained.

"This was done for Will and you. Let them help you, Maeve."

I was silent for a minute. Then I reluctantly agreed. "Fine." It was starting to hit me that Will really could be in danger. But I couldn't help chafing at the gesture. Private security. Of course, the Kensingtons would not stand for less. They probably had a division of Navy SEALs on retainer. On the other hand, I had to admit that it was a privilege I was grateful for at this time.

Meg smiled at me and started to leave the guest room. "I know you need to get ready. There is makeup in the bath. Shelley will bring a few outfits for you to choose from to wear today."

"Meg, you know I will never fit into your clothes."

"Don't worry—I am having her bring things that will look great on you. You won't wear Spanx, will you?"

"Spanx? For every day? No, only if I'm going to a wedding and probably not even then."

"That's a shame." Meg shook her head with obvious disappointment. "Breakfast will be waiting. In the meantime, I'll have Shelley bring coffee with the clothes."

The rainforest showerhead was divine, and afterward, I could not resist trying a few of the deliciously fragrant creams as well as the top-shelf makeup and fragrances. When I had finished drying my hair, I stepped into the bedroom and saw that another coffee service and a few scones had been left, and four different outfits were hung around the room.

Julia Roberts in Pretty Woman *has nothing on me.*

After a few misses, I settled on black Eileen Fisher slacks with a forgiving waist and a long-sleeved, silk Dior shirt in a rich burgundy color. Not quite my style, but still very presentable. I felt a bit like mini-Meg, albeit minus the jewels and hair, and let's not forget the manicured nails.

Henry and Meg were seated at the long white granite island in the kitchen. Shelley was at one end of the island writing a shopping list. Brady jumped up to come over and get a head scratch. Clearly, despite all my beautifying efforts, I was still trailing more than a whiff of "Eau de Fenway."

"Good morning, Aunt Maeve." Henry reached up to hug me.

"Good morning, Henry."

"How's Uncle Will?" he asked, a look of concern clouding his face.

"He'll be fine, Henry. He just needs to rest for a while."

"I'll be able to help, Aunt Maeve."

"You'll be a great help. I'll tell Uncle Will that you said hello."

"Can I get you something to drink, Maeve?" Shelley asked.

"I had your wonderful coffee and scones upstairs, so I'm fine, thank you."

"How about a kale smoothie?" Meg asked. "Please make her one for the road, Shelley." Then, eyeing my outfit choice, she added, "Well, you look very professional. I know you usually tend toward embroidered tops, but I have to say this is quite becoming on you. I have a large black statement necklace that would be perfect with that."

"Meg, this is great. I don't need the jewelry. Thank you for everything."

She pouted in disapproval. "Well, all right. What time do you want to leave?"

"As soon as you're ready."

"Your wish is my command. Have a great day at school, Henry. Don't miss the bus. Shelley, I'll check in with you later."

Meg and I kissed Henry, and we were off. On the way, Meg asked, "What time are you meeting Dr. Schofield?"

"Seven fifteen, so I should be fine."

"Have you talked to Will?"

"No, I decided to let him rest."

As Meg pulled onto the drive to the carriage house, I saw a black sedan parked at the side of the road with two imposing-looking men in the front seat.

The driver gave me a wave, and I rolled down my window.

"Hello, Mrs. Kensington. We're private security hired by William and Lydia Kensington. Our operatives will be here around the clock. Please rest assured, your safety is our priority."

"Th-thank you," I stammered.

"Just go with it, Maeve," Meg whispered.

Meg pulled to a stop in front of the house. "Thanks for everything, Meg," I said as I slid out of the car, trying to act as nonchalant as possible and hoping Meg was not paying attention.

"Here," she said. "Don't forget your smoothie."

I stifled a sigh of resignation and went into the house, heading straight for the kitchen. I emptied the kale concoction down the sink, thinking about what I'd give for an Egg McMuffin. Then I gathered my purse and car keys and headed for the back door. As I passed the back hall mirror, I gasped. For a moment, I thought there was an intruder in the house. Then I realized it was my reflection. I was a mini-Meg.

Will was sitting up when I entered his hospital room.

"Well, you look nice," he said. "Very different, but nice."

"Meg's wardrobe," I said.

He smiled. "Ah, yes, I do see shades of Meg."

"How are you?"

"Well, I am feeling sore but clearer-headed, although I still need the pain medication."

"Great," I exclaimed. "Well, not about the pain, but I am glad you feel at least a little bit back to normal. Honey, you know that you will need pain medication for a while."

Will didn't respond. I could tell this would be a continuing battle, but I changed the subject for now. "I noticed that Gabe left."

"Yes, he came in to say goodbye at about seven. Maeve, I still can't remember anything about my fall."

"Don't try too hard, Will. The memory will come back, or it won't."

Dr. Schofield knocked and entered the room. "Good morning, Maeve and Will," he said. "How are you feeling today, Will?"

"The rest did me a world of good."

"My physician's assistant, Rachelle, will stop by in a few minutes and go over immobilization and pain relief with you. I would like to see you in my office in one week. Remember, you need to rest. Walking, taking a shower with assistance, and light paperwork is fine, but nothing more than that."

"I'm a chef, Dr. Schofield. How long before I can get back in the kitchen?"

"Are you right-handed?"

"Yes," Will said.

"Let's see how you are in a week. I think you will need to delegate some duties for a few weeks, and absolutely no driving. You need to be off the opioids to drive, and then you need to wait until that shoulder heals."

"Will do, Dr. Schofield."

I could tell that Will was keeping a stiff upper lip, but having his independence curtailed was a new blow to him. "Will," I tried to reassure him when we were alone, "we have plenty of family and friends to help. This is just a speed bump in the road."

Will looked at me and managed a weak smile.

By the time we got detailed instructions from Rachelle, were formally discharged by the nursing staff, collected Will's few belongings, and visited the pharmacy, it was late morning. When we got back to our house, two security guards nodded hello from their car as I pulled into our driveway.

"Will..." I began.

"I know. My father called me this morning about the security. It's fine, Maeve." He let out a deep sigh. "I feel like an old man. I'm ready for a nap."

"You should be ready for a nap. I can set the bed up for you." The bed would not be the easiest place for Will to get up from, but I would add a lot of pillows to make him more comfortable.

As we entered the house, the enticing aromas of cinnamon and walnut greeted us. We followed them to the kitchen, where homemade loaves of bread were neatly stacked on the island, along with a note from Nora saying she had placed dinner in the refrigerator for me to reheat later. Baskets of treats and floral arrangements from hospital staff covered the kitchen table. I smiled and motioned to the living room.

"Come on. Let's get you settled on the couch, and I'll bring you samples to try."

The living room had also seen visitors. Our couch was moved to one side, and a large leather recliner was next to the fireplace in prime viewing distance of the TV.

"Grand," we both said at once.

I settled Will into the recliner, and he put his feet up. He smiled appreciatively. "This is perfect," he murmured. "Now I can get up by myself again."

Barking came from the side door. I opened it and saw Fenway straining at her leash with Oscar, Grand's driver, trying to hold her back.

"Hi, Maeve. She's been walked, fed, and done her business, and now she's desperate to see the two of you."

"Thank you so much, Oscar," I told him as I took the leash. "And thank you for your kindness yesterday."

"Let us know what you need, Maeve. Mrs. Kensington said to call her when you get settled."

Fenway was trying to climb up my leg, so I picked her up and got a furious tongue bath in return. "I know, I know, little bug. We missed you, too."

"Hi, sweet Fenway," Will said.

Fenway tried to leap from my arms to his, but I held on to her and just let her kiss him. "These strong little legs would put you in a world of pain if you held her," I said.

I put Fenway down, and she began her rounds to make sure her toys, food bowls, and bed were all in the same places she had left them. Then she settled on her cushion directly beside Will's chair. Curling into as tight a circle as she could manage, Fenway shut her eyes and sighed. Her pack was home, she was home, and all was well with the world.

I went upstairs to change into sweats and came back down with a throw to cover Will. Snores from both Will and Fenway greeted me.

Settling on the couch, I started a list of things that needed to be done in the days ahead. I needed to get organized since I was planning on going back to work tomorrow. Grand had already arranged for Henry and Nora to check in on Will frequently and arranged a home health aide. Although I hated leaving Will alone, so many things were happening with the midwifery practice that I didn't want El Cid and Evelyn to use my absence as another weapon.

Looking at my notebook, I realized that I had started doodling names of suspects and questions in the margins with question marks beside them.

El Cid?
Mrs. Whitaker?
Evelyn?

Ava?
Kevin?
Whitaker children?
Someone else?
Were all the events connected? Did the murderer also attack Charlotte and Will?
Was Will even attacked?
What was the thread that connected all three events?
Was there a thread?

Sometime later, I awoke and realized that I had been napping along with Will and Fenway. I got up and went to the kitchen to begin heating the pot roast left in the fridge. Luckily, the instructions were taped to the aluminum foil covering. Turning on a sports radio talk show, I began to set the table.

"Well, how the tables have turned," Will said from the doorway. Fenway was at his feet.

"Did you nap okay?" I asked.

"Yes, I did. I am going to need another pain pill, though."

"Absolutely. But before I get it, let me help you sit." I guided him to his usual place at the table. "Fenway, out in the yard with you before dinner."

Fenway quickly did her business and raced back in the door. She was never one to miss a meal.

The aromatic smell of pot roast filled the kitchen when I opened the oven door. "Who made that?" Will asked.

"Nora," I said, filling his plate.

"That woman is amazing. Fresh ingredients, delicious seasoning, all well prepared. I like her style." He took a bite. "Delicious," he pronounced. "So, honey, work tomorrow?"

"Will you be alright here?"

"Maeve, you need to be at Creighton. Don't worry. I'll be fine."

"Once the medication kicks in after dinner, let's cover your dressings and get you in the shower. I think a warm shower and fresh sweats will help you sleep better."

"That would be wonderful," Will agreed.

"Plus, you get an assistant to help you shower."

"Sounds great, except I can't even hug you."

"You can still kiss me," I said.

"Yes, I can," Will said, lifting my hand to his mouth and gently kissing it. I loved this man.

CHAPTER TWENTY-FIVE

Approximately fifty percent of twins and ninety percent of triplets are born before thirty-seven weeks of gestation.

Will spent the night in the recliner with Fenway, his guard dog, on the floor beside him. I tiptoed out at six a.m. so I wouldn't wake them. I knew Oscar and Nora would be over at seven with breakfast, and the home health aide would arrive at eight.

After grabbing a mocha coffee and a cinnamon bagel with cream cheese at the Dunkin' drive-thru, I headed to the labor unit. I got reports on two of our patients from Winnie, who informed me that she was off to meet with Madeline.

"Aren't you tired, Winnie? You've been up all night."

Stretching to her full height of five feet three inches and putting her hands on her hips, she looked at me with her eyes narrowed and said, "I'm tired, all right. I'm tired of Dr. Cydson. I'm tired of Evelyn. And I'm especially tired of fighting for midwifery rights. Foolishly, I thought some battles were behind us, but apparently, they are not. But we will not be destroyed, Maeve. We will fight back."

With eyes blazing, she headed to the elevator.

Who knew Winnie was Olivia Pope in disguise?

I was about to check on my patients when my cell rang.

"Hi, Maeve, it's Pat."

"Hey, Pat."

"I need to talk to you about Will."

"What about Will?" I asked, my throat clenching up.

"One of our patrol officers was checking the Langford fairgrounds and found a 1966 black Chevy pickup with damage to the right fender in one of the stalls."

My heart skipped a beat. "Did you find out who owns it?"

"It belongs to Louise Aikens. She's eighty-three years old and hard of hearing. She lives way out in West Langford in a farmhouse and was at her gardening club when Will was injured. Neither she nor any of her neighbors saw anyone drive the truck, but the houses are far apart out there. The truck belonged to her late husband. She kept it in their barn with the keys in the ignition. She often lets neighbors borrow it for moving items. Supposedly, though, no one's used it for the last month."

"Gosh, Pat, I guess someone was trying to hurt Will."

"It is pretty suspicious," he agreed.

"Were there any prints on the car?" I asked, knowing that Pat would have already had the truck gone over from top to bottom.

"Wiped clean."

"Oh, no."

"Yeah, and probably done by the driver. That truck is so old there should have been a multitude of prints on it." Silence hung in the air for a minute. Then Pat filled the void, "Maeve, I have to talk to Will again."

"About what?"

"He must be careful. Someone clearly tried to hurt him."

"Or kill him," I added, beginning to shake a little.

"I know the Kensingtons have hired a private security firm. They cleared it with me. But if he needs us, we will be there quickly."

"Pat, he is still weak and slow."

"I know, Maeve. But that security team is excellent, and you and Will are welcome to stay with us if you want."

"No, we will be fine. But thank you."

"Think about it, Maeve. Or consider staying with Meg."

"Pat, we need to find Dr. Whitaker's killer and soon."

"We, as in the police, Maeve. Not we as in you and Meg."

Ignoring Pat, I continued, "Dr. Whitaker, Charlotte, and Will. Somehow there is a connection."

"I'm going to interview Charlotte again to see if she remembers anything from the wedding or the attack," Pat said.

"Kevin Reardon is still in custody," I pointed out.

"He is. That's because there is evidence linking him to one crime if not two."

I knew this wasn't the time to argue. "Okay, Pat."

"I'm going to swing by and see Will," he said.

"When you do, tell him I'll be there as soon as I am done here at the hospital."

Thankfully, the small family conference room was empty. I went in, closed the door behind me, and dialed Meg. Answering the first ring, she almost sounded out of breath as she said, "Everything okay?" We were all living on the edge.

"I'm at work, and Will is fine, but the police found the truck."

"Did they find the driver, too?" Repeating to Meg what Pat had told me somehow made it sound so much worse. "Maeve, there must be some connection here. What are we missing?"

At that moment, the pager on my left hip started vibrating wildly. "Meg, I am getting paged. I need to call you back."

The message read, *Your patient in room four is starting to push*. The patient in room four was Simone Bellia. She was a lovely thirty-two-year-old woman who had been with the midwife group for the birth of her first daughter, Magdalena, now three years old. I headed for the birth suite.

"Simone and Joel," I said as I entered their labor room. "Let's have a baby." Simone looked directly at me and nodded. I could see she was in full concentration mode, with Joel standing behind her rubbing her shoulders.

Shirley, one of the labor nurses, had the delivery table ready. "She's fully dilated and zero station," she said.

I scrubbed my hands while talking to Simone in a quiet voice. "You're doing great, Simone. When you get a contraction, give some nice gentle pushes, and we'll see this little human soon."

Positioning myself at the side of the bed, I quickly set up the instruments I would need and watched while Simone began to push. "Wonderful, wonderful," I said as I saw the top of the baby's head advancing downward. Then the contraction ended, and Shirley checked the fetal heart. It was one hundred and thirty beats per minute, which was perfect.

"Simone, I think you'll have a baby with your next push."

Simone nodded. As the next contraction started, she gave a big push, and the baby's head emerged. After the next push, the infant's body rapidly followed.

"It's Sam," Joel cried.

"Lift your gown, Simone, so I can put Sam on your chest," I told her.

"Oh, baby," Simone said as she reached for Sam. She was beaming.

"Sam looks great," Shirley said. "He's a definite ten."

The placenta delivered smoothly, and I checked Simone for any lacerations. "No stitches needed," I said.

Joel and Simone were kissing and admiring Sam.

"You both were magnificent," I told them. "What a team."

"Maeve, thank you. I couldn't have done this without the midwives."

I cleaned up the delivery table, examined Sam, checked the placenta, and said my goodbyes.

"Thanks so much, Shirley," I said as I left the room.

At the labor desk, I ran into Madeline. "Hey, Maeve," she greeted me.

"Hi, Maddie. Good to see you."

"Nice birth?"

"Wonderful! What a lovely couple. Simone and Joel could star in a childbirth video."

We walked over to the staff kitchen, and I made a strong cup of Earl Grey tea. Madeline poured herself a cup of coffee. "Let's find an empty call room so that we can talk," Madeline said.

We were reduced to finding private space wherever we could now that our offices had all been repurposed.

"Madeline, that coffee will rot your stomach. Who knows when it was made, and it's always so strong and so bitter."

"I'm used to it, Maeve. My taste buds don't know any better." I grimaced, but she ignored me and went on. "How's Will?"

"Improving."

"That's great. Thanks so much for coming in today."

"It was my shift, Madeline," I pointed out.

"I know, but we try to cover for each other in times of need. We rearranged the schedule so you can have some time off."

"Madeline, thank you so much. That means a lot." I was both surprised and touched by everyone's generosity and understanding.

Madeline hugged me.

"What about the midwifery issues going on?" I asked.

"Don't think I'm letting you completely off the hook," Madeline admonished. "I'll text and email you with updates, and I'll want your thoughts."

We talked a bit longer and then got on to the rest of our work. When the day was over, and I finally got back to my car, I leaned back while waves of exhaustion washed over me. Thankfully, it was a short drive home.

"Bottom of the second. All tied up," the television murmured as I entered the unlocked door to our home. I called out, "Hi, honey. I'm back." Will was sitting in the recliner watching the game with Fenway on his lap. "Oh, so you're letting the princess on your lap now?"

"Fenway is being very gentle. I think she knows I am wounded. How was your day?"

"My day was fine. How are you?" I leaned over to kiss him and to pat Fenway.

"Getting by. Better today. Nora was here for a few hours, cleaning and cooking. Grand stopped by. Nico, the health aide, is a great guy. My parents stopped in, too."

"Oh? How did that go?"

"Less painful than my shoulder and ribs," he said with a laugh.

"Did you tell them we're so grateful for the private security? We need to keep those guards until you are back on your feet and the police figure out what's going on."

"I did," Will said. "Pat stopped by, too."

"He called me," I acknowledged. "You know about the truck then."

"Yes." He sighed deeply. "I just don't remember anything, honey."

"Maybe you didn't see anything. There might be nothing to remember."

Will was silent. He patted Fenway and shook his head, primarily to himself.

I did my best to sound reassuring. "We are going to get through this."

"I know, but someone wanted to put me out of commission or worse."

"We don't know that."

"Well, love, they weren't inviting me for a drink." He laughed again and then grimaced from the pain.

"Do you need some pain medication?"

"I just took some Advil. I'm trying to space out the narcotics."

"Good idea. We can also alternate that with Tylenol."

"Okay, Maeve."

"Please don't forget that you are very well-liked in this town. Pat will get to the bottom of this."

Will was suddenly incredulous. "Am I hearing you correctly? You and Meg are hanging up your crime-fighting badges?"

"Um, don't hold me to that." He smiled but remained silent. Taking his hand in mine, I asked, "What else, honey?"

"I'm worried about the business. I see it's so easy for everything to slip away."

"What events do you have coming up?" I asked.

"The Johnson and Pearlstein weddings are next weekend, and we are catering two engagement parties this Sunday."

"Can Ella handle the events?"

"I think so. She is on top of everything. She's bringing the head chef and servers over here tomorrow to go over final details."

"That sounds positive," I pointed out.

"But Maeve, I should be there checking on them, getting new business, visiting suppliers, and selling our services to new venues. The new loan did not come through yet."

"You'll be back in the saddle plenty soon enough. For now, though, you need to take it easy. I'm sure you've prepared Ella well."

Will stared at his hands.

"What?" I demanded.

"Maybe my father is right. Maybe this is a ridiculous dream. Look at me. I'm out of commission, and the business could easily be lost. That wouldn't happen if I worked in finance."

I pulled up an ottoman and sat facing him.

"Will Kensington, you look at me. This catering business is your dream. You are never happier than when you are cooking, creating, and making every event memorable. If you want to go into finance, I will support you. But I don't think this is a good time to make that decision. Right now, you're tired, and you've been badly hurt. But you will also get stronger every day, and we will get through this together. Don't even think about making any decisions for the next few weeks."

Will looked directly at me. "Is this my transition talk?" he asked.

I stared back. "Your what?" I asked back, although I smiled because I knew what he meant. Transition is the final phase of the first stage of labor before pushing begins. It brings many physical and emotional changes, and women often need to be guided through it. At this point in labor, many women doubt their ability to give birth successfully. They often need encouragement from someone they trust fully.

"You're an excellent midwife, Maeve," Will said with a slow grin. "I see how you get women through labor. And you're right. I am not in a place to make any big decisions yet. So onward and upward. Upward, that is, if you help me to the table."

I put Fenway on the floor and helped Will up. "Caution, Will. This means I get to cook for you."

"Maeve, open the fridge."

I did. "Oh, my gosh," I muttered. Every shelf of the refrigerator was packed with labeled plastic containers.

"Nora was a very busy woman," Will said.

I started reading off the labels. "We seem to have a choice of veggie lasagna, grilled chicken with rice, or turkey with all the trimmings."

"You know," mused Will, "I may try to entice Nora to switch her career to catering."

We settled on turkey. I set the table, and we sat down. "This is so good," I said between mouthfuls of roast turkey.

"Should I be worried about the competition?" Will asked.

"Both of you are fabulous cooks. But look at me, I can't even make a decent cookie."

"Baking is a specialty unto itself, and it's hard always to get it right. If you want to bake, why not start with a quick bread, like maybe a lemon bread?"

I put my head down and started sobbing.

"Maeve, what is it?" Will asked, reaching over to hug me with his one good arm. I couldn't stop crying. Will rubbed my back as I attempted to get myself together.

He kissed my head and my neck. He began, "I know this has all been a lot on you. My injury, the murder—"

"No, Will, it's not any of that," I stopped him. He was quiet then and let me talk. "How can I be a mother if I can't bake a simple cookie?"

"Oh, Maeve."

"Mothers bake cookies."

"Maeve, think about it. Has Meg ever baked a cookie in her life?"

"She's different. This is important to me. You know, cookies for the kids when they come home from school."

"Oh, honey, you are so much more than just a cookie."

I dried my eyes and looked at him.

"Maeve, talk to me. Is it the fertility appointments? We can put everything on hold."

"I want a baby more than anything, Will. I thought if I could make a decent cookie, then I could get pregnant."

Will started smiling. "I love you. Think about it. If you had to be a baker to have kids, there might not be a need for birth control."

"I know it's crazy. In my head, I know it's silly. It's not really about the cookies. It's the fact that I might be infertile."

"Maeve, we are a team. It's not you, not me. It's us."

"I love you, Will."

"Love you more. Do you want to put the baby-making on hold for now?"

"No, I don't."

"Well, my little baker. I have a book of quick bread recipes. Try one and see how you do. Then, when I'm healed, we'll make cookies together."

"That might be an idea," I allowed.

We finished dissecting the Red Sox game, just happy to be in each other's company. Will put down his glass and yawned. "I'm going to lie down."

"Feeling okay?"

"Yeah, I'm just tired. Thanks for a great dinner. Love you."

I watched him go back to the recliner. *He is still in recovery mode.*

Cleanup was simple since everything had been pre-cooked. When I was finished, Fenway and I went to look at the ocean for our usual walk. Staring out at the water, I thought again about how grateful I was for Will…and the person who invented simple baking recipes.

CHAPTER TWENTY-SIX

At term, approximately three percent of fetuses are in a breech presentation.

The next few days settled into a quiet, comfortable pattern. Will continued to get stronger, and the two of us took short walks with Fenway. Nora supplied meals, which were always delicious. Will's catering managers dropped by daily, and I saw the excitement in his face as they painstakingly went over the details of upcoming events. Amazingly, I had no trouble sleeping.

There were no new leads about the truck or its driver. Things at Creighton Memorial were also in a lull. Even so, Madeline sent the midwife staff daily messages about strategies to preserve our practice.

I had to keep myself occupied, so I decided to take Will's advice and research quick breads. Sitting on the deck, I decided to search for chocolate bread since that was one of Will's favorites. Googling chocolate bread and cakes produced a flood of hits. Overwhelmed, I changed the search to simply chocolate cakes.

I clicked on a promising heading for a "really simple chocolate cake." The recipe called for just a few ingredients and a Bundt pan. I wasn't sure what a Bundt pan was, but I knew how to Google. This was going to be my signature dessert. I could just feel it.

"Will," I called out, "I'm going to run to the store for a few things."

"Okay, Maeve." He was seated at the desk writing menus.

"Anything you need before I go?"

"Honestly, Maeve, I feel so much better. If I don't require surgery, I am ready to start back at least part-time."

"Well, I don't want you to push yourself before you're ready. Your appointment is tomorrow at three."

"And our appointment is coming up."

"Our appointment?"

"With Dr. Chisholm."

"Oh." I had forgotten entirely. "Do you think we should push it back a few weeks?"

"Because of my injury? Don't let this stop us, Maeve."

"We do have a lot on our plates right now," I suggested.

"When don't we?" Will countered. "Let's keep to the schedule. That is if it's alright with you."

"It's fine," I agreed. "I think I'm just worried about the findings."

"Whatever we face, we do it together, Maeve."

I smiled and kissed him. "Love you," I said.

"Love you more."

Driving out, I saluted the security team and made my way to Langford Center. It was sunny and bright, and with calm seas, it was a perfect July day. Not surprisingly, the grocery was crowded with mothers, a few fathers, children, seniors doing the weekly shopping, and summer people ordering sandwiches for the beach.

I quickly purchased my items, including a cake mix that might horrify Will. I would have to keep this undercover at home. After I scanned the aisles a few times, the helpful cake decorator at the market helped me find a Bundt pan. I also purchased three packages of slice-and-bake chocolate chip cookies. Will was right. Cookie baking was so overrated!

I was loading the Jeep when my phone pinged. It was a text from Aidan. We're bringing dinner tomorrow night. What time is good?

I texted back. How about six?

The reply was immediate. See you then.

I loved when Aidan and Sebi came to visit, and I appreciated their offer. Will truly enjoyed spending time with them and Chloe, so it would be a fun evening no matter how his appointment went.

Before I could pull out of the parking lot, Meg called my cell.

"Hi, Meg."

"Hey, Maeve, I have some news from Artie. He put his minions to work investigating the PTD Foundation."

"And?"

"The PTD Foundation is not listed on any charitable foundation list. It was incorporated two years ago and has a post office box in Wellford, Massachusetts."

"Wellford?"

"Wellford," Meg repeated. "It's a small town on Cape Cod, about forty-five minutes away. There is only a president and vice president listed in the documents. Any guesses?"

"El Cid?"

"El Cid and Mrs. El Cid. And its current holdings are three and a half million dollars."

"Wow. What does the foundation do, and why have I never heard of it?"

"It looks like it doesn't do much of anything. Artie thinks it is a dummy organization to funnel money."

"From Creighton Memorial? El Cid would be crazy to do that," I pointed out.

"Now we must find out how El Cid is getting money from Creighton's OB/GYN department to his foundation."

I thought about that. "Did Dr. Whitaker know?"

"His name isn't on any of the foundation's papers," Meg said. "Come to think of it, do you think anyone knew about this?"

"We should start with Evelyn. She knows everything that goes on at Creighton."

"But we know nothing is going to escape those thin, tight lips."

"You've got a point," I agreed.

"I'll leave the next steps up to you, Maeve. My resources are running out."

"Okay, Meg, and thank Artie, too. By the way, Aidan, Sebi, and Chloe are bringing dinner tomorrow night."

"I thought family dinner this week was canceled."

"It was," I explained. "But Aidan just asked if they could come and bring dinner, so I thought that you and Henry might come, too. I asked Patrick and Olivia, but Penelope's team has a soccer game scheduled."

"Henry has a friend's birthday party, but I'll be there."

"Great. Will has an appointment with the orthopedist, and we'll get the final word on surgery."

"How is he today?"

"He's much better than I thought he would be by now. I think getting back to work, even though it's from home, has helped a lot."

"He's strong, Maeve. He'll be okay."

"See you at dinner," I said, ending the call.

As I started the car, my mind began turning over the implications of what Meg had told me. *What was El Cid involved in? What did his foundation do?* Unfortunately, by the time I got home, I was no closer to answering either question.

As I pulled into our driveway, I saw that Will was in the yard with Fenway. "It's a beautiful day out here, Maeve," he observed as he watched me get out of the car and cross the yard.

"Why don't you stay out here while I make you lunch?" I offered.

"Perfect. You know I love being catered to."

"Is turkey and provolone on wheat with honey mustard, okay?" It was a safe bet. That was one of Will's favorites.

"Sounds wonderful."

I made the sandwiches and brought them outside with a pitcher of iced tea and some Cape Cod chips.

"Thanks, Maeve. This looks perfect," Will said.

We sat in our Adirondack chairs, looking at the garden and the ocean in the distance. Fenway was patrolling our feet for any dropped crumbs.

"Here, Fenway," I said, giving her a chewy dog bone. She scuttled off to a corner of the yard so that no one could take it from her.

Will reached over and took my hand. I looked over at my strong but wounded husband. "Maeve, I want you to know how much I love you. I don't know how the business and the police investigation is going to play out, but I am so thankful to have you by my side."

My eyes filled with tears. I wanted to make everything better. "Will, we are always in this together. It's how we roll."

Will was quiet and then looked at Fenway. She was finished with her bone and now sat expectantly between us. She whined. "I would say there are three of us in this marriage,

Maeve," Will pointed out. We both laughed. When we stopped laughing, we continued our lunch and talked about adding a small greenhouse.

All in all, it was a perfect lunch date. Afterward, Will stretched out on the blue denim lounger. Soon he was asleep with Fenway curled up on his lap. Best buddies.

I went back into the house and reread the chocolate cake recipe. With a sense of confidence that I fervently hoped wasn't misplaced, I preheated the oven and began to assemble the ingredients. When I was done and my new hope was in the oven, I set the timer and went off to do laundry and get ready for tomorrow's dinner.

A few hours later, the house was shining, the laundry was done, and the cake was cooling. "Do I smell chocolate?" said Will, coming into the kitchen, followed by Fenway.

"Yes, you do. But no tasting until dinner tomorrow night."

"Ouch, that's just mean, sweetie."

"Well, I just hope it tastes good."

"Everything chocolate tastes good. Your cake will be no exception. I am so proud of you."

Previous experience kept me from buying into the flattery. "Hold your praise until after you taste it."

He just ignored me and went on. "Look at the house. It's sparkling. I'm so sorry I couldn't help."

"You still need to recover, and cleaning was a good distraction for me." I filled him in on what Meg had told me about El Cid and the PTD Foundation.

"Wouldn't the OB staff know about the foundation?" he asked when I'd finished.

"Maybe that was the reason for hiding the checkbook, to keep the whole thing a secret."

"Who knows? We are going to have to call Nora off soon. Her food is delicious, but I eat too much of it." He made a show of patting his torso.

"Ha! You are doing just fine. We'll be back to our routine soon."

CHAPTER TWENTY-SEVEN

Cesarean birth is a surgical procedure that delivers a baby through an abdominal incision and is usually performed when a vaginal birth puts the mother or baby at risk.

Wednesday afternoon found Will and me in the waiting room of Dr. Schofield's office. Dark brown woodwork and maroon walls sported framed pictures of sailing ships. The roster of the department's physicians listed by the door was made up entirely of male physicians. It gave me the distinct feeling that orthopedics was long overdue for a female influx.

"Will," called the medical assistant.

Will and I got up and were led to Dr. Schofield's exam room. Will undressed and sat on the exam table.

"We got this, honey," he said, smiling at me.

Dr. Schofield entered the exam room wearing the whitest, most starched lab coat I had ever seen. It looked like it could stand and walk around the office by itself. Apparently, those crisp white coats were reserved for surgeons but not for lowly midwives.

Washing his hands, Dr. Schofield said, "Let's see how you are doing."

I watched as Dr. Schofield examined Will. Rachelle, his physician's assistant, typed his comments into a computer. Although I knew nothing about orthopedics, Will's range of motion looked pretty good to me.

"Well, you are coming along very well," Dr. Schofield said. "It helps that you were in good shape before the injury. At this point, I would say no surgery. Are you still on narcotics?"

"Advil and Tylenol only."

"Wonderful. I know you still have pain, but I am glad it's controlled with those medications."

"What about driving?" Will asked.

"I would advise no driving for another few weeks." Will's face fell.

"It's a safety issue, Will," Dr. Schofield said.

"I understand," Will reluctantly agreed.

"You are progressing very quickly. Let's meet again in two weeks and reassess. In the meantime, Rachelle will show you some exercises and set up your next appointment."

Hmm, how lovely to have someone else chart and handle all the patient's follow-up for you. Maybe I missed my calling.

We left the office, and by the time we pulled into the carriage house, it was almost five p.m.

"How about if I walk Fenway while you set the table, Maeve."

"Okay, honey. Good news, huh?"

"It was, but I still think I could drive."

"William Kensington!" I went for my most intimidating glare.

Will threw up his right hand. "I know, I know. I'll follow the rules." He quickly ducked out to the yard with Fenway, leaving me to get the table ready for guests.

Ten minutes later, I heard the familiar purr of the Jaguar coming up the driveway. "Hello, all," Meg called as she got out of her car. She went over and gently hugged Will and patted Fenway.

"Hey, Meg," I said when she came into the kitchen. She was carrying a bottle of wine and a carefully chosen cheese and olive tray.

"What's the verdict?" she asked.

"No surgery," I said.

"No surgery!" she exclaimed while setting down the bottle and tray. "How great is that?" Her eyes rested on my latest baking effort. "Look at that cake, will you," she said. "Is it from Nora?"

"No," I replied, barely concealing my delighted smile at her mistake. This cake might be my breakthrough.

"Well," Meg said, suddenly somewhat cautious, "I know Will can't bake right now."

I smiled and pointed to my chest.

"Wow, you baked a cake! Is it for Fenway or humans?"

I rolled my eyes and frowned. In return, she laughed and hugged me.

Aidan and Sebi's black Cadillac SUV pulled up to the house. Aidan sat in the back with Chloe while Mom was in the front with Sebi. Will, Meg, and I went out to greet them.

"Hi, Mom," I said. Mom was in a turquoise and silver sequin top with navy pants. Her hair was styled and sprayed. As usual, every finger had a different ring.

"Hello, Maeve. How is that wing doing, Will?"

"Getting better." Will gave Mom an abbreviated hug.

"Come to your favorite aunt!" Meg said as she unbuckled Chloe from her car seat. Chloe was dressed in a pale pink, sleeveless, smocked linen dress with white sandals and a white ribbon in her hair. "Precious lovebug."

"She's ready for the cover of baby Vogue," I agreed as Aidan and Sebi beamed and began unloading the car.

"Do you think you brought enough?" Will asked.

"We know how to do dinner." Aidan laughed.

Sebi handed me a gorgeous bouquet of dark blue hydrangeas. Then he and Aidan unloaded bags and bags of food, which they began to prepare.

"Will, we brought you a gift," Aidan said. Unwrapping a large silver box from Nordstrom, Will pulled out two shirts. One was a classic blue oxford long-sleeve shirt, and the other was blue-and-white striped.

"Trying to spruce my wardrobe up?" Will asked.

"Queer Eye for the Straight Guy," Meg said.

"These are special shirts," Aidan said. "We know you'll be back to work next week but will have restricted arm movement for some time."

Sebi nodded eagerly. "And these shirts are meant to be worn untucked. It's the latest thing. They have a straight hem so they will look neat, and hopefully, they will be easier on your shoulder."

"Thank you so much," Will said sincerely. "They will be a huge help, and they do look very professional."

"Time for dinner." Meg finally put Chloe down in the highchair that her dads had brought.

Two hours later, we were sitting in the family room digesting. Chloe was sitting on the floor with Aidan. Fenway was enamored with her and snuck in a lick whenever she could. Chloe shrieked in delight every time.

We had feasted on Langford Bay oysters, grilled shrimp and scallop kebabs, new potatoes, braised brussels sprouts, and corn on the cob. And all of this had been paired with a crisp Napa sauvignon blanc. I had my own entry on the menu, and it was finally time to spring it.

"Everyone better have saved room for dessert," I said.

"What did you buy?" Aidan asked.

"Betty Crocker made a cake," Meg said.

"Maeve! Are you sure it's cooked?" Mom asked.

"Wait and see," I said.

"I'll serve," Meg said. "What is this delight called?"

"Triple fudge cake," I replied. "And I also have Friendly's vanilla ice cream to go with it."

"À la mode, please," Mom said.

Plates were filled with slices of cake and generous scoops of ice cream. When everyone had their serving, I crossed my fingers while they tried the cake.

"Delicious!" Sebi said.

"Awesome," Aidan chimed. "Look at Chloe. She loves it." Chloe's face was covered in chocolate cake and vanilla ice cream.

"It's magnificent," Mom said.

"It's amazing," Meg said. "I'm going to bring a piece home to Henry."

"You've got a winner," Will said, grinning. "I'm very proud of you, Maeve."

Even I had to admit the cake was delicious.

We were all quiet for a moment, watching Chloe eat. Then Aidan broke the silence with a new topic. "Hey, Maeve, what do you know about Dr. Theodore Cydson?"

Meg and I exchanged curious glances. "Well, he's the new acting chief of Obstetrics," I explained.

"He approached my firm about tearing down an existing home on the Point and building a modern house in its place," Sebi said.

The Point was an enclave of large, historic homes built initially for shipbuilders and merchants in Langford long ago.

The houses all faced Langford Bay, and many had been lovingly restored. They rarely went to market.

"Really?" Meg said. "Well, someone did their homework and knew the best builder around."

"Thanks, Meg," Sebi said. "I'm just not sure about the project. The size and design of the house will overwhelm the neighbors. Plus it's a historic district, and all projects require special approval from the Langford Board, the Historical Society, and the Conservation Guild."

"It will never get approved. Size and design restrictions are by the letter of the law. Also, where is El Cid getting that kind of money?" Meg asked.

"El Cid?" Aidan asked.

"A nickname only uttered behind his back," I said.

Aidan shook his head, smiling.

"He seemed very confident," Sebi said. "Although he was less interested in my firm when I told him I needed to do research and that we're booked for the next year. But I certainly don't want to get into a battle with any town, and I object to the destruction of historic communities."

"I agree," Meg said.

"Hey. Look at Chloe and Fenway now," Will said.

Chloe was asleep on her blanket beside a very pleased Fenway, who was pressed as close to her as she could possibly be. We all took out our phones and got our fill of photos. Then Aidan and Sebi carefully separated them, bundled Chloe and Mom into their SUV, and said their goodbyes.

As they drove off, Meg looked at Will and me. "We need to find out what the heck the PTD Foundation is. I smell a rat," she said. "Building a new house on the water? Tearing down a historic home? Where is he getting that kind of money? The PTD Foundation?"

"I think you two should tell Pat and let him handle this," Will said.

"Oh, please, Will. What fun is that?" Meg demanded. "This discussion will continue at a later date. Thanks for dessert tonight, Ina Garten. You outdid yourself. I'm taking another piece for later. Hey, are you two coming to the parade and fireworks tomorrow?"

Will and I looked at each other. We both knew we wanted a quiet holiday.

"We'll watch the display from our yard," Will said.

"Okay." Meg smiled. "But remember, a Langford 4th of July celebration is small-town living at its finest."

We hugged her goodnight and then went back into the kitchen. Will smiled broadly and said, "I loved your cake."

"You know, don't you?"

"Know what?" He tried hard to suppress a grin.

"You know my cake is made from a mix with a few added ingredients."

"Who cares?" Will said. "Everyone loved it. Just wait until you make it for the midwives."

"I knew a true chef would be able to tell."

"Maeve, I am proud of you for baking a wonderful cake. Don't you see it doesn't matter how you did it, but rather just that you did? And it did taste terrific."

"Thanks, Will." I almost gave him a friendly poke in the ribs but caught myself. "You better watch out. I may expand my repertoire. By the way, I also bought slice-and-bake cookies."

"I love that. See, there is more than one way to skin a cat," he said, kissing me.

We surveyed the pile of dishes at the sink. "Let me load the dishwasher, and I'll be right up," I said.

"Thank you. Fenway and I will warm up the bed."

While cleaning up the kitchen, I kept going over suspects and angles, and I realized that, as usual, I had more questions than answers about Dr. Whitaker's death. Where did El Cid get his newfound wealth? Was he guilty of murder, or did I just want him to be? Why would he attack Charlotte? Did she have a connection to the PTD Foundation? My head was spinning with possible motives when I shut off the lights and headed to bed.

CHAPTER TWENTY-EIGHT

Vacuum extraction is performed during the second stage when there has not been sufficient progress toward delivery. The vacuum provides gentle suction to guide the baby's head. It may be used if the baby needs to be delivered quickly.

After a quiet holiday weekend, Monday morning felt like a bad dream when my alarm went off at five-fifteen. I fought my way awake, though, because I wanted to grab a coffee, get to the hospital early, and check my email and schedule for the day.

Arriving at the hospital, I brought my large Dunkin' coffee with two shots of caramel to the labor floor nursing station. It was early enough that I had my choice of unused computer terminals, so I logged in to the nearest one. I felt the caramel and caffeine doing wonders for me as I waited for the screen to boot up. When it finally did, I took another sip and opened my email. The top message was highlighted in red and had been sent out at five a.m.

> To: Creighton Memorial nurse-midwives
> As of August 1st, the midwives will no longer provide care for prenatal patients. Midwives will provide assistance to the resident and attending physician staff on the labor unit.
> Dr. Theodore Cydson
> Acting Chief OB/GYN
> Creighton Memorial Hospital

What? I felt my breath rush out of me. *What?* He couldn't do this. Could he? What about the rest of the faculty? Were they on board? I had to see Madeline now.

At that second, my beeper went off.

Meet me @ Cydson's old office. Mayday! was the message from Madeline.

Madeline was pacing back and forth in the empty clinic office. Her scrubs were bloodstained, and a mask dangled from her neck. Pieces of hair peeked from under her scrub cap. Her eyes were wide and unfocused, and she was visibly shaking.

I walked in and hugged her. "Maddie, sit down."

"I can't sit."

"Talk to me," I urged.

"How can we stop him? He will destroy the midwifery practice."

"Then let's strategize."

"Strategize what?" Madeline demanded. "He's dismantling everything so fast that it's like we never existed."

"Madeline, you must get a handle on this. You are our leader, and we need you now more than ever."

She let out a long sigh and sat down. "Leader, huh? How does a leader let this happen?"

"Madeline, you know this is not about you."

She looked at me. "You're right. I need to pull myself together. I was up all night. Diana Chang had a long labor and finally delivered vaginally just a little while ago. She had a previous cesarean section for a breech, so she and her wife are thrilled."

"She couldn't have done it without your expertise," I assured her. "Now, come on. It's list time."

Madeline flipped open her laptop and stared at me.

I prompted her. "Who on the medical staff will support us?"

"Well, yesterday, I would have said almost everyone, but now I'm paranoid. I don't know what to think," Madeline said.

"We know John Armstrong will. Bev told me that he has already had discussions with a lot of the medical staff about El Cid's draconian treatment of us. Sanjay Patel and all the maternal-fetal medicine staff will support us."

"What about the rest of the obstetricians?"

"Well, I think most of them support us in spirit, but will they support us if it means going against El Cid? Remember, he assigns operating room times and can make their lives miserable if he wants to."

"Maeve, let's think positively. We can at least reach out and ask for their support."

"Agreed. Then there's Evelyn, who would love to see us gone."

"I knew she did not like us personally, but I thought she would want to see the nursing profession, and thus midwifery, succeed. But I see I guessed wrong," Madeline said.

"Evelyn goes with the power. She would like nurses to be under her total control."

"She's always wanted us to be subservient to her," Madeline agreed.

"On the other hand, Dr. Whitaker supported us. Don't you think Evelyn would want to continue his legacy?"

"I think she wants to stay in her position," Madeline said. "She will do whatever Dr. Cydson wants. Plus, she would love to have a young and inexperienced nursing staff that she can dominate."

"You're probably right." That led to a sudden realization. "You know, we could enlist the support of the nurses."

"Yes, we could. But remember, we have no union, and it's hard to buck the powers that be. The nurses will be very supportive up to a point, but people need their jobs."

I sighed. "True."

Then it was Madeline's turn for inspiration. "I'll tell you who can't and won't be intimidated—our patients. They can make their voices heard."

"Yes!" I enthusiastically agreed.

Madeline turned to the computer. "I'm going to send an email to all the midwives about approaching their patients." She brought up the email program and stared at it for a moment. Then her eyes widened all over again.

"What?" I demanded.

The confidence Madeline had just a moment ago went draining out of her, and her voice shook as she explained, "I just got an email from Evelyn. It says that if we do not have an active labor patient, then we can be loaned out to any other nursing unit in the hospital."

"Oh, no, no." Beyond those three words, I found myself speechless. Madeline, though, recovered quickly.

"That witch. She's helping El Cid to sabotage us," Madeline said.

I walked to the window, thinking. "Madeline," I said slowly. "Don't write back yet."

"What! I want to rip her pinched little face to shreds."

"Let me go speak with her."

"What good will that do?"

"Trust me. I may have something on El Cid." I told her about the checkbook and the foundation.

"You think he's been diverting funds? You think she is in on it?"

"I doubt it. She has always been sitting at Dr. Whitaker's right hand. But let me go and talk to her, and maybe this will let her see the evil side of El Cid."

"If she is a part of this, you could be in major trouble. There has already been a murder, and both Charlotte and Will have been injured. You need to be careful, Maeve."

I nodded. "Her executive assistant gets in early. I'm going to see if I can make an appointment for today."

Taking the back stairs, I tried to put my thoughts in order as I walked to Evelyn's office. I was about to open the door to the administrative suite when my cell phone rang. Glancing at the screen, I answered on the first ring.

"Hey, Meg."

"Maeve, Shelley just came in, and she brought me some dirt on Ava and the Whitakers."

"Tell me, quick."

"Both Ava and her husband are undocumented. He works at The Country Club under a false name and social security number. Ava also falsified her green card, but when Mrs. Whitaker found out, she decided to keep her on. Apparently, the Whitakers were difficult to work for and went through a number of staff. Ava needed the job and was a hard worker, so she put up with all their demands. Ava and her husband have a six-year-old daughter, living with Ava's mother in Mexico."

"What does that have to do with anything?" I asked, genuinely puzzled.

"Ava found out about Mrs. Whitaker's affair with Zabalon. She tried to blackmail Mrs. Whitaker for money to bring her daughter here, but Mrs. Whitaker knew about Ava and her husband and threatened to call the police."

"Ava must have been desperate, thinking that she and her husband might get deported."

"The plot thickens. Shelley says Dr. Whitaker knew of the affair and forbade Mrs. Whitaker from calling the police on Ava and her husband."

"What? He knew?" This was getting confusing.

"Yes. She says he wanted to get a quiet divorce after the wedding."

"Maybe Mrs. Whitaker is the killer," I mused.

"But the peanut oil was in Charlotte's glass," Meg pointed out.

"Do you think maybe it was Ava's husband?" I suggested. "You know, a daughter for a daughter."

"And maybe he also assaulted Charlotte."

"But what about Will?" I asked.

"Maybe someone connected to Kevin hit him."

"This is so confusing," I complained.

"Any idea on where to go next?"

"Well, I'm trying a direct approach right now. I'm about to see if I can meet with Evelyn."

"Do you plan to tell her about El Cid and the foundation?" Meg asked.

"Yes. She's helping him try to put the midwives out of business, and I'm going to try to get her to see reason."

"Well, be careful, Maeve. You don't want to get fired." Meg's voice held genuine concern.

"Thanks. I will. Talk later." I clicked off the phone, my head swimming. *Ava? Mrs. Whitaker? Kevin? El Cid? Evelyn?*

CHAPTER TWENTY-NINE

A biophysical profile (BPP) measures the fetus's health by ultrasound. It measures heart rate, movement, breathing, muscle tone, and the amount of amniotic fluid.

I gritted my teeth and opened the door to the administrative suite. Evelyn had relocated here when El Cid became acting chief. Jeanine, Evelyn's executive assistant, was typing away at her desk as I entered. Glancing at me from under her black fringe and cat-eyeglasses, she said, "May I assist you, Mrs. Kensington?"

"Good morning, Jeanine. I'd like to make an appointment today with Evelyn."

Jeanine looked at me as if she had tasted something very bitter. "Miss Greyson is booking appointments for next week. She is not available today."

"This is urgent, Jeanine."

"Perhaps to you, dear, but her schedule is her schedule. Shouldn't you be on duty?"

I glared at her. "Please tell Evelyn I must speak with her today."

"Maeve, what are you doing here?" Evelyn asked, coming up behind me.

I turned around quickly. "Hello, Evelyn. I must see you today."

"If this is about the midwifery practice, you can save your breath," she said.

"It's not about the midwives."

Evelyn narrowed her eyes and glared at me. "What's so urgent?"

I cast a glance at Jeanine and said, "I would prefer to speak in private."

Walking briskly to her office, Evelyn snapped her fingers and said, "Five minutes, Maeve, just five minutes. Jeanine, please watch the clock and buzz me when time is up." Evelyn closed her office door. Then she sat stiffly behind her large oak desk and crossed her arms.

"The clock is ticking."

Sitting across from her in a high back, glossy black chair with the Creighton Memorial seal on the seat, I froze. *How to begin?*

"Evelyn, I wanted to ask you about a foundation at Creighton."

"A foundation? This was your urgent business?" Evelyn started to rise from her chair.

"The PTD Foundation," I said. Evelyn sat back down, and her cheeks had the slightest shade of pink to them. She knew something.

"I don't know what you are talking about, Maeve," she said, a bit too quickly.

"Evelyn, I know about El Cid, I mean Dr. Cydson's, PTD Foundation."

Fake it until you make it.

She tried to look at me blankly, but I could see her breathing had quickened, and she was tapping her fingers against her suit jacket. I pressed my opening.

"Dr. Cydson has a secret foundation here at Creighton."

Evelyn sat up straighter in her chair. "As acting chief of Obstetrics, Dr. Cydson has several foundations and committees under his oversight at Creighton. He does not need to explain them to you."

"I have reason to believe that the PTD Foundation may not be aboveboard."

"Ridiculous," Evelyn said.

"Do you know what the foundation does, Evelyn?"

"That's none of your business, Maeve."

"Would Dr. Whitaker approve? Would it harm his legacy?"

"How dare you," she hissed.

"Time's up," came Jeanine's voice from the intercom.

Not taking her eyes off me, Evelyn raised her eyebrows and pointed toward the door. "You heard her," she said.

"Think about it, Evelyn," I said.

Heading back to the labor unit, I felt ill. What had I done besides play my only card for nothing in return? When I arrived, Madeline was sitting by herself at the labor desk, waiting for me.

"What does the other guy look like?" she asked.

"Maddie, I blew it. I accomplished nothing, and Evelyn is incensed," I said.

"Evelyn's incensed. Gee, that's a change."

Sinking onto a stool, I buried my head in my arms. "I made things so much worse," I moaned.

"No, Maeve, you tried. We were already at rock bottom."

"But what will we do now?"

"I am off to make calls and get the word out. The best thing you can do today is to continue providing excellent care. Show them what midwives do." Madeline hugged me. "Stay calm, and call the midwife."

I smiled weakly. "Yes, ma'am."

Luckily, triage was very busy for the day and kept my mind occupied. Between Evelyn's reaction and my upcoming fertility appointment, I welcomed all the distractions I could get.

When I finally arrived home after the long day, I skipped dinner and was already asleep when Will came home. Surprisingly, I didn't wake with nightmares. But then again, my nightmares were all coming in the daytime.

CHAPTER THIRTY

Lightening is the descent of the fetal head into the pelvis in preparation for labor.

The week progressed, and on Friday morning, Will gripped my hand tightly as we walked to our reproductive endocrinology appointment. "How are you doing?" he asked.

I gave a weak smile.

"Maeve, whatever it is, we are in this together. Please remember that."

I squeezed his hand.

We were fifteen minutes early and were still taken right away. *Is this a bad sign?*

"Good morning, Maeve. Good morning, Will." Dr. Chisholm looked at her computer screen and then at the two of us. "Well, so far, all the tests have been normal. The semen analysis is within the normal range, and, Maeve, your ovarian function tests are all fine. We know you are ovulating. At this point, we don't have a reason for your fertility issues. You said that your mother had a history of endometriosis and fibroids, and you have a long history of painful periods, so I think, given your age, we should be proactive. What I recommend is a laparoscopy including a hysterosalpingogram to make sure that your tubes are open and clear and to see if there are any abnormalities in your uterus."

She explained the surgery to Will. My mind went into shutdown mode. *I am now a fertility patient.*

"Sounds good," Will said.

"Well…uh…okay," I stuttered. "But my schedule is pretty packed."

"I can work around your schedule, Maeve."

"Okay," I repeated.

"Do you have any questions about the process?" she asked. We both shook our heads. "Fine. See Adeline on your way out, and she will book everything." She stared at Will a moment and then said, "Will, I have to ask. What happened?"

Will shrugged. "Just a tumble."

The doctor looked at him for a moment. "Off a galloping horse, maybe? Well, I hope you heal quickly."

As we stepped outside the medical building, I stared at the parking lot. I could not remember my plans for the rest of the day. *Where did we park?* Taking a few steps forward, I stumbled over the parking lot's curb. Will grabbed my arm.

"Is everything okay, Maeve?"

"Yeah, I guess everything is just going so fast," I answered, still unsteady.

"But this is what we want, isn't it?"

"Yes, yes. It is." I tried to sound reassuring. "I'm just a bit overwhelmed right now."

"Honey, I'm right here for you. You know that, and you know I want to do what you want."

"It is what I want. I don't know—everything seems to be here before you know it."

"And maybe a baby, too?" Will suggested as he smiled and put his arm around my shoulder.

I leaned into him and smiled. As we stood there, Ella pulled up in the catering van. Will waved goodbye as they left.

I went to get an iced coffee before my session. Then at the clinic I took two extra-strength Tylenol for my headache and looked over the schedule. In room A, there was Gretchen Sanborn, a lovely school psychologist. She had given birth to a beautiful seven-pound daughter six weeks ago.

"Hello, Gretchen," I said as I popped into the exam room and gave her a quick hug.

"Hello, Maeve. I brought Harper. Look how big she's gotten."

"She's beautiful," I said with enthusiasm. She was a cutie with large brown eyes, a tiny bit of peach fuzz, and deep brown skin. "How has it been going at home?"

"Pretty well. I'm tired, of course, but I finally got the hang of breastfeeding. Thanks for that referral to the lactation consultant. She was terrific."

"She's helped many women," I agreed. "Are you enjoying motherhood?"

"I am."

"How much parental leave do you have?"

"I'm off until October fifteenth."

"That's great," I said with a nod. "What are you doing for childcare?"

"Jack's mother will care for her two days a week, and my mother will take her one day. She will be in daycare at my school the other two days."

"That's terrific, Gretchen!"

"I know. I'm lucky to have both grandmothers to count on as well as having the school, and I get out at two p.m."

"How are you feeling physically?"

"I still have fifteen pounds to lose," Gretchen admitted, her eyes lowering for a moment.

"You remember what I told you?" I prompted.

"I know," she said. "It took nine months to grow her. I know the weight *will* come off, and I need to eat sensibly and exercise."

"It does work," I said, as gently and reassuringly as I could.

Gretchen sighed. "I'm just impatient."

"Let's put Harper in her stroller while I examine you. You did extremely well in labor. Jack was a great coach."

"Thanks, Maeve. I didn't think I could do it but taking one contraction at a time helped. You were wonderful to us. I tell all my friends that they should go to midwives."

Taking a breath, I said, "Gretchen, the midwives need help from satisfied patients."

"What do you mean, Maeve?"

"Things are a bit difficult right now. The hospital needs to know that women and their families want us at Creighton."

"What? Of course, we do. Tell me what you need. I will get the word out. There is a great mom's blog that many women in Langford read. And we have a Facebook group."

"Letters to the Board would help."

"Don't say another word. I'll mobilize everyone. Is that why you're in this drab office?"

I shrugged and sighed.

"I got this, Maeve."

"Thank you so much."

I finished the exam, sent a script for birth control pills to her pharmacy, and hugged Gretchen and Harper goodbye.

As my final patient left, I suddenly realized that I had forgotten entirely about my family commitment for this evening. If I didn't hurry, I could miss it completely, in which case I might as well leave town.

Jumping into my Jeep, I hurried home to find the dinner Will had left me to eat before tonight's event. It was a lobster roll, made just the way I liked it: chilled lobster meat with lots of claw, celery, and a tiny bit of mayo on a toasted hot dog roll. Heaven! Along with it, there was a sketch of a lobster swimming in a sea of hearts, mouthing the words, "Love you so much."

I took the roll with me and managed to finish the last bite as I pulled into the town's recreation center at six forty-five. I found a parking space, but it was one of the last ones left at the far edge of the lot, so I had to run to make it to the entrance on time. Passing through the door, I suddenly had that familiar sense of combined excitement and pit-of-my-stomach fear. But it wasn't fear for my sake. It was for Henry. His wrestling meet was starting at seven.

When I got inside, I scanned the bleachers until I saw Meg. She was decked out in white slacks and a navy-and-white striped sweater with gold buttons. "Looking shipshape," I said after climbing up the bleachers and taking a seat next to her.

She glared at me. "Well, what does one wear to a fight, anyway?"

"A fight? Meg, this is wrestling, not MMA. It's a sport, not a fight."

"Semantics," she sneered.

Oh boy, this is going to be a great night. As I looked around at the crowd, I saw that sweats and tee shirts were the dominant fashion notes for this event.

"Not the Chablis and Brie crowd," Meg said rather pointedly.

"My type of crowd," I said.

The wrestling meet began with the lightest weight class and advanced to the heavyweight division. The lightweight matches were always very dramatic. The compact bodies seemed to fly across the mat when they weren't contorted into pretzel shapes. Unfortunately, I had no idea how the score was being kept, and I decided once again that I needed to learn more about the sport.

I got progressively more nervous as we moved up the weight classes toward Henry's. *What would happen to Henry, and could I bear to watch?*

Suddenly, one of the one-hundred-and-forty-five-pound wrestlers, a handsome boy with short red hair, walked to the side of the bleacher and proceeded to vomit what appeared to be orange Gatorade into a bucket.

"How lovely," Meg said. "You don't see that often in tennis."

I turned my back to her and looked over at Henry. He had his headgear on and was listening to his headphones. He was pacing back and forth on the floor behind his team's side of the mat.

Let his competition be small and weak. Or have the flu.

The announcer called Henry's name, and he walked to the center of the mat. He looked long and lean in his singlet. A much shorter, very round, blond-haired boy came out to face him from the other side of the mat.

"Now, does this look evenly matched?" Meg asked with all pretense of sarcasm replaced by genuine alarm. "It looks like the other boy outweighs him by thirty pounds at least!"

The referee signaled the start of the match, and Henry's opponent dove forward and grabbed him by the legs. Henry looked like a giraffe who had been lassoed as he went down.

Only a few seconds had passed before Henry was on his back. The ref slammed his hand down, and the match was over. The crowd broke into applause.

"That's it?" Meg asked with shocked disbelief. Henry was still on the mat.

"Well, at least it was quick," I observed, trying to sound philosophical.

"Maybe now he'll see this isn't his sport," Meg retorted.

Henry, a bit wobbly, got up and shook hands with his opponent. He walked back to the bench with his head lowered, but his teammates and coaches surrounded him and patted him on the back when he got there.

"Well, that trouncing should end this nightmare," Meg commented with cold satisfaction.

"Let's get coffee and let Henry come to us," I said. We headed over to the concession stand.

Looking over the selection, Meg said, "Well, if you like hot dogs and pizza, you're in luck."

"I love a good hot dog." I grinned. "Especially one with mustard, onions, and relish."

Meg gave in. "Well, make it two, then."

The dogs were delicious. I didn't even care that I had already eaten a lobster roll for dinner.

As we sat back down in our seats, Henry approached with a broad smile on his face. "Hi, Mom. Hi, Aunt Maeve. Thanks for coming."

"Are you hurt, Henry?" Meg inquired as she looked Henry over from top to bottom for signs of damage.

"I'm great, Mom. That was Jake Smith. He's rated number one in the state in this weight category. He rocked me, but I'm going to get better. I can't wait till next week."

"You mean you want to keep on..." Meg started, her face betraying an arduous struggle between a volcanic eruption and the proverbial deer caught in the headlights.

"We'll be cheering you on," I said.

"I just need to take a shower, Mom. Be back soon."

"Oh...my...He likes this," Meg said to no one in particular after Henry left.

"Yes, he does," I agreed. "So we'd better get on the wagon."

"Perhaps," Meg said. "Time will tell."

I decided the time was ripe to share my news with Meg. "Meg, I'm going to have a surgical procedure next week."

Meg looked at me but did not ask any questions.

"Just part of the fertility journey. It's day surgery. It shouldn't take long."

She nodded. "Have you told Mom yet?"

"I'm going to call her tonight. I hate to burden her, but she'll want to know."

"That she will. Plus, you need to give her time to get the prayer candles lit, say some rosaries, and enlist Gaby's prayer circle."

We both smiled, thinking of Mom and Gaby doing their own preparations for my surgery.

Changing the subject, I said, "Hey, are you still up for spying on Evelyn?"

"Sure, I'm game. But remind me again what the deal is and why me."

"Evelyn's cool demeanor slipped for a moment when I told her she was seen at Hanville Grove. I can't put my finger on it, but I feel like we need to know more about her, between that and our foundation conversation." I filled her in briefly about my encounter with Evelyn the day before, as well as the moves against the midwives. "What if you check out the assisted living center Tuesday as a daughter of a potential client? Maybe you can discover what she does there."

"Great idea. I'm sure Evelyn doesn't remember me. We only met briefly, one time, and I'll dress like a PI."

"Come on, Meg."

She threw her hands up. "Just kidding. Actually, it sounds like the best shot we have right now."

"Good," I said. "I'll pick you up Tuesday at nine."

"I'm synchronizing my watch as we speak."

CHAPTER THIRTY-ONE

Placenta previa occurs when the placenta partially or totally covers the mother's cervix.

The following Tuesday morning, I pulled into Meg's driveway and waited. Within a minute, she came out in a black-and-white houndstooth suit with a large-brimmed, black hat and huge black sunglasses.

"Audrey Hepburn lives," I said.

Meg scowled and took a long look at my car. "Leave the Jeep here. We'll drive my Jag."

I took the keys, and we got in. When the Jag hummed to life, I steered onto the street.

"It's a good thing we tipped Mom off that you're coming," I said," Or else she would tell the entire building she saw you on TV."

"Only if she could recognize me, dahling. Now let's get going."

Oh, brother. Meg is really into this disguise mode. I wondered if she might get a little too into it and blow up the whole thing. All I could do now was sit in the car with my fingers crossed.

We didn't have to wait long before Evelyn arrived. She parked her car and got out. Evelyn strode purposefully toward the building without pausing and looked every inch like she owned the center.

Meg opened her car door. "I'll be back."

"I feel like the getaway driver," I muttered as Meg slammed the door. I watched her head toward the Hanville Grove Assisted Living Center like a woman on a mission. A minute later, my cell phone vibrated, and I quickly opened it without looking at the caller ID.

"Maeve," came a raspy whisper.
"Who is this?" I asked.
"It's Mom. How is the operation going?"
"Why are you whispering?"
"Because it's top secret."
"Is anyone with you in your apartment?"
"No, but the phone could be bugged. I watch *CSI*. I know about these things. I saw that woman go in the door to the assisted living center."
"Are you watching on your TV?"
"Of course, I'm watching. Meg looks great."
Maybe I could get Mom a gig at Rotten Tomatoes. "Mom, I'll call you later."
"I'll say a rosary." She hung up.
No doubt to the patron saint of impersonations. I settled into my seat to wait. Forty-five minutes later, Meg swept back into the car.
"Drive," she commanded.
"Yes, Miss Daisy," I replied.
"Thankfully, we took my car. If they're looking outside, at least they'll see the Jag and not your battered Jeep."
We pulled into the local Dunkin' Donuts drive-thru a few miles down the road. We both ordered large coffees and jelly sticks.
"This is so good," Meg said while trying to swallow a mouthful of strawberry jelly.
"Did you see where Evelyn went?" I asked.
"She wasn't in the lobby, but I saw the guest book while I was waiting. E. Greyson visited Room 318."
"Strong work," I said.
"Oh, and here's my loot." Meg smiled, holding several glossy brochures. "It's a pricey little place, with two hundred thousand dollars required for the initial payment."
"Wow!" I blurted out. "That explains why Mom always said she'd never set foot in the place. I always thought it was just stubbornness about not leaving her friends and her apartment."
"The senior residences where Mom lives charge rent on a sliding scale. The assisted living wing is under separate management. Everyone pays the same high fees. The prices go even higher if you end up in the nursing home."

I whistled. "When did you make our appointment?"

"Tomorrow at ten a.m. And don't worry. I will sell this more easily than an overpriced colonial on a cul-de-sac."

The first strains of "When the Saints Go Marching In" came from Meg's cell phone. "It's Miss Marple." Meg grimaced as she answered the phone. "Hello? Hello? Mom, are you there? Why are you whispering?"

I laughed to myself.

"Yes, Mom. You're on for tomorrow at ten a.m....Yes, Mom...Yes, Mom...Yes, and I'll talk to you later." Meg ended the call. "Well, I'm sure that she's starting to get ready now."

"That's no surprise. But tomorrow could be crucial, Meg, even if it's a long shot. I don't know where else to look for leverage against Evelyn and El Cid."

She smiled at me. "Tomorrow and tomorrow and tomorrow…"

CHAPTER THIRTY-TWO

A nonstress test (NST) is a prenatal test used to check on the well-being of a fetus. During the test, the heart rate of a fetus is monitored to see how it correlates to fetal movement. The term (NST) refers to the fact that nothing is done to stress the fetus during the test.

Meg roared into my driveway on Wednesday morning, right on time as always. She was dressed in a winter white Chanel suit with black Christian Louboutin heels and a red Birkin bag. She wore a ring with a Chiclet-sized emerald on one hand and South Sea pearls draped around her neck. She was a woman with the resources to afford the Hanover Grove Assisted Living Center.

"Wealthy, caring daughter reporting for duty," she announced with an over-the-top salute.

"You certainly look the part," I said.

"You don't look half bad yourself. A bit like a studious librarian, perhaps, but you'll blend in easily."

"Easy with the compliments," I objected. But Meg had a point. I had a J. Jill fitted black check jacket over my standby black skirt. My hair was pulled into a tight bun.

"I hope Mom is ready to go," I said.

"Are you kidding me? She's been ready for this all her life," Meg pointed out.

We went around to the back entrance to avoid the lobby and climbed the stairs to Mom's apartment. On entering, we saw that some tony Boston Back Bay matron had changed places with Mom overnight.

"What have you done with our mother?" Meg asked.

I took in the Pendleton beige tweed suit and pearls, toned-down makeup, and pink pearl nails. A pair of white kid gloves were next to her black clutch. "Gloves, Mom?" I asked incredulously.

"I can't actually wear them because of the arthritis, but I thought it was a nice touch."

"Well," Meg said, "This is right out of *Invasion of the Body Snatchers*."

"Stop, you two," Mom objected. "I want to look the part. I know how these people think, and I want to look like the Dowager Countess of Grantham from *Downton Abbey*. Well, a modern-day version of the Dowager Countess. I wish that show was still on television."

"Where did you get the suit?" I inquired.

"Gaby got it from the Langford Thrift Shoppe. You can get great things there."

Gaby was Mom's neighbor and her partner in crime in almost everything these days.

"And the pearls?"

"They're on loan from Dottie. I told her it was a special luncheon."

"Okay, Countess, we're off." Meg took hold of the wheelchair and pushed it out the door and down the hallway.

"Do you remember the plan?" I asked.

"I am going to distract them with a million questions," Mom said serenely, "while you and Meg scope out the joint."

"Correct, as usual," Meg said.

Mom beamed.

We took the back elevators to avoid inquiring eyes. Then we wheeled Mom down the brick pathway to the assisted living entrance.

"Alright, team, here we go," whispered Meg.

Stepping through the door was like entering a whole new world. The foyer was pale green with a white marble floor and a large crystal chandelier as the centerpiece. The sound of a New Age instrumental piece emanated from invisible speakers.

"Serious money," Mom said.

"Hush," I said.

We rolled up to the white marble reception desk and were greeted by a professionally made-up twenty-something blonde dressed in a form-fitting hot pink suit and three-inch heels.

"This must be Mrs. O'Reilly," she practically cooed. "Hello, dear, and welcome to Hanover Grove."

Mom sat up straight and leaned forward. I was suddenly afraid this would be a very short-lived trip.

"Hello, darlin', and what's your name?" Mom asked in a thick Irish brogue.

"I'm Tiffany, your guide today."

"Of course you are!" Mom said. She needed to dial back her method acting. I dug my fingers into Mom's shoulder. She gave me an icy stare back.

"I'm going to give you a tour, Mrs. O'Reilly, and then we can have tea in the sunroom. Give me just a minute while I get Brittany to relieve me at the front desk."

As she clicked away, Mom hissed, "Nursing home Barbie."

"Rein it in, Countess," Meg whispered.

"Do you have to be named Tiffany or Brittany to work here?" Mom asked as she folded her gloves in her lap and sat smiling sweetly.

"Watch it, Mom. She's coming back," I warned.

"Here we go," Tiffany said after retrieving her fellow Barbie to mind the store while she gave the grand tour. "Now that you have seen our lovely foyer and lobby, let's start in the gorgeous Eden wing." She made a sweeping Vanna White gesture as she pointed down the hall.

"Buy this girl a vowel," Mom mumbled. I gave Mom's shoulder another big nudge.

"This wing houses our activity rooms, swimming pool, and bowling alley, as well as our in-house movie theater." She gushed on, nearly overcome with enthusiasm over all the facility's amenities.

When I stopped in the foyer to admire a gorgeous and almost obscenely large artificial flower arrangement, Tiffany kept on moving and talking without missing a beat. Her radar was calibrated to follow the money, and my Marion-the-Librarian persona wasn't registering with her. I listened as Tiffany's voice trailed down the corridor. Then, as Mom and Meg followed along while coming up with a constant stream of questions, I headed for the stairs and Room 318.

CHAPTER THIRTY-THREE

The first stage of labor is from the onset of regular contractions until the cervix is dilated ten centimeters.

On reaching the third floor, I looked around quickly to get my bearings. There was a nurses' station down the hall to my left, and it appeared that Room 318 was located to the right. The hall was quiet. Apparently, most patients on this unit were bedridden.

I stepped out into the thick steel blue textured rug and speed walked to the room. The large white metal door was closed. *Oh great. There is probably a nurse or medical assistant in the room.* I tried to listen, but the door was too thick. *Oh, well. In for a penny, in for a pound.* I held my breath and opened it.

Pink! All I saw was pink! The walls, bedding, and curtains were various shades of pink. Pictures of ballerinas hung on all the walls. Vases of pink roses adorned the dresser and the windowsill. "Teddy Bears' Picnic" was playing softly in the background. This was the ultimate little girl's room, and it was empty.

I slipped into the room, closed the door, and walked to the sitting area, where two armchairs were covered in pink silk. I saw a pile of children's books from Langford Library was neatly stacked on a small table. It hit me that those holds I saw must have indeed been Evelyn's.

Who is this girl? Is she Evelyn's niece? The daughter of a friend? Evelyn's daughter? As I mused, the door started to open. Panicking, I jumped into the bathroom and ducked behind the pink, ruffled shower curtain. Standing quietly to avoid knocking over the various lotions, shampoos, and conditioners, I strained to hear the conversation in the main room.

"Here you go, Rebecca. Let's get you all settled after your walk."

Though there was no response from Rebecca, I could hear someone being transferred to a bed, presumably from a wheelchair.

"Okay, sweetie, you take a nap now, and I'll check back in a little bit."

I waited until there was no further noise and quietly crept out of the shower. I tiptoed to the bathroom door and looked back at the bed. What I saw stopped me in my tracks. A small, disabled woman was nestled under the coverlet.

"Hello?" I whispered.

There was no response, so I stepped closer. She was fast asleep. Her tiny, beautiful face was unlined but not a child's. She was petite and couldn't have weighed more than sixty or seventy pounds. She wore a lovely pink velour top and pants, and her thick, dark-blonde hair was in two braids tied with pink satin ribbons.

This girl, or woman, was considerably older than she appeared. *Why is she in a wheelchair? How old is she? What happened to her, and what is her connection to Evelyn?* I glanced at my watch and realized that it was well past time to meet Meg and Mom. I quietly left the room since I did not want a search party looking for me. As I reached the main floor, I heard fast moving footsteps and loud voices coming from the lounge at the end of the hall.

"Get the oxygen!"

"Mrs. O'Reilly, do you have an inhaler?"

I saw Mom, Meg, and a group of nurses in a tight knot. Mom was having an asthma attack.

I quickly took over. "Okay, Mom, nice and easy. Everyone, please stay back." I found Mom's inhaler and knelt by her wheelchair. She winked at me. I blinked.

Winked?

Suddenly, Mom's wheezing began to improve rapidly.

"Let's get her home. This tour has ended," Meg said.

"Thanks so much, Tiffany," I said, reaching out to shake her hand. Her hair was falling out of its chignon, and her suit was wrinkled.

"Please, let's be in touch," she replied. "When your mother gets better, of course."

Mom gave a queenly wave, and off we went. Once we got back to Mom's apartment, Meg went nuts.

"Where the heck were you?" she berated me. "Did you forget what time we were going to meet? Tiffany got antsy, and they started looking everywhere for you. I was sure our goose was cooked."

"I saved the day," Mom piped up.

"What do you mean?" Meg asked. "You got so upset you had an asthma attack."

"Fake news, my dear."

"Faked?" Meg nearly choked.

I shrugged and laughed a little. "I knew when she winked at me."

"I need a drink," Meg said.

"Wine is in the fridge, dear," Mom said.

"Drinks all around, please," I added sweetly.

"Okay, Maeve." Meg sighed as she brought out the glasses. "Talk."

"Yes, ma'am," I replied. We all settled in, and I relayed my findings.

"That's more than a little strange," Meg said when I was done.

"How old was the poor dear?" Mom asked with some concern.

"I don't know. I thought she was a child at first, but then I realized she could be in her twenties. Her name is Rebecca."

"Last name?" Meg asked.

"Don't know."

"I do." Mom pulled out a lab sticker. "Rebecca Greyson. Date of birth August 10, 1995. Room 318."

"Where did you get that?" I asked.

"People in wheelchairs are ignored," Mom said. "I grabbed it when Meg was talking to Miss MBA-in-Healthcare. Rebecca is twenty-six years old."

"Could it be Evelyn's niece?" I wondered aloud.

"Could it be her daughter, and she kept her hidden all these years?" Meg mused.

"That's a hard one to swallow," I said. "I can't imagine Evelyn getting pregnant without being married."

"Are you actually a midwife, Maeve?" Meg asked.

"You know what I mean, Meg. She's so straitlaced."

Meg shrugged. "The harder they fall."

"And," I continued, "where does she get the money for the assisted living center?"

We all sat silently for a few moments and looked at each other.

"I need to get home," I finally said. "My surgery is tomorrow, and I have to put this out of my head for now."

"I'll pray to St. Jude tonight. Have Will call when it's over." A note of concern returned to Mom's voice.

St. Jude was getting a workout from Mom.

"Have Will call me, too," Meg added.

I kissed Mom. "Bye, Mom. Love you. Good job today, ladies. Come on, Meg."

We snuck out the back door and settled into the car. "Do you think Rebecca was born at Creighton Memorial?" I wondered.

"Probably," Meg replied.

"You know, I could check out her delivery record now that I have her birth date."

"Maeve," Meg said with a sigh, "You need to concentrate on your surgery. We'll worry about this next week."

"I just want to tie up these loose ends and find the killer quickly. Remember, Kevin Reardon is going to trial."

"I know, but your surgery comes first," Meg stated flatly.

"You're right," I said, as the whole fertility issue suddenly leaped back onto my shoulders.

"You'll be fine tomorrow," Meg reassured me.

"Yeah," I nodded. "But I just kept hoping it wouldn't come to this."

"Hopefully, it will be something small."

"And not something large," I said glumly.

We looked at each other. *As Daniel Patrick Moynihan once said, "To be Irish is to know that, in the end, the world will break your heart."*

CHAPTER THIRTY-FOUR

The second stage of labor is from full dilatation until the baby's birth.

I slept fitfully. At eight, Will and I kissed Fenway goodbye and headed to our appointment at Creighton Memorial.

"It's so strange checking in as a patient," I said as we entered the lobby.

"I know, honey, and I wish it were me. I do. I promise I will pamper you tonight."

"You always do."

My procedure was scheduled for ten a.m., and I was on a stretcher in the pre-op holding area at nine-thirty. Instead of my usual scrubs, I was wearing an open-backed hospital gown; and in place of my nametag, I had a plastic ID bracelet. I felt tethered to the stretcher by the IV in my arm. It was odd feeling so vulnerable in a place where I usually gave directions. Becoming a patient certainly did change your perspective on health care.

Dr. Chisholm walked up. "Good morning, Maeve. Hello, Will," she said as she picked up the chart at the foot of the stretcher. "How are you doing, Maeve?"

I smiled as best I could. "I'm fine. I'm ready to get this over with."

"Being on the other end is disorienting, but you are going to be fine," she assured me with a smile. Then she checked off a few items in the chart and set it back down again. "Will, you should go get a coffee or a snack, and I will find you in the surgical waiting area when we are done. Do either of you have any questions?"

Neither of us did. She gave us one last warm smile and headed off in the direction of the OR.

Will gave me a quick kiss. "I love you, Maeve. I'll be right here when you wake up." Then he was gone.

A nurse in blue scrubs and a hat and mask pulled the curtains around the cubicle. She picked up the IV tubing in one hand. My eyes focused on the syringe she was holding.

"Did you find what you were looking for?" a familiar voice asked as I watched the medication being pushed down the IV tubing and into my arm.

"What?" I recognized the voice, but whatever was in that syringe had spread instant fog through my head.

"At the assisted living center?" the voice prompted me.

"What?" The fog had become a swamp, and my head was slipping beneath the surface.

"You need to mind your own business," the now disembodied voice said.

It was the last thing I heard.

I awoke in a haze. *What day is it? What time is it? Where am I?* Then a wave of nausea swept through me. As I turned on my side, my lower abdomen started cramping severely. "Oh," was all I could get out.

Then I heard Will's voice. "Maeve," he said, "you're just waking up. You had quite a time coming out of anesthesia."

I began to dry heave. Then I heard another voice say, "I am going to give her something for nausea."

I was so groggy and dizzy that I could not open my eyes without the room spinning. My mouth seemed unable to form words. I closed my eyes, and Will was holding my hand when I came to again.

"Maeve, it's six p.m. Dr. Chisholm says you're going to have to stay overnight," Will said.

Six p.m.? I should have been home and in my bed by now. Instead, I was staying in the hospital overnight. Then something began to come back to me, something about an IV injection before the surgery. I remembered getting some medication and hearing the nurse who injected it say something odd. But there were no details to the memory that I could grab hold of.

The recovery nurse must have seen that I was awake again. She came over to my stretcher and said, "Time for Will to go home and get a good night's rest. We'll be taking you up to your room shortly. You'll see him when he comes to pick you up in the morning."

"Goodnight, sweet Maeve," Will said as he kissed me on the forehead.

"No, don't go," I said. *Or did I?* I still could not keep my eyes open, and I must have fallen asleep again.

Much later, I woke up, aware of someone standing over me in the dark. I lay in my bed and listened but did not open my eyes.

"Sleep, Maeve," she crooned softly. "We have time before your devastating event. Such a shame that a young, healthy woman will die after a simple surgery, but that will come in a few hours. I'll be back to inject you with your special sleepy time drug."

This time I placed the voice immediately. It was Evelyn's. She must have leaned over me to see if I was awake because I could hear her breathing. Then she pulled back, and I watched her leave my room through slit eyes.

What had happened to me? I'd never reacted to any medication before, so why now? I tried to focus on what had happened in the pre-op holding unit, but it was still a fuzzy memory. Then I turned suddenly cold as I realized that it was Evelyn who had medicated me before my surgery. What had she given me? And what had she said? I tried to wrestle with those questions, but exhaustion and nausea came over me in a wave, and I slipped back into sleep.

When I awoke again, a clock on the wall said eleven-thirty p.m. I slowly sat up. I was still a bit dizzy but otherwise, not too bad. My lower abdominal cramping had subsided a bit but still let me know it was there. The rest of my body felt like a truck had hit me. *So much for same-day surgery. Or was it Evelyn's drug concoction?*

I reached for the phone. There was no dial tone, and I saw that the wall cord was hanging loose. *Had it been cut? Why did I leave my cell phone at home? Come to think of it, why wasn't I at home? Okay, enough of that.* I shook my head. That set me spinning, so I stopped and let the sensation settle down. It was clear that Evelyn had a secret and that I had to find out what the mystery was. This meant I needed to unearth that delivery record now.

I slowly got to my feet and arranged the pillow under the sheets to resemble a body. It wouldn't fool anyone for long, but it might buy me a few minutes. I inched along the utility table next to the bed, but then quickly realized that I wouldn't get very far attached to an IV. I unwound the elastic dressing, pulled the catheter out of my arm, applied pressure with a washcloth, and then re-wrapped the elastic around the entire site. It made for a huge, unwieldy Band-Aid, but it would have to do.

Taking baby steps to the door, I crept along. *Maybe the drugs are finally leaving my system.*

Holding on to the doorframe, I peered out. There was no one in the hallway. I needed to get to the stairway as quickly as I could manage. Grasping the railing in the hall, I took a shallow breath, held my abdomen, and made my way shakily to the back stairs that led to the old basement. Some old records and birth certificates may still be there. *Wow, this cramping hurts.*

Slowly, I tried the first step down. It didn't feel too bad, so I descended more quickly. A searing pain gripped my pelvic region. When I got to the bottom, sweat was pouring down my back. I had probably come too fast, but what was done was done. I shut my eyes, concentrated on my breathing, and let the pain recede.

Tentatively, I opened the heavy metal door leading to the basement. After looking around, I stepped into the empty corridor. Moving as quickly as I dared, I rounded the corner and entered the oldest and least used part of Creighton Memorial. My bare feet were soundless, but I had to hurry. I wished I had some hospital socks, but it would have hurt too much to try and bend over to put them on. Also, someone would soon discover I was gone from my room.

Straight ahead was a set of automatic doors. I pushed the metal plate on the wall, and both doors opened with a loud creaking noise. I hit the wall switch, and an old fluorescent light hummed to life. *Let's just make a little more noise, Maeve!*

Two doors down, I saw a yellowed, stenciled sign that read Records Room. I turned the handle. Locked! This section of the hospital was built long before the days of key cards. *Oh, I should have thought of this. How am I going to get in? I don't need to add breaking and entering to my resume.*

Continuing to walk down the corridor, I opened a door and saw I was in one of the old operating rooms. Glass-doored cabinets lined the far wall. I started opening cabinet doors and looking for any small instrument to use as a makeshift key.

A pair of dust-covered forceps was sitting on a bottom shelf along with a package of long-expired 4x4 surgical sponges. When Creighton Memorial expanded, cleaning out the old operating rooms had been a low priority.

A sudden wave of cramps stopped me again. *Let it pass—let it pass. Keep breathing, Maeve. You've got this.*

As the pain receded, I saw that the operating room had an observation gallery on one wall. Three stairs led up to it. *Is there something I could use on the other side of the gallery?*

I inched along the bench seating in the observation deck. Opening the door at the end of the row, I found myself in a small hallway. There were two identical doors, one on each side. *Make a choice, the lady or the tiger?* I tried the one on the left and stumbled into the back of the records room. *So much for HIPAA. Things were so much easier in the old days. What's a little privacy anyway?*

Six large wooden cabinets lined the walls. *Where do I even begin?* On close inspection, I saw that each cabinet was labeled by years. Walking over to the one labeled *1995*, I pulled open the heavy wooden drawer. A sweet, musky smell permeated the air. Spreading apart the tightly packed folders, I found one for August. I rapidly went through all the names but could not find a chart for Evelyn. *Could I be wrong? Had she used a different last name?*

As I shut the heavy drawer, I saw cartons labeled *Birth Certificates* against the wall. Creighton wasn't going to win any medals for safe record keeping. Maybe there would be a copy of a birth certificate with Evelyn's name on it. There had to be a record of Rebecca Greyson's birth somewhere.

As I lifted the top carton, a wave of dizziness overtook me. I sat down amid the cartons and saw *1995*. Inside, there was a folder for August, and there I found the birth certificate form. There were no other records, just a copy of a birth certificate for Rebecca Greyson with her mother's name listed as Evelyn Greyson. The father's name had been left blank. Dr. Whitaker had delivered Rebecca. The time of delivery was listed as two-thirty a.m.

This was very strange. There were no hospital notes, just a birth certificate.

I folded the certificate to prove that Evelyn had a daughter, although I was still unsure of the meaning of this piece of information.

Another wave of nausea overtook me. I needed to get to a phone. I also needed pain medication and a bed. And I needed to talk with Meg.

I crossed back through the observation room and looked out the doorway down the hall to the new building annex. The hall looked a mile long to me, which meant I was more exhausted than I'd thought.

Whack! I fell forward into the doorframe and slumped to the floor. I had been struck in the head and knocked flat. I heard a moan escape my lips. Groggily, I looked up.

"Evelyn!" I gasped, and a chill ran through my body.

CHAPTER THIRTY-FIVE

The third stage of labor is from the baby's birth to the delivery of the placenta.

Evelyn looked at the floor and spotted the birth certificate. "I knew you were trouble when I first saw you. We should never have hired you," she spat. "I went to give you your special medication, but you were not in your room. Are all your questions answered now, my dear?"

My mouth opened, but nothing came out. *Does she mean to hurt me? Kill me? I need to get help.*

"You are too much of a snoop for your own good," Evelyn sneered.

"I, I…"

"Cat got your tongue, dear?" As she said this, she dragged me a few inches back into the operating room by my leg and closed the heavy metal door. My head banged against the floor. She was much stronger than she looked.

"Don't worry, Maeve," she said with a condescending smile. "Your pain will soon be over."

Fear gripped me. *I need to keep her talking. I need to escape.* "Evelyn, I didn't mean to intrude on your privacy."

"Do you take me for a fool?"

"No, no, I was just curious," I stammered. My head was spinning.

"Curiosity killed the cat, dear," she sneered again.

I felt nauseous. Did I have a concussion? Why had I thought this was a good plan?

"What does your daughter do?" I asked. "Does she live near Langford?" Maybe playing dumb would buy me some time.

"What does she do? You saw her, Maeve. She's helpless," Evelyn shrieked. With that, she started pacing up and down.

"I didn't know that was your daughter," I said. What was I going to do? We were so far from the main hospital. I needed a weapon.

"She *is* my daughter," Evelyn hissed. "Her name is Rebecca."

"Well, that's nice," I said and attempted a smile. Maybe I could appeal to her mothering side.

"Nice? Nice? Don't be such a fool," she said with a wicked grin.

I shuddered involuntarily.

"Do you think I was never in love?" Her eyes glazed over, and she swayed a little as she started talking. It was as if she was speaking to herself.

"I'm sure you were, Evelyn."

"I know what you and the other midwives think of me. Poor, uptight, unloved Evelyn."

She is unhinged. Correct, but unhinged.

She closed her eyes and continued. "Harrison and I were madly in love, but we had to hide my pregnancy until the time was right. We were meant to be together. It was love at first sight. We were perfect soulmates."

Yeah. It was that or Dr. Whitaker being horny. But horny for Evelyn?

"We were keeping our relationship quiet until it was the perfect time for him to leave his wife. Rebecca and Charlotte were born in the same year. Rebecca arrived in August and Charlotte in November."

Didn't old Harrison ever hear of condoms or the wisdom of pregnancy spacing?

"How did you manage to hide your pregnancy?" I asked. Maybe I could keep Evelyn talking while I gathered my strength and made a plan.

"Maeve, women have hidden pregnancies for many, many years. I was lucky. I carried very small, and I wore a tight girdle."

"That must have been very uncomfortable." My eyes searched the floor for anything metal.

"Comfort was not something I was worried about."

"Did you have prenatal care?"

"Harrison followed the pregnancy closely," Evelyn all but sniffed. "As you know, he was a world-class obstetrician. He only wanted the best for Rebecca and me."

Oh, gag me.

I saw something silver poking out from under a table to my right. Hoping it was an old instrument, I started slowly moving toward it. "I'm sure he did," I said with another shaky smile. "Did your pregnancy go well?"

Evelyn began to pace again. As quietly as I could, I edged toward the table. Suddenly, she turned around with her eyes narrowed and arms wrapped around her torso, almost as if she was attempting to protect herself.

"My pregnancy was perfect. Harrison and I decided that no one could ever know or suspect anything about the birth. Unfortunately, Rebecca was almost three weeks overdue, and we realized we would have to intervene to get her born safely."

Three weeks overdue? What a recipe for disaster!

"Were you induced?" I asked. *Keep her talking. Just keep her talking.* I was only inches from the silver object, and I didn't think Evelyn had noticed my movement.

Evelyn continued her narrative. "Harrison induced me at my home. I labored for thirty-six hours before I started pushing."

"That must have been so difficult, Evelyn," I commented.

"Mind over matter. Mind over matter. It was our mission, Harrison's, and mine. He went back and forth to the hospital during my labor."

"Laboring alone takes a lot of stamina and resolve."

Compliment the maniac. Let's try to defuse the situation.

Evelyn returned a look of pure disdain. "It's what had to be. Not that your generation would know anything about that. I pushed for seven hours, but Rebecca just would not come out. I made no progress. She was occiput posterior and did not turn no matter how hard I pushed. And I tried every position."

Seven hours of pushing with no progress? That's just crazy!!

I inched my hand toward the metal object.

"Evelyn, occiput posterior can be very challenging, especially with a first baby." In the occiput posterior position, the baby's head faces the mother's front and is harder to get through the pelvis.

"I could have done better. I should have done better." Evelyn's eyes opened, and she glared at me.

"What happened?" I asked.

With that, her gaze softened, and a faraway look came into her eyes. "We decided to go to the hospital after midnight so that Harrison could do a forceps delivery. Harrison called and made sure the staff had gone for the night. In those days, the obstetrics department was very small. The staff was on call and stayed at home if there were no patients. We knew we had to avoid a cesarean section. How could that be explained to the operating room team? Everyone would know our secret. Harrison decided to rotate the baby with forceps. It was complicated, but he managed to get Rebecca born."

I pictured a forceps delivery with rotation of occiput posterior to occiput anterior. One needed to be highly skilled with forceps on the one hand, but one also had to know when to throw the towel in and resort to surgery on the other.

"Did you have any anesthesia?"

"Of course not. We needed to get in and out of the hospital as fast as we could."

Oh my gosh, she must have been in severe pain.

"Rebecca had an Apgar of one and was blue and not breathing, but Harrison got her going."

I wondered what her actual condition had been at birth. "What about you, Evelyn? Were you okay?"

"I had many vaginal lacerations, which Harrison repaired. I lost about a liter of blood, but I knew I would recover."

"Oh," I gasped.

"We had a beautiful daughter, and it was our special secret. Harrison took Rebecca and me back to my house as soon as possible. No one ever knew." Her eyes narrowed at me.

"Did you have any help at home?"

"I arranged for vacation time while I took care of myself and Rebecca."

"What did you do for childcare when you went back to work?" I asked. *Keep her talking. Buy time.*

"Such an inquisitive young woman, aren't you, Maeve? Well, what does it matter? The dead can't speak."

Chills ran up my back. I realized that she intended to kill me. I had to attack first.

Evelyn continued. "I eventually hired Marion Ventura, an older woman I met at church. She had been a nanny for many years but had fallen on hard times. She needed a place to live. She was very discreet and kept to herself. Marion had no family in the area and no close friends. I never told her who Rebecca's father was, and she never asked. It was quite a symbiotic relationship. She needed me, and I needed her. She loved Rebecca like a daughter. Marion told anyone who inquired that Rebecca was her cousin's child."

My hand closed on cold metal. It was an old surgical clamp that was still somewhat sharp. This particular clamp, called a towel clamp, was used to secure drapes around a patient in order to create a sterile field. The handles locked the two pointed ends together. Care had to be taken to keep these away from the patient's skin, or they could cause a significant injury. It wasn't much of a weapon, but it was better than nothing.

"Did it take you and Rebecca long to recover?" *Keep her going. I must keep her going.* Could I take her in a fight? I was younger and stronger, and adrenaline was helping me cope with my pain and fatigue. I needed to get on my feet to level the playing field.

"Rebecca seemed fine at first. She was so beautiful. She looked like her handsome father." Evelyn sighed and suddenly looked all of her sixty years. Sweat made her face glisten. "But then she didn't reach any milestones. She couldn't sit, never spoke, had continuous seizures, and her growth was severely impacted. We eventually discovered that she was blind."

Evelyn stopped and looked away. She collected herself and continued. "Harrison was just inconsolable. He arranged for us to see specialists in Chicago and New York so that no one could trace anything back to Massachusetts. He wanted the best for her. The verdict was that she had severe damage from the traumatic forceps delivery. Harrison went into a terrible depression. He thought about closing his practice. But what could he do? It wasn't his fault. We were both trying to hide my pregnancy. I should have pushed harder to get her delivered. I just know I could have done much better. It was all my fault."

"Evelyn," I started, but she put her hand up to quiet me. Tears ran down her cheeks.

"Harrison was very, very good to us. He provided for all of Rebecca's needs since she was an infant. He financed my condo. He was a wonderful man."

Yeah, right. Protecting his reputation and marriage.

Evelyn pulled a gold chain from inside her blouse and rubbed something on the end of it. "Harrison gave me this when Rebecca was born, this beautiful stork with the pink bundle. I have worn it every day since Rebecca's birth. He treated me the same as his wife."

Matching wife and mistress gifts? Harrison had been such a jerk, and an unimaginative jerk at that.

Evelyn was so delusional. I looked around the operating room to see how I could escape. As I looked, I gently pushed myself into a semi-reclining position.

Evelyn was standing in front of the OR door. There was no other way out. I would have to go through her. She turned and looked at me as her lips curled into an evil smirk.

"But then, my dear, I had to watch twenty-six years of the lovely Charlotte. Twenty-six years of tea parties, lavish birthday celebrations, and ballet lessons. She went to Rushton Prep and then to Brown, and I watched it all knowing that my Rebecca would never have any of it."

"Evelyn, did you think Dr. Whitaker would get divorced after Rebecca was born?" *Oh, no. Why did I blurt that out?*

Her eyes narrowed, and she nearly spat at me. "Do you think I was the stupid other woman, Maeve? I had a child to protect. I couldn't provide what Rebecca needed on my salary. If anyone found out about our love affair and Rebecca, I was afraid his income would dry up. So I was caught in a horrifying catch twenty-two. I had to remain the loyal assistant."

She paused to catch her breath. I sat up and hid the towel clamp under my right thigh. I tried to look as if I was giving Evelyn my full attention. I tried to look as empathetic as possible while Evelyn continued as if I wasn't present. Maybe she had forgotten about me. Perhaps I could use the element of surprise in my attack.

"Charlotte's wedding was too much. All those beautiful pink flowers and her extravagant wedding dress and veil. She had those fancy, beautiful bridesmaids and her exquisite diamond ring. There was her handsome Ivy League husband. On top of all of that, I had to listen to how much everything cost," Evelyn said bitterly. "Charlotte and Harrison danced to 'My Girl.' But he had *two* girls."

Strands of Evelyn's hair had come undone from her tight chignon and were sticking straight up. This only added to her psychotic appearance. "The boys—his boys—didn't bother me," she continued. "But Charlotte—she was everything my Rebecca wasn't. So I decided to ruin her perfect day. I had it all planned. But then, dear Harrison drank the wrong champagne."

"What do you mean?"

"Don't play dumb with me, Maeve. You must have figured it out."

"No, I don't understand, Evelyn," I told her.

"You see, no one notices older women. Our time has passed. So it's effortless for an older woman to plan a murder in plain sight. After all, who even noticed loyal old Evelyn? How much harm could I cause? Well, I knew all about the pink pearl in Charlotte's wine glass. I'd heard about every single aspect of her ridiculous wedding."

"You put peanut oil in Charlotte's drink?" I gasped. *How I wish I could record this conversation.*

"Of course. I wanted her happiness to stop. I was so sick of it. I wanted to ruin the happiest day of her life. Just a few drops of peanut oil in her champagne would do the trick."

"Ruin her day? You planned to kill her!"

"Well, Maeve, she had twenty-six years of bliss while my Rebecca had none. It was a fair trade, I think."

"But you knew that Dr. Whitaker also had a nut allergy."

A sudden scowl clouded her face. "Harrison was given the wrong flute. It was that stupid, stupid boy. He was supposed to give Charlotte the flute with the pink pearl. I am sure he was told that. It was all *his* fault."

I was up against the wall now. So far, Evelyn seemed not to have noticed my movement.

"But what about the EpiPen? Did you know it was defective?"

"Of course, Maeve. Why give Charlotte peanut oil and then let her be saved. I took a defective EpiPen from Creighton and saved it for the wedding day. It was simple to pilfer it from the mailroom."

"But Larry Smith, the pharmacist, is getting blamed for that."

"Into every life, a little rain must fall," Evelyn jeered.

Chills ran down my spine. *She is such a monster.*

"How did you slip it into Mrs. Whitaker's purse?" I bent my knees slightly, getting ready to spring up quickly.

"Haven't you realized yet, Maeve? I am the loyal Whitaker family assistant. Who else would hold Mrs. Whitaker's purse? I switched EpiPens during the family photo session. Everything was planned down to the last detail," she said with a satisfied smile on her face.

"Wasn't Dr. Whitaker going to get a divorce? He knew about Mrs. Whitaker's affair. You two could have finally been together."

"Harrison was going to divorce Audrey, but he said the time wasn't right for us. He didn't want anyone to know about our past."

Hmm, just as I thought. Old Harrison was a world-class sleaze. As Ann Landers famously said, "If you marry a man who cheats on his wife, you'll be married to a man who cheats on his wife."

I suddenly realized that this was my chance to find out what else she had been up to. "Did you attack Charlotte, too?"

"I couldn't stand the thought of Charlotte having a happily-ever-after life. I knew that the police were focusing on Kevin Reardon. It was easy to steal that bat from his pickup and attack Charlotte."

I was numb. I could only stare at Evelyn as she went on.

"But I didn't hit her hard enough. So once again, I failed," she sighed. "I keep making mistakes."

"And what about my Will?" I asked in a quiet voice.

"Yes, your dear Will," she smiled. "You just couldn't mind your business, could you, Maeve?" She leaned over me. "I thought that by injuring Will, you would be so busy that you would stop meddling in *my* business. But even that didn't stop you, did it?"

"You hit Will with that truck?"

"Yes, dear. I met Mrs. Aikens when her daughter inquired about placing her in the nursing home. I often do admission assessments for the assisted living center. When I visited her farmhouse, she showed me her truck in the old barn. It was perfect to use on Will. It also helped that he is a creature of habit. He always runs the same route and always at the same time."

"You could have killed him!" I cried out.

"I was hoping to kill him," Evelyn admitted.

The towel clamp was in my hand. I knew now that I had to stop Evelyn from killing *me*.

"And then, dear Maeve, you found out about the PTD Foundation."

"So you and El Cid were in that together?"

"El Cid? That's Dr. Cydson to you."

I lowered my gaze and pretended to look embarrassed.

"It turned out that Dr. Cydson is a very greedy man, which is what I needed. I was afraid that when Harrison retired, there would be less money, and Rebecca would get shortchanged yet again."

Evelyn stopped pacing and stood again in the OR doorway. I decided that I would attack her with the towel clamp when she approached me again.

"So when I discovered Dr. Cydson's little foundation, I made him agree to provide me with ongoing payments in exchange for my silence. Of course, I secretly told Harrison about the foundation. That was why he decided not to retire and had planned to turn Dr. Cydson over to the authorities when he had gathered all the evidence."

Well, well. The plot thickens yet again.

"Now, with my dear Harrison gone, Dr. Cydson's continued cash influx will come in handy."

I was ready. My knees were bent. My pulse was pounding. I could do this.

"Well, dear, now you know the whole story, and so your time has come." Evelyn stared intently at me.

It's now or never. I pushed myself up while clutching the towel clamp. I ran to the door and shoved her out of my way, hitting her left arm with the sharp end of the towel clamp, but it slipped before I could lock the handle. As I passed her, I felt a jab in my upper arm. I turned back and swung out wide, trying to hit Evelyn again.

My legs. My legs sagged under me, and I melted to the ground. Evelyn stood over me.

"Seriously, Maeve, a towel clamp? Did you think that would save you?"

"What did you give me?"

"I injected you with a shot of rocuronium, dear. First your legs, and then your chest muscles will be paralyzed. You won't be able to breathe, and you will die." She picked up the towel clamp and attached it to my leg. It hurt like crazy, but my leg didn't even twitch.

"See? It works rapidly, doesn't it?"

I could see blood dripping down my thigh from the towel clamp. Panic gripped me. *What could I do?*

She stood over me.

"Sweet dreams, Maeve. For the record, you were a decent midwife."

And with that, Evelyn opened the operating room door and left.

No, no, this can't be happening. I was alone in a long abandoned operating room. I had to get help! But my legs were leaden. I didn't want to die!

My eyes swept the room. I saw the emergency wall plate with the red code button above me. But could I reach it?

I put my arm up. It felt as if it had a fifty-pound weight attached. I stretched my arm as high as I could, and my fingers just reached the button. I pushed. I pushed again. Nothing happened. There were no sounds, no alarms going off. I realized then that it must have been disconnected.

I slumped to the floor. *What about Will? My family? Is this it?* My arms stopped working. My chest felt like it was being crushed. Everything began to turn black.

I laid my head back and tried to picture Will.

As I drifted off, I thought I heard the thundering hooves of horses.

"Come on, Maeve, stay with us."

What? Someone opened my eyelids. I saw blue scrubs and faces staring at me. *What is happening? Why can't I speak?*

"Maeve, you're intubated. You cannot speak. You're okay, but we are taking you to the ICU."

I'm alive. The code staff had somehow heard the alarm.

"Why is she paralyzed?" I heard someone ask. I wanted to tell them but couldn't.

"Why is there a towel clamp on her thigh?" That's when I remembered that Evelyn was getting away, but there was nothing I could do.

We'd barely arrived in the ICU when I heard, "Maeve, we have reversed the effects of the muscle relaxant." A tall, raven-haired attending physician was standing next to me with a syringe in her hand. She gave me a warm smile. "You'll be able to move your arms and legs in just a minute or two."

"Just hang on, Maeve," Madeline whispered in my ear. She stroked my hair. "You'll be better very soon." *Madeline! If only I could tell her to stop Evelyn.* I could feel my strength returning, but I still felt so helpless.

Suddenly, I got movement back in my hands. I tried to pantomime writing with a pen.

"What is she doing?" Madeleine asked. "What does she…Oh, she wants a pen and paper."

Yes! Someone handed them to me, and I scribbled as quickly as I could.

"What is she writing?" someone asked. "I can't read it."

I tried again.

"Give it to me," Madeline said. "I've read her chicken scratch for years. Looks like an *E* and a *W*…No…*E-V*…Wait, Evelyn? Evelyn did this to you?"

I smiled around the breathing tube.

"Get security."

And with that, I finally felt calm. I leaned back and let exhaustion overtake me.

CHAPTER THIRTY-SIX

The postpartum period is from the baby's birth until six weeks afterward.

I opened my eyes to see Will sleeping in a lounge chair. *Where am I?* Looking around, I realized I was at Creighton. Memories came flooding back. Awful memories, starting with…Evelyn! *Evelyn!* I sat bolt upright in the bed. The movement caused Will to wake up.

"Honey," he said, coming over to wrap his good arm around me, "everything is fine. You are out of the ICU. You've been awake off and on for the last day."

"Evelyn?" I croaked. I had a sore throat, probably from being intubated. Will passed me a glass of water.

"Sip slowly, Maeve."

"Evelyn?" I asked again after a sip.

"Evelyn was arrested. She broke down and confessed everything," Will said.

"What about her daughter?" I asked.

"She's doing fine. Your mom has rallied the troops, and everyone at the center is doting on her. Brittany and Tiffany were horrified by Evelyn's deeds, and now Mom is their new best friend."

"Mom's really doing well? It's been a lot of chaos."

"Mrs. O'Reilly has never been better. Just give her a cause."

We both smiled. Then I added, "Mom was on the right track about the murderer. Evelyn was a disgruntled patient, after all. Hey, how did they find me?"

"That old emergency call button was still active, and once they realized where the alarm came from, the cardiac code team got to you just in time."

"Wow, I can't believe it!"

"Double wow," Will said and smiled. Then he slid into bed beside me.

"Be careful of your arm and ribs," I admonished him.

"I am much better, Maeve. Now I get to take care of you."

I leaned back. "What a pathetic pair we are." Then something else came back to me. "Will, Evelyn tried to kill you," I said.

"I know, but she didn't. We are going to be alright."

Then he leaned over and kissed me. That was the cue for the loud knock at the door. Without waiting for an answer, Patrick walked into the room.

"Hi, Pat," Will greeted him.

"Hi, Will. Maeve, I am so happy to see you awake and well."

"Thank you, Patrick. I cannot begin to tell you how happy I am to be alive."

"Well, you brought Evelyn to justice. She spilled everything and took El Cid, um, that is Dr. Cydson, down with her. He and his wife have just been arrested for embezzlement."

"Amazing. Who's running the department?" I asked.

"Dr. Patel has just been named acting chief," Pat said.

"Also, Creighton Memorial has been flooded with calls and letters extolling the excellent midwifery care," Will added.

"Our wonderful patients!" I enthused. The midwives would be back to their usual practice in no time.

"What about Kevin Reardon?" I asked.

"Kevin Reardon has been released, and his family is singing your praises," Pat said.

"What happened to Ava and her husband? Are they in trouble?" I asked.

Pat looked at the floor and then looked at me. "Ava committed no crime. Her husband committed no crime. My deputies had enough to do without following up on alleged stories about them. So, Maeve, I'm just letting it go at being glad you are okay. That was a close call."

"Tell me about it, Pat. I intend to stick to midwifery in the future and leave detective work to you."

Pat grinned. "I'll let you off by saying you did a great job and then skip the lecture. If you two need anything, call."

"We will. Thanks, Pat."

As Pat started to leave my room, Meg burst in with shopping bags in each arm and greeted everyone.

"I'm just leaving, Meg," Pat said, giving her a quick kiss on the cheek.

"What is all this?" I asked as she set the bags down on every available table and chair.

"Maeve, you can't leave without makeup, perfume, and a going-home outfit."

Will and I burst out laughing. "Thank you, Meg," I finally got out.

"I'm not staying," she replied. "You are looking at the real estate agent for Mrs. Whitaker's manse. I have to supervise the photo shoot."

"She's selling?" I asked.

"She and the car king are leaving for an extended European vacation."

I shook my head in disbelief.

"Call me," Meg said as she headed out the door.

"She and Zabalon? Really?"

Will nodded. "But the best news is that Ella called, and the check for the balance of the Whitaker wedding was hand-delivered to the shop by Mrs. Whitaker's driver."

"Will, that is wonderful! No new loan then?" I asked.

"No new loan," he beamed. "And a hefty payment was made to the existing loan."

I snuggled up against Will and looked around the room.

"Look at all these flowers. Peonies, hydrangeas, and lilacs—all my favorites."

"You know Grand and the midwives. You have a fan club, Maeve."

"What about your family? They must be out of their minds over all of this."

"Well, the security detail is gone. However, I now have a car and driver at my beck and call for two months. Let's say they've adjusted in their own way."

"Will, I forgot to ask. What did Dr. Chisholm say about my surgery? What did she find?"

I held my breath, waiting for him to answer.

"She said that you have a fair amount of endometriosis. She did some cauterization and removed a few polyps. She'll see us in a few weeks to discuss the next steps."

Endometriosis. *I had always suspected this. Okay. I'm ready for the next steps now.* "Will, let's get out of here," I said.

"Easy, easy, easy, woman. You'll be discharged soon. And it's a good thing because Fenway is beside herself waiting for you."

"You know, Will, looking back on it all, two things keep coming back to me. The first is I never thought Evelyn was so deranged, and the second is I should have listened to Dame Agatha."

"What do you mean?" Will asked, looking genuinely puzzled.

"She always said that poison, or in this case peanut oil, is a woman's weapon."

He smiled and gave me another kiss.

That night I was nestled on our couch with Fenway resting on my legs while Will was in the kitchen reheating one of our many casserole gifts. I had enjoyed calls from Mom, Meg, Henry, Aidan and Sebi, and all the midwives. I heard that Macey Cunningham was living with her sister and doing very well with her new daughter. Now I just wanted to rest, love Will and Fenway, and enjoy life.

I adjusted the pillow I was lying on and felt a hard object beneath my hand.

"Be ready in a minute, honey," Will called from the kitchen.

I looked down and saw I was holding a book. It was titled *Being a Great Dad for Dummies*.

"Can't wait," I answered.

RECIPES

Will's Pasta Shrimp Salad

1 lb. pasta shells
2 lbs. large cooked frozen shrimp
1 cup petite green peas
½ cup diced sweet red pepper
½ cup diced yellow pepper
½ cup diced purple onion
1 cup sliced black olives
1 tablespoon fresh or dried basil
4 tablespoons lemon juice
½ cup olive oil
Salt & pepper
Breadsticks

Cook pasta & drain.
Defrost shrimp.
Put pasta, shrimp, peas, peppers, onion, and olives in a bowl.
Whisk basil, lemon juice, and olive oil together.
Pour over salad and toss to combine.
Add salt and pepper to taste.
Serve immediately, or salad may be refrigerated and served chilled.
Serve with warm breadsticks.

Will's American Chop Suey

1 lb. lean ground beef
1 tablespoon olive oil
1 large yellow onion, chopped fine
1 clove garlic, crushed
3 carrots, chopped
½ teaspoon ground allspice
1 teaspoon ground cinnamon
3 teaspoons tomato paste
3 cups chicken stock
salt & pepper
8 ounces medium shell macaroni
8 ounces shredded mozzarella cheese
¾ cup grated Parmesan cheese

Set oven to 400°F.
Cook meat in an oven-ready pan on the stove and then remove from the pan.
Add the olive oil and heat until hot.
Add the onion, garlic, and carrots. Reduce the heat, cover the pan, and cook the vegetables for 10 minutes.
Return the meat to the pan and stir in the allspice and cinnamon. Cook for 30 seconds and stir in the tomato paste, chicken stock, and salt and pepper to taste.
Bring the sauce to a boil, reduce the heat, and stir for 15 minutes or until the liquid has reduced.
Cook the pasta, drain, and stir into the meat sauce.
Top with the mozzarella and Parmesan cheeses and transfer the skillet to the oven.
Bake for 5 minutes and serve at once.
It's also great as leftovers.

Nora's Pot Roast

4 lbs. bottom round roast
2 teaspoons black pepper
3 tablespoons olive oil
3 cups beef stock
(Additional beef stock may be needed.)
2 cups red wine
1 teaspoon salt
1 package onion soup mix
3 cups yellow onions, chopped
2 cups peeled one inch carrot chunks
8 Yukon Gold potatoes, peeled and cut into thirds
2 cups canned Italian plum tomatoes with juice

Preheat oven to 350°F.
Rub the roast with black pepper and sear on all sides in olive oil in the frying pan.
Put the meat in a large ovenproof pan. Pour in 3 cups of beef stock and wine.
Add the salt, onions, carrots, potatoes, soup mix, and tomatoes with juice.
Bring to a simmer on the stove.
Cover and bake in the oven for three hours.
Uncover and cook for two more hours. Add more beef stock if needed.

Mary Margaret Callahan O'Reilly's Date Nut Bread

1½ cups chopped dates
4 tablespoons butter
½ cup sugar
1 cup boiling water
1 egg, beaten
1¾ cups all-purpose flour
1 teaspoon baking soda
1 teaspoon vanilla
½ teaspoon salt
½ cup chopped walnuts

Preheat the oven to 350°F.
Grease and flour a 9x5-inch loaf pan.
Combine the dates, butter, and sugar.
Pour the boiling water over them.
Let stand until cool.
When the dates have cooled, stir the mixture.
Mix in the egg, vanilla, flour, baking soda, salt, and walnuts.
Pour into the prepared pan.
Bake for 50 minutes or until a cake tester inserted into the center comes out clean.
Allow to cool for twenty minutes before removing from pan.
Enjoy with cream cheese and tea!

Maeve's Triple Fudge Cake

1 box (15.25 oz.) chocolate cake mix
1 package (3.9 oz.) chocolate instant pudding
4 eggs
1 cup sour cream
¾ cup water
¾ cup vegetable or canola oil
1 teaspoon vanilla
10-oz. bag mini milk chocolate chips
 Chocolate shell topping

Preheat oven to 350°F.
Except shell topping, mix together all ingredients well (can use a hand mixer), and pour batter into a well-greased Bundt pan.
Bake on the middle rack for 40-50 minutes.
Use a cake tester to check if done.
Remove from oven—let the cake cool completely in pan.
The cake *must* cool completely before unmolding.
With a knife, loosen the cake around the outside and inside edges.
Tip upside down onto a platter.
Cover the cake with chocolate shell topping.
Refrigerate the cake, and remove it 20 minutes before serving.
Top with your favorite ice cream. Friendly's brand is the best!
Don't tell anyone how you made this cake.

ABOUT THE AUTHOR

Christine Knapp practiced as a nurse-midwife for many years. A writer of texts and journal articles, she is now thrilled to combine her love of midwifery and mysteries as a debut author. Christine currently narrates books for the visually impaired. A dog lover, she lives near Boston.

To learn more about Christine Knapp, visit her online at: https://thoughtfulmidwife.wordpress.com/